Buried in the Mississippi Mud is a work of fiction based on true stories. Although its form is that of an autobiography, it is not one. Any references to historical events, real people, or real locales are used fictitiously. Other names, characters, places, and incidents are the product of the author's imagination, and any resemblance to actual events, locales, or persons, living or dead, is entirely coincidental. The opinions expressed are those of the characters and should not be confused with the author's opinion.

All rights reserved.

No part of this publication may be reproduced, stored in a retrieval system, or transmitted in any form or by any means, electronic, mechanical, photocopying, recording, or otherwise without the consent of the author.

For my children, your children,

for us, for them.

To pass the heirloom of continuous healing,

From the inside out.

-Chinna Dunigan

Table of Contents

Letter to the Readers

Chapter One: Dirty on the Inside

Chapter Two: Children Can Be So Cruel

Chapter Three: The Blue Construction Paper Book

Chapter Four: Curiosity Killed More Than Her Cat

Chapter Five: I Flushed the Hope of Love Down the Toilet

Chapter Six: Traded the Big Coward for the Little Liar

Chapter Seven: Your Suffering Don't Mean Nothing to Me

Chapter Eight: Old Bats and Young Cows Don't Give You a Break

Chapter Nine: Don't Insult the Comeback Queen

Chapter Ten: The First To Tell a Story Is Not Always the Truth

Chapter Eleven: Welcome to the Mud

Chapter Twelve: At the Crossroads with the Delta Devil and God

Chapter Thirteen: The Unholy Pastor and Dishonorable Mayor

Chapter Fourteen: False Restart

Chapter Fifteen: You Can't Get Apple Juice From an Orange

Chapter Sixteen: All Truths Don't Set You Free

Chapter Seventeen: The Lonely Road of Freedom

Author's Bio

Acknowledgements

Letter to Readers

Dear Reader:

As you read this book, please forgive me if I make you angry. Please forgive me if I make you cry. Excuse my words if they offend you and hold on to the words that touch your heart. Know that the story of the main character is a blend of experiences and stories experienced by many people, especially black women.

So many of us are heirs to damage and hurt, resistant to healing. Then others are heirs to being accusers and abusers, ignorant to how our words and actions bruise the spirits of others, especially those closest to us. The sad reality of it all is that we inflict wrongs on each other as much as others exploit us. I hope you can take from these pages the ability to only judge yourself for the inability to understand, the inability to empathize, and inability to sympathize with others that appear to be unlike you. May you be enlightened to know that we all have more in common than we care to acknowledge.

    The black woman has been and is still being subjected to so many atrocities by other people, by her people, and other black women. For years, religion has been used to excuse it, ignore it, and cure it. Hence, the reason you can find so many black women buried in the place of worship looking to remedy their traumas.

    Like the cotton fields of the Mississippi Delta, please pick from these pages all of the consideration and compassion needed to reverse the systemic, traditional, and religious conditioning that still hold us in a bondage that we didn't even realize existed. Let us stop being slaves to ourselves and masters of slaves of ourselves. May your hidden, personal insecurities be banished through enlightenment and make way for an open-minded, authentic soul. Enjoy and may you be set free.

Sincerely,
-Chinna

Chapter One: Dirty on the Inside

I'm lying here in my bed. I hear a soft bump at the door so I get up to look out of the peephole. I'm sure it's probably one of my neighbors coming in late. They make a lot of noise at these apartments. I just know they're staggering in from the club. I glanced at the clock while walking to the door to check the peephole; and it was 2:11am. As I look out, I see instead, it's someone at my door, William , my estranged husband. Everyone calls him Will. I was surprised and startled because I didn't know he found where I live. I cracked the door just enough to hear why he was here and what he had to say. I whispered, "yes?" "What are you doing here?" He overpowers me and forces his way in the door. My heart is beating fast. My mind is racing. What is he going to do? Should I scream? Should I keep quiet because my four children are in the bedroom? Will whispers in my ear, "Take me to your room". He grabs my arm with this unyielding grip, pushing me, even though I was leading the way. I had this sick feeling that he was going to beat me again. Maybe even kill me this time because I finally mustered up the strength to leave him. I just pray, God please don't let my children find my body. Better yet, please God don't let him hurt my children. I'd rather they find my body than him hurt them.

He pushes me on the bed and climbs on top of me. He whispers in my ear, "Who've you been   sleeping with? Have you been letting James get it?" I said, "no". He got louder and said, "I know you've been sleeping with him." "If not him, then who because I know you're sleeping with somebody." I said, "I promise I'm not." "There's no one else. You're still my husband. I wouldn't do that to you." I thought by acknowledging that he was still my husband it would diffuse the situation and he would feel my loyalty to him.

Then Will puts his hand on my throat and starts to choke me. With the other hand, he reaches underneath my nightgown and pulls my panties to the side. I started pushing and trying to pry his hand off of my neck. I tried to turn over and block him with my knees so that he would not penetrate me. He forced his weight down on my body, held down one of my legs with his knee, and entered inside of me. He continued to hold my throat with one hand resting his elbow on my arm so that I could not move; and held down my other arm with his other hand. He starts thrusting hard. Grinding and thrusting so hard that it begins to hurt my pelvis. I tried to wiggle and twist to get loose. I couldn't breathe very well because he was still holding my throat. The entire time he's saying with a hot, breathy voice, "I know you've been sleeping James." "You're just a whore; but you belong to me." "You're my whore." "I'm gonna mess you up." "I'm gonna tear your insides up so that no other man will want you." "I know you're sleeping with him and you're just trying to protect him by lying to me." "When I get done with you, he won't want you." "Nobody will want you."

I stopped fighting. I knew I wouldn't be able to get loose from the grips of this demon. I, once again, relinquished my control to him. I just lied there and let him finish. I felt like it was going on forever. My body just rocked back and forth. He just kept pumping and grinding on my body, all the while cursing in my ear calling me all kinds of horrible names. "You're a nasty hoe. Don't nobody want you. Nobody will ever want a hoe with four kids. That nigga just sleeping with you cause you easy. He at home right now with his wife while your stupid ass laying up here protecting him. Just tell me the truth about you and him and I'll leave you alone. I'll leave; but I just can't understand y'all stupid girls."

Suddenly, he changes. It was like a switch flipped. He transforms from this agitated, angry monster to a man with a calm intonation. He whispers softly in my ear, "baby, you know I love you". "I just want you to admit to me that you've been sleeping with him so we can move past this and get back to the way we used to be". "I want my family back." I finally muttered a response in a soft rattling voice, "I didn't sleep with him. I promise I didn't. I would never betray our vows. You are my husband and my loyalty is to you." He chokes me harder, and starts speaking in a low mutter in my ear. It sounds somewhat like a growl, speaking through his teeth, from his frustration with me. "Your stupid ass is gonna protect him to the end, aren't you?" I can feel his blood boiling because he wants me to oblige his demands and say I had an affair with James. I refused to say that.

    I just turned my head to the side and focused on the glare of the street light that I could see shining through a space in the blinds of my bedroom window. It took my attention from the low, steady knocking of my bed against the wall. I can now feel the warmth and wetness on my right cheek from my tears starting to soak my pillow. On the other side, I could feel his hot prickly skin rubbing back and forth on my left cheek and his smoldering breath burning straight through my soul. I just sobbed. Hoping and praying it would stop. He would stop. With every agonizing thrust of him inside of me, it was like him stabbing my soul. I could feel my soul crying out in despair, but I had no more tears left to cry. I died more and more every second he entered my body. Every time he pulled out, he took another part of me that I could never get back. I suffered in silence, so my children wouldn't wake and see me like this. I see my alarm clock on the dresser and it is 5:26 am. He's been on top of me about three tortuous hours. No normal man can go for that long. I'm sure it's the hateful demons inside of him that's fueling his stamina. Finally, he ejaculates, leaving his evil darkness inside of me, taking the last morsel of my dignity, respect, and worth with him. He pulls out, climbs up my torso and spits in my face. Then gets up, puts his uniform on, and walks out the door to go save everyone else from people like himself.

    I lie there in my bed, body helpless, spirit broken, with the remnants of his semen on my thighs, the symbol of disdainment by his spit on my face, and dry tears on my cheeks from mourning the death of my soul.

There's still silence in my apartment because my children remain asleep. So, I get up and walk to the bathroom to wash this pity off of me. I turn on the shower with the hottest water that my skin can bear. Next, I grab the bottle of spray bleach that I have resting on the floor beside the toilet. I sprayed the bleach on my towel, and began to vigorously rub my face, chest, and thighs. While standing under the steamy water streaming from the shower head, I began to spray the bleach directly on my body. I was trying to scour away the dirt he left on me. I scrubbed and I scrubbed until the skin started to peel away from my body. When I looked down in the tub at my feet and saw the trickles of blood mixed with the shower water. I realized that I had scrubbed the skin from my chest and I started to bleed. The dirt that I was trying to scrub away was not on my body; it was inside of me. I was dirty in places that I could not wash with my hands. The feeling of being unclean and dirty was a familiar one that was inflicted on me as a child. That demon in Will was the same murky demon that visited me before. At that moment I realized that this situation and this feeling has repeated itself. How did I get to this helpless place again? Surrendering my power to another person that took advantage of me? I need to start at the beginning and see how I got buried so deep in a place that I can't seem to find my way out.

Chapter Two: Children Can Be So Cruel

It is 4:30 am. I love waking up early before everyone gets up. Well, almost everyone. I go wash my face and brush my teeth. I walk back into my room where my sister is sleeping in her bunk bed. Even though they are bunk beds, we have them side by side. I look on top of the plastic bin that separates our beds to find my orange t-shirt, which is my favorite color to wear and my denim shorts. I slip them on quietly to prevent waking my sister. I don't have a dresser to place my clothes in because there's no room in the bureau for my clothes, my sister's clothes and my mama's clothes. After carefully and quietly getting my clothes out and on, I'm now almost fully dressed but I'm barefooted. I'm sure it's about 5:00 am. I didn't look at the clock but my grandfather usually leaves around five to meet with the other old men around town. These older men congregate at the gas station at around the same time every week day to buy coffee and talk about the local gossip. That's the same gas station that the young folks around town go to after high school football and basketball games to hangout and talk also.

My grandma is cooking breakfast for when my grandfather returns home. I'm just waiting for the sun to come up so that I can get a smell of the crisp morning dew on the withered grass outside. That smell is my inspiration for waking up early every morning. I love the outside. When I get in trouble, I sometimes beg my mama, "please whip me, please". I will even go get a keen switch from the plum tree in the back yard and pull all of the leaves off with the exception of a couple of leaves that I was taught to let remain on the end. Because the alternative to a whipping is the punishment of being forbidden to go outside. I cannot live if I can't go outside.

As I patiently wait on the sun, I sit and watch as my grandma fries thick sliced Wrights' bacon and bakes biscuits from scratch. It's like my grandfather smells the biscuits coming out of the oven because he arrives back just in time for them to come out of the oven. She fixes his plate first and sits the Brer Rabbit molasses on the table beside him with a tall glass of cold water. He usually only drinks water on the weekdays. He saves a Coke or a strawberry Fago for the weekend to accompany a meal when he doesn't have his whiskey. I sat at the table beside him and watched him eat. He eventually asks if I want some; but not with words. While sober, my grandfather was a man of few words. He grabs a handful of biscuits, holding the morsels between his fingers and thumb, and rubs the bread in the molasses. Then he urges them toward my face and I open wide and eat from his hand. That's how I always saw him eat biscuits, cornbread, and greens, with his fingers. My grandma tells me to fix myself some and eat before it's time for me to leave for school. I obeyed her request.

    The only part of my wardrobe that was missing was my shoes. I only had one pair of gym shoes for school and they were "talking to me". The front of the sole had come off of the shoe so it was flapping when I walked. I went to my grandparents' room to get the gorilla glue. I saw it there when I was snooping around the other day. I just looked to see what I could find so that I can reenact a scene from an episode of MacGyver that I saw. I loved MacGyver. He is so ingenious; he can make something out of nothing. I believe I am the female version of him; or wish I was. I found the gorilla glue. Now, I'm gluing the bottom front of my shoe back on. I'm going to go ahead and put them on so while I'm walking to school, the pressure from me walking will make it stick more. So, I know it will be fine according to my logic. I don't know that strategy to be tried and proven but I imagine it will work.

    My mama combs my hair at night, ties it up with a scarf, and puts a pair of my old stockings on my head so that I won't mess it up while I'm sleeping. I am usually gone to school by the time she makes it home from work because she works at night. I leave just as the sun is rising at about 6:50 am. My grandfather worked from home as a mechanic so he could actually take me to school but he believes that if your feet aren't broken you walk or take the bus. We were always told that your mama, aunts, and uncle walked to school; they turned out fine; so you all can walk too. Whether rain, sleet, or snow, my sister and I walked to school.

Well, I've left my grandma's house now. I'm trucking down the road, walking along the curb because there are no sidewalks. I'm in my element. The sun is up, shining bright, warming the back of my head like a furnace and the air smells like perfumes of grass, rose bushes and honeysuckle. I get to a point about a mile away from the house and I'm also about a mile away from the school. Then, the unthinkable happens. The shoe comes apart. The glue was not dry. The plan I conjured up to put pressure on my shoe to make the sole stick back on while walking did not work. I am too far from home to turn back and get my sandals. If I do, I'll be late for school. I have another plan for fixing my shoe when I make it to school. I'm going to exercise my MacGyver ingenuity. Meanwhile, I flipped and flopped the remaining way to school.

When I arrived at school, I stopped by the cafeteria to get breakfast because I wanted to make sure I had a full stomach. This will be like a snack since I ate before I left home much earlier. I hate walking in the cafeteria by myself in the mornings because everybody looks at you. My clothes are always clean and neat because my grandma and mama make me iron them at night before school. After ironing them, I just laid them back on the box with my other clothes to prevent wrinkling them. They are not the newest clothes sometimes. My sister or cousin probably wore them first and handed them down to me but I think they look pretty good. I do have a few new pieces since school started a couple months ago. I got these shoes then too, but my mama says that I am so hard on shoes. I don't try to be. They have to understand that kickball is tough on a pair of Keds.

I'm done eating the country ham and biscuit and departed the caf' for my homeroom. I've finally made it to class. I came up with the bright idea of stapling the sole back on my shoe. I asked my teacher to borrow her stapler; she said yes. I opened it like I've seen teachers do when they are decorating bulletin boards. I took my shoe off and my sock was black on bottom like I had been walking on the ground. I stapled the sole back on. It was a success; but I'm going to wait until after I walk in the shoe and test it out before I get too happy.

The morning has passed pretty fast and lunch is upon us. So the teacher, Mrs. Lee, lines the class up to go to the cafeteria. We walk single file like little army ants marching to the cafeteria. When walking into the cafeteria, it's like walking on a stage and everyone sitting down with their lunch trays are like the audience. All eyes are on the next class walking in. Just as we turn the corner and enter the cafeteria, the sole of the shoe comes off again and the staples are poking the bottom of my foot. I start to limp because I'm dragging my foot to keep the sole from coming off completely. It seemed like the lights went out and the spotlight was shining on me because everyone in the cafeteria was looking at me and my shoe. Everyone was laughing and pointing. I was so embarrassed. When I got my tray and sat down, I just gave my food away because I couldn't eat. My appetite left with my pride. April, who I thought was my friend, made a joke about me in front of everyone. As she got up to take her tray to put in the garbage, she said, "hey Leia, I got some shoes at home that I can bring for you; because we know your foot is not broken, it's your raggedy shoes." "It's cool, we all know, you can walk straight, now." Everyone started laughing.

This day could not be over fast enough. When school got out, I walked home with my neighbor from across the street. April used to be one of the children that walked home with me because we lived in the same direction. I could not stand to be around her anymore that day because of what she said in the cafeteria. I took my shoes off and put them in my backpack. I just walked in my socks. It was more comfortable than the staples sticking my foot. Besides, with the sole missing, I was practically walking on the ground.

After I arrived home, there wasn't much time to play outside because we had to go to the Kingdom Hall for the Tuesday night meeting. We don't go very often because my mama is not a Jehovah's Witness but my grandmother is. It's kind of tradition to attend the Kingdom Hall. My grandmother told me that she has been a Jehovah's Witness since around her mid twenties. So, the Kingdom Hall is the only religion we know. I like going there because everyone is so nice. They show so much love to each other.I remember the scripture John 13:35 that says, "By this all people will know that you are my disciples, if you have love for one another".

I always hear them giving my grandmother compliments on how well she dresses. They always tell my sister and I that we are pretty and smart when we give comments on the microphone. It's the total opposite of the ridicule and bullying I get from school. Even though my attendance is scarce, I look forward to the encouragement I get when I go there. There is also a girl, Makayla, that goes to school with me and her mother and grandmother attend the Kingdom Hall as well. I know she wouldn't be mean to me because the Jehovah's witnesses are taught to be polite christian people. However, she and I are not in the same class. I wish we were then maybe I could have one friend on my side.

We've made it home now. It's about 9:15. This is the only time I stay up this late on a school night. I'm usually in bed by 8:30. My mama has a strict schedule for my sister and I. If it's summertime and it gets dark later, the neighborhood knows that we have to be in the house when the streetlight comes on. When it's Fall like now, we have to be in by 6:30 pm. We always know because the Wheel of Fortune comes on and that's the cue to start taking our baths. My mama maintained the very strict schedule of taking baths at 6:30, eating dinner by 7:30, and going to bed by 8:30. So, tonight I was glad to be up a little later than usual. I didn't eat before we left for the Kingdom Hall. I'm going to eat now before bed. I have a choice of what my grandma cooked for my grandfather, cornbread, field peas, that we shelled the other day, and hog maws. I don't like any of that; but I could eat the spaghetti with wieners cut up in it. I don't like that either but it's the better choice. My mama always says, "eat what's cooked or don't eat anything". I was a picky eater but I did not want to go to bed on an empty stomach again. Spaghetti and wieners was the choice tonight.

Now, I have to prepare for tomorrow. I am not trying to reconstruct this shoe again. They are beyond repair. So, I will get my cute sandals to wear to school tomorrow. My mama combs my hair at night and places a scarf and a stocking cap made from grandma's old pantyhose on my head because I have torn up the one made from my stockings . I sleep wild and will wake up with my hair all over my head. The pantyhose are the extra protection for my hairstyle, which are four ponytails this time. I like to wear my plaits because people can see how long my hair is. My long pretty hair is a distraction from my clothes and shoes sometimes. My clothes are always clean and neat but they are not the style and brands that the other kids are wearing. That's why they make fun of me. I climb in my twin bed adjacent to my sister and try to go to sleep. My mind is all over the place because I'm excited about tomorrow and the opportunity to redeem myself from this embarrassing day.

I'm up early like usual, still sleepy though. It took me forever to fall asleep. I'm ready to get to school today. I have on my black biker shorts, my white t-shirt with a multi-colored zebra on the front, and my green jelly bean sandals. I threw on my London Fog coat and some white socks because the weather is starting to turn cool. I pulled the shirt to the side on my hip and put a big rubber band on it because that is the style.

    I practically ran to school this morning because I walked so fast. I was ready to get to school to show off my outfit and show that I do have the ability to dress well. I walked so confidently, with my head and shoulders held high, ponytails swinging with my matching black, white, and green ribbons and barrettes. I sashayed into the cafeteria to get my breakfast. Unfortunately, I was so early, there weren't many people in the cafeteria to see my outfit. I hung around in the cafeteria, eating slowly like a turtle, waiting for somebody to come in and look at me, waiting to get some attention for my fly outfit. Nobody noticed.

    As I leave the cafeteria and walk down the hall to my classroom, I see April again. She looked at me in awe and rushed down the hall to the classroom. I know she was impressed with my outfit. When I walk near the classroom door, I overhear her telling the class, "y'all not gonna believe what Leia has on". "She's wearing green jelly beans with white socks, biker shorts, and a coat!" Everyone bursts out in laughter. Then April said, "when she walks in everybody needs to joke on her". "We will all take turns". I could hear everything that was said and the kids agreeing to make jokes about me. Before they saw me, I ran into the restroom; then ran into the stall and broke down crying. I thought my green jelly bean sandals were nice and it was just logical to me that since it's getting cool outside,put on socks and a coat just in case I got cold. That was a huge mistake. I looked like a fool and didn't even know it before I left home. I cried as hard as I could so that I could get it all out and put on my tough face when I walked into the war zone of insults. I don't want to appear like it bothers me even though it eats me alive. I can't let them know that they affect me. I cried and cried some more. Then, I walked out of the stall and to the sink to splash cold water on my face to relieve the red face and swollen eyes on my pale skin. I want to appear normal though I already know the devices that await me.

My heart is beating fast; but I hold my head up high and walk into the battle with my facade of strength and normality. They let me have it. "Green bean jelly bean", said April. "Leia doesn't know if she is hot or cold", Robert said. Keshia walked up to me and pulled my hair and called me Pippi Long Stockings. Ivory pointed out that my shoes were falling apart yesterday. They gave me blow after blow of verbal insults. I was so humilitated. Finally, the teacher said, "alright, alright, that's enough noise". "You all need to settle down now". But the damage was already done. This added to the list of one of the worst days of school. I couldn't wait to go home and end this day.

Chapter Three: The Blue Construction Paper Book

Mrs. Lee is one of my favorite teachers. I love to finish my work early because she lets us do crafts, color, and draw in the spare time. My classmate Kenya, sits beside me. Mrs. Lee often pairs us up together because she says that we are the smartest students in the class. I think Kenya is pretty too and like to pretend that she is my sister.

Today, Kenya and I finished our work early like usual. So Kenya and I pulled our desks
together to draw and color. Kenya decided that we should make a book. So, we wrote stories, illustrated pictures, and made covers from construction paper. We punched holes in it and bound them with yarn to make them look like real books. Kenya finished before me and showed hers to Mrs. Lee. Mrs. Lee was so impressed and happy after seeing Kenya's book that I knew I had to make mine great. It was fulfilling to get that admiration from Mrs. Lee. She gave me something that I did not get at home. I always felt like nothing I did ever pleased my mother. I was a straight "A" student but I never got commendation from my mother. My mom always seemed numb. I never saw her smile or laugh. She was always stern and melancholy. Nothing I ever did seemed to make her proud of me. When I did something extraordinary in class, Mrs. Lee always praised me and that's what I needed. I needed to feel important to someone. So, I crumbled my book up and started over. I had to make my story and my book more exciting than Kenya's book. I wasn't competing with Kenya to make a better book. I just wanted to make Mrs. Lee the most proud.

So, I finished my book. I used blue construction paper for the front and back covers, a red sheet of construction paper for the inside, and I glued a sheet of typing paper on each page of the red construction paper to write my story. I drew a picture of pink flowered panties on the front and back covers, a television, and a stuffed black and white polar bear. These depicted images that correlated to my story. When I finished, I handed my book to Mrs. Lee and awaited the gratifying countenance on her face. To my dismay, she had a look of shock. I asked her, "is there something wrong?" "Do you not like my story?" She called me outside of the classroom and asked me to tell her all about my story from the beginning to the end. So, I did.

I started at the beginning. My mama, sister and I finally got our own place to live. We moved into Blue Manor Apartments. My mama's boyfriend moved in with us as well. My mama worked at night as a janitor, so we usually still stayed the nights at my grandparents' house on the nights that my mama had to work. This particular night, I lied down in my mama's bed because I had a headache. I told her, "if I fall asleep, wake me up". "Don't leave me". She said, "Ok". I fell asleep. When I woke up, I had a worst headache and it hadn't subsided. Stan, my mother's boyfriend was in the bedroom. He was sitting in a chair in front of the television. I noticed a naked white man and naked white woman on the television lying on top of each other kissing and grinding. I asked where my mother was and he said she was gone to work. I asked if my sister was there and he said she was gone to my grandmother's house. My mother had left me there. I told him that I had a bad headache and he said he would give me something to make it go away. He came back to the bedroom with a glass of something. He said, "this will make your headache go away". "Drink it all and drink it fast". I asked, "what is it?" He said it was milk. It did kind of look like milk but with maybe water added to it.

As I started to drink it, it burned my throat and had a very strong, pungent smell. It definitely was not milk. I told him, "it burns; I can't drink it". He forced the glass up to my face and made me drink it all. My throat and chest burned from whatever was in this glass. The burning of my chest and throat distracted me from the headache. When I finished, he told me to lie down, go back to sleep, and I would feel better. I actually started to feel a little dizzy and light headed after lying back down. I never felt like that before. Whatever was in that drink made me feel dizzy.

When I woke up again, it was from the elastic on my panties popping. I felt pain in my vagina. It was his fingers going inside of me. I grabbed his hand and told him to stop. He sat up, grabbed my hand and continued to put his fingers in and out of my vagina. It was dark with the exception of the light shining from the bathroom. I could not see him but I knew it was him because I could smell his cologne and he had a unmistakeable keloid scar on his hand that I could feel. He also had a distinct smell of Brut that seemed as if he bathed in it. I begged him to please stop and that it hurt. I said, "my mama told me to never let anybody touch me there". He said, "it's okay". "I do it to your mama all of the time". I said, "but I'm not my mama". "I don't want you to do that to me; I'm only eight years old". He said, "somebody has to do it some time in your life". "It might as well be me". He continued to push his fingers inside of me and I started to wiggle and scoot away from him. I scooted until I got to the opposite side of the bed but I could not go any further. He said, "I'm trying to open you up". Then he climbed on top of me and tried to penetrate. He said it hurt him because I was still too tight so he just rubbed his penis inside the lips of my vagina until he got tired and fell asleep on top of me. I could smell his breath; it was the same smell of whatever he gave me to drink for my headache. When I knew he was asleep, I scooted from underneath him because he was so heavy I could hardly breathe. Since I was at the edge of the bed and could move no further on the bed, I scooted on the floor between the bed and the wall so that I didn't have to be next to him. My mama had a stuffed polar bear in the corner that he had won for her at the fair. I grabbed the polar bear and put it between the bed and me and curled up in the corner for the rest of the night. I did not go back to sleep. I just watched the clock as the minutes turned to hours and the morning came. My vagina burned from him manipulating it. That was the only feeling that I had. I didn't know how to feel emotionally.

When the morning came and he woke, he told me to get out of the corner, bath, and get dressed. He was going to take me to my grandmother's house. As we rode in his truck to my grandparents' house, he told me how special I was to him. He said I was his daughter and that what happened last night was our little secret. When we pulled up in the driveway of my grandparents' house, he put his arm around me and reiterated, "remember, this is our little secret and you can't tell anybody". "This Sunday I'm going to take you to church with me, because I'm the new pastor at church". I told him ok and that I would not tell. I got out of the truck and went into my grandparents' house.

As soon as I walked into the house, I told my grandmother what had happened. She asked was I okay and did I need anything. I told her that I needed to shower, despite having just taken a bath before I left home. She asked why. I told her because I felt dirty from what he did to me. It just so happened that the day before, my grandmother was watching the Oprah Winfrey talk show. Her guests on the show were women telling the stories about having been raped. I remembered that one lady said, "if this happens to you, you should tell someone right away". She said, "she felt dirty and wanted to shower". That was why I told my grandmother right away; and that was why I thought I was dirty. I thought I was supposed to be dirty and that I was supposed to shower because of what I heard the woman say on the show. My grandmother ran me a hot shower and I washed and scrubbed just like that lady said she did. However, the feeling of dirtiness didn't go away. It didn't go away because I was dirty on the inside. Little did I know that I would feel dirty for many years to come and would get even dirtier before I figured out how to get clean .

After finishing my story, Mrs. Lee was crying. I couldn't understand why. I didn't think people should be sad over someone getting dirty. She sent me back to the classroom only to return with someone else. It was a tall black lady very well dressed with heels on. Mrs. Lee said she told her my story and would like me to reaffirm it. She said that this lady was a social worker and that they were going to remove me from that house and send my mama and her boyfriend to jail. When she said jail, it scared me so bad. I didn't want my mama to go to jail; besides, she was pregnant. So, I recanted my story and said that I made it all up. Mrs. Lee was so disappointed in me. That hurt more than being molested. I hated letting down someone that cared so much for me.

My mama always warned us that she did not condone us staying the night at other children's houses because too much goes on at people's houses. I had more going on in my own house than I could imagine was happening at other people's houses. I guess that's why she kept her children and our secrets at home.

Chapter Four: Curiosity Killed More Than Her Cat

This is one of the few times that my mama let me go somewhere. I had to get my friend Leslie to ask my mom if I could go to Jackson to the Colosseum for the state basketball championship game. Our high school advanced to the finals. The entire town is going to Jackson to support our team. A lot of the ninth graders in my class were going as well. I really wanted to be there. So, I had my friend to ask for me because I was scared my mama would say no. She will tell my friends, "no", as well; but my chances are better when my friends ask permission for me.

While we're at the game, I see this handsome boy with olive colored skin and curly hair. He wore his hair in kind of a small afro but it was mostly curls, black Nike shirt, freshly pressed dark jeans, and Timberland boots. I kept my eyes on him. I didn't really watch the game. My purpose for being there was actually to socialize with my friends anyway. I noticed that my friend's cousin, Necy, spoke to him and his friends. So, I asked her, "hey, does Necy know that boy in the black Nike shirt?". Leslie said, "Yeah, I know him too". "We're in the same grade, he's actually my cousin on my dad's side but he's from Natchitoches, the same place Necy lives". I asked Leslie to introduce me to him. She said, "okay, if you want me to". "I can't believe you like Bud's little silly butt. He plays so much." She introduces us. We sat together the rest of the game. When we were leaving, he asked for my number. I gave him my grandparents' home number. I was at their house during the day time, I went home at night because my mom works the day shift now.

We started talking everyday. I really liked him. He was my first real boyfriend. I thought I was doing something because he was a grade ahead of me. I had it going on with a tenth grade boyfriend that didn't live in our town. He attended the same high school as me because Natchitoches and the other surrounding town, Coldwater, did not have a high school. This was common in the Mississippi

Delta. Many small towns did not have high schools. Students were bused to a larger town, within that county, that had a high school in close proximity. After the eighth grade, all the children were bused to my town in Lafayette to attend high school.

I became friends with my friend Leslie 's cousin Necy. I really loved their entire family. They treated me like I was their family. Necy was also an alibi for me to get to Natchitoches and see Bud. I would have Leslie 's mother or sister take us down there and he would come pick me up from Necy's parents' house. He and I started talking on the phone everyday. Every other weekend I was trying to get to Necy's house. He introduced me to his parents. His mother was a beautiful woman. She told me that I could pass for her daughter. She acted like she really loved me. His father was a handsome man as well. During the time that we started dating, his parents split up though. Bud remained living with his father.

His father started letting him drive a red, two door, 1990 Honda Accord. It was his father's old car. He started driving to Lafayette to pick me up from my grandparent's house. Of course, he couldn't come by himself. He would have Necy and Leslie in the car with him so that he would look inconspicuous.

One Sunday, I told my mama that I had to finish a project with Necy and needed to go to her house. My grandfather drove down to her house and dropped me off. I lied. I didn't have a project. I just wanted to get down there to be with Bud. I had something else on my agenda. I called him from Necy's house when I arrived. He came to pick me shortly after and took me to his house. His father wasn't home and Bud said it would be a while before he was to return. Bud told me that he loved me. I told him I loved him back; but I didn't mean it.

I knew I didn't know what love meant. I didn't grow up in a family that said I love you. My mother never told me she loved me. My grandfather or grandmother never told me they loved me. However, my daddy did say he loved me each time he would hang up the phone. He would always say, "You know daddy love you".

I talked to him maybe three times a year and I saw him maybe once a year or every other year. My dad lived in Fort Chapel, Alabama. He was in the military. The army was the ship that sailed him out of little bitty Lafayette, Mississippi. He did visit Lafayette more often than when he came to see my sister and I; but he came to party and gamble with his friends or to see his lady friends when his wife wasn't with him. I sometimes would not know he's even been in town until I run into someone that says, "oh, I saw your daddy this weekend." "We sure had a good time with your dad". Now, if he heard that I was getting an award, he would show up and cheer all loud like he contributed to some of my accomplishments.

I liked the support but all his visits would end with a threat like, "you better keep up the good work so I don't have to come back and tear your ass up". As if my accomplishments were a result of me trying to circumvent a whipping. I didn't see him more than I saw him. That didn't bother much because I didn't like to see or talk to him anyway. He was so intimidating. He talked very loud and had a deep voice. I trembled at the sound of his voice. I hated to call him. My mother usually had me to call him only when I needed school clothes or money for something. "You need some school clothes, call your daddy". The other times I would call him was when I was in trouble. Then she would threaten me that she was gonna call my dad when I acted up. So, really his purpose was to make some ends meet when my mama couldn't and to menace me to correct unfavorable behavior. I really didn't know the man; so, his "daddy love you" meant nothing to me. It sounded like it came from a stranger.

      Poor Bud didn't know that the motive behind my visit was not about love. We planned to lose our virginities to each other on that day. His motive was because he loved me. My motive was because I was curious about what consensual sex felt like. The closest thing I had ever experienced was my mama's husband forcing himself on me. It was her boyfriend when it happened. I found out three years later, during a conversation, when my mother informed us that she bought her first home. I wrote her a letter informing her of my desire to not live with her and Stan. She told me that it would really hurt her if I didn't move in with her and her husband. I replied, "what husband?" She said, "Girl, Stan and I are married". I was dumbfounded. I whispered in a low tone to my grandmother who was sitting near me, "I didn't know that".

      When my mama left for work, I said to my grandmother, "Did you know that my mama was married to him?" She said, "yes, where have you been?" "Didn't you see the wedding band on her finger?". I replied, "I saw a ring but I thought it was a fashion ring." "I'm only eleven years old." " How was I supposed to know that ring meant marriage?" I never saw my grandparents wear wedding rings either, so I didn't know to recognize something that I never noticed to look for. "I can't believe she married him after what he did to me!" "She must not have asked him." Do you remember you convinced me to tell her, that same day it happened when she arrived home from work?" "She never told me that she asked him".

      My grandma said, "I called both of them over here and asked him, myself, in front of her". I asked, "So, what did he say? What did my mama say?" My grandma replied, "He said that he didn't do that, that you must have dreamed that, that happened". My grandma said, "ain't no child that young, gonna dream up nothing like that." "She not gone come up with no story, that detailed and just make it up." "If I hear of anything like that happening again, I'm gonna go to the police myself". She said, "your mama didn't say anything". At that moment I knew, she believed that man over me. She married a man, lied in bed beside him every night after knowing he slept with her child, and didn't say a word in defense of her child. I knew she did not love me.

At the same time, I knew that my grandmother and grandfather were the only people that did love me. My grandmother had to persuade my grandfather from going to shoot him. After she convinced me to tell him what happened, he got out of bed only wearing his boxer shorts and a white v-neck t-shirt. He grabbed his shotgun and tried to leave to go shoot him. I watched her be dragged by my grandfather, holding on to his arm and then his leg to keep him from going to kill Stan. Then I told my grandfather, he was my only protection. I didn't want him to go to jail. Let God handle it. I recited this scripture to him Romans 12:19, *"vengeance is mine, I will repay, says the Lord"*. I'm okay granddad. Then he went back to bed.

That was how I found out that she had married that man. Just in casual conversation. She married a man that had been with her child. After that situation, my heart was hardened. I didn't love anybody. Sex was not associated to emotion for me. I was only curious about what consensual sex felt like to do it. Most of my "friends" had been sexually active already. I hadn't. Bud was just an opportunity to quench my curiosity.

We went into his father's room; he pulled out a bag of magazines. He said, "these are my dad's Playboy magazines. You want to look in them to get you in the mood?" I replied, "I came here in the mood. I know what I came to do. I just need you to go ahead and get naked." I wasn't aroused. I was just determined to be in control of losing my virginity and not having anybody taking it from me.

He climbed on top of me and tried to push his penis inside. He screams, "ouch, it hurts". I said, "well spit on it then to make it wet. Maybe it will slide in then." It hurts me too; but the pain does not deter my goal of losing my virginity. Spitting on it didn't work. So, I told him to get the Vaseline and I'll rub it all over to make it work. He gets the Vaseline from the bathroom; and we move to the living room so we can hear or see anybody that may come over. I told him to lie on the couch and I rubbed Vaseline all over his penis. I said, "just keep it hard and hold it up; I'm gonna jump on it to make it go in". I lined up his penis with the opening of my vagina and sat down as hard as I could. He screeched in pain. I told him, "toughen up, it will feel better in a minute", as if I knew what I was talking about. I was successful. We got it in and I continued to rock back and forth on his lap. Then I told him to get a condom. When he stood up, I was bleeding. I heard girls say that was to be expected.

He was alarmed. I wasn't. He started apologizing, "I'm so sorry. Are you okay?" "Should we stop?" I said, "no." "I'm fine. Get me a cold towel, wipe us off, put on the condom and let's finish this". This time he got on top. We continued to have sex until he ejaculated. He kissed my lips and told me he loved me. I said it back but I didn't mean it. When he pulled out to take the condom off, he looked at me surprised and said it was gone. I asked, "where could it have gone? Is it inside of me?" Then he looked down at himself and only the rim was left wrapped around the base of his penis. The condom had broken.

We both were a nervous wreck for the next few days. We talked about the what if's for the next couple of weeks. Then Bud's phone calls started getting few and far in between. It was a big transition from the phone calls everyday, for hours at a time, to maybe a fifteen minute call once or twice a week. I was calling him. He was no longer calling me; and he was suddenly so busy now that he always rushed me off the phone. When I see him at school, he goes the other way. He was avoiding me.

    About a month has passed now, and I can count on one hand how many times he has called me. The only purpose for the call is to check on my status and see if anything has changed that he needed to know about. Today, I chose to walk to my mama's house after school; this was a bit out of the ordinary. I usually ride the bus from Magnolia Junior High School to my grandmother's house in the evenings after school. It was just part of the plan I conjured up to get downtown so I could buy a pregnancy test from Bill's Dollar Store. I bought two just in case I messed up one. I waited another week before taking the test just to be sure because my period was late. I hid the tests in the bottom of my backpack underneath my books. The following Saturday, I went into the bathroom at my mama's house and took the test. I felt like I may have messed it up because I peed all over the little screen that gives the results and all the lines are blue. So, I took the second one. This time I peed in a little cup and placed the testing stick part inside of the urine to make sure I didn't spill it on the incorrect part. All the lines were blue again. I got the package to decipher what those results meant. Two blue lines meant that it was positive. I called Bud and told him that I was pregnant. He said, "I never want to talk to you again. Don't call me anymore". I was fifteen, pregnant, and alone.

Chapter Five: I Flushed the Hope of Love Down the Toilet

It's so hot out here. This Delta heat could cook an egg on the sidewalk. By the time the first football game arrives, all of us majorettes look like burnt toast. It's the beginning of band camp and we're all out here baking. I also have something baking inside of me. It's July and I'm five months pregnant. I can't wait until we go inside for individual section practice. Then, I can get in some air conditioning. I know it's not good for the baby; but I can't tell anyone that I'm expecting. I was chosen from the final cuts before school got out last year so I knew band camp was coming. It would be suspicious to my family and my friends if I quit something that everyone knew I wanted so badly.

Our high school band is one of the best in the Delta. Everyone knew it was always my dream to be a prancing tiger in the baddest band in the land, the Lafayette High School Marching Band. Since I was a little girl, I had pictured myself in the red and gold sequin suit, gold knee boots, with my long black hair hanging down marching down the field to the cadence of the drum line. My heart beat fast in anticipation of the half-time show to buck, flip, slip, and dance to the sounds of the mighty Tigers Band. I couldn't wait to see the crowd cheer at seeing us dance and entertain. Only thing holding me back was this big bump in front of my stomach. I'm wearing a big navy blue faded t-shirt with Devine Family Reunion in white letters printed on the front; underneath the oversized shirt, pink and purple tights are cutting the circulation off below my growing belly. I keep rolling the tights down below my stomach to avoid the uncomfortableness and the tightness on the baby nestled inside of me.

One of the majorettes points out, Leia, your skin has gotten so pretty and your hair has gotten so long. Then, everyone started looking at me and examining my appearance, each nodding and gesturing in agreeance. Erica another majorette said, "you ain't pregnant are you?". I replied, "only a fool would be out here in this heat and be pregnant". She said yeah you're right; I was just playing. Guess I was a fool because I was out here in it. However, I was not ready to tell my family because I knew that I would be in big trouble and that I would really disappoint my mama and grandmother. I also anticipate that when my mama finds out she will make me drop out of the band. I really don't want to lose that opportunity either. I'm stuck between a rock and a hard place. There is no other choice but to keep this secret for as long as I can. I never wanted to put my unborn baby's life in jeopardy.

After practice, my friend Leslie and I were walking home together and she asked me, " Leia, let me see your stomach?" I dropped my head in shame and lifted my baggy t-shirt. Her eyes nearly popped out of her head. She gently touches my bulging stomach with skepticism. After the long awkward silence. She continues with being inquisitive about everything. "Oh my goodness, Leia; what are you going to do?" "Have you told Bud?" "What did he say?" "Have you told your Mama?" "Well, I know you guys will have a beautiful baby."

She finally paused with her questions to allow me to begin to respond to what I had few answers. I said, "I don't know what I'm going to do." "I haven't told anyone but Bud; he said he didn't want to talk to me anymore and he acted like he didn't know me before school got out for the summer break." Leslie got angry. She said, "Now, he's so wrong for that." " He grew up with both of his parents in the same household and should want his child to have the same." "He was raised better than that; I can't believe he would do you like that!" "I am so sorry." "I am here for you, whatever you need." "You don't have to go through this alone." I really appreciate the support from Leslie. Even though I was afraid to share my pregnancy, it was a relief to get that burden off my chest to somebody and not carry all that weight on my shoulders all alone.

Leslie was the captain of the majorettes. She took it pretty easy on me for the rest of the week at practice. However, today, Friday, I have succumbed to the consistent days of prolonged hours in the delta heat at band practice. I've started feeling really weak and tired. I've pushed through to the end of practice and now we're walking home. Leslie asks, "Are you feeling ok?" "You don't look so good." I uttered in a faint voice, "I'm not feeling well." "If I can just make it to my grandma's house, I'm gonna lie down".

I could barely drag my flaccid body up the driveway and into the house. I was like a car cruising on fumes of gas left in an empty tank. I went straight to what we call the front room and got in bed. I slept almost three hours. When I got up, I still did not feel much better. It was an exhaustion that I just could not shake. I proceeded to the bathroom to pee. As I pulled down my panties, I discovered that I was bleeding. I was so shocked, disappointed, and relieved all in the same moment. I was shocked because I read everything about pregnancy. I had been reading about the stages of pregnancy and times that a fetus is more susceptible to miscarry. I was well beyond that stage so I thought my baby would be okay. I know I should have been at least five months pregnant because I had only had sex once and I remember exactly when it happened; but this has surprised me. I must have missed something in my research of the Childcraft Books and Encyclopedia.

If this is really a miscarriage, I'm very disappointed and hurt because I was actually looking forward to, for once in my life having someone that loves me. I know that my baby will love me and I really wanted my baby to be okay. I was in anticipation of the experience of love because nobody ever told me they loved me and supported it with actions that proved what love really meant. I didn't know what love meant; but I felt the discovery of love was impregnated inside of me and birth would introduce us. This appearance of blood could be the symbol of death of the opportunity to ever know real love. I am devastated at the idea of losing it.

I'm ashamed to admit to myself that I am a bit relieved, though. I wouldn't have to give up my dream of being a prancing tigerrette. I wouldn't have to give up my plans to go to college and have a career. Regardless how handsome Bud is, I wouldn't be having a child with a sorry joker that thought it was okay to turn his back on us, either. The baby isn't even here yet and he has disappeared at the idea of it. I would definitely be saved from dealing with him for the rest of my life; someone that runs from accountability. The biggest relief of all, is that I wouldn't have to tell my mama what I've done. Sex was not something we talked about in our family. We couldn't watch people kiss on tv, read about it in books, or even listen to songs with sexual innuendos. My sisters and I couldn't wear any nail poilsh that wasn't clear until we were 18. My mama always said that colored nail polish was for women and girls are "fast" that wore colors on their hands. So, how could I say that I had gotten pregnant? That's the extreme opposite of colored nails. If I am having a miscarriage, I won't have to worry about explaining anything.

I just put on a pad and went back to bed. I tried to stop thinking about all of the "what ifs". When I woke up again, it was 4:36 am and I was covered in blood and in excruciating pain. I thought my pelvis was separating from my body. I've never felt pain like this before. I snuck the linens and mattress pad off of the bed and placed them into the washer. I got fresh linens and made the bed. Then, I got two garbage bags, split them in half, lined my bed with them, and got back into bed. My stomach and back hurt so bad. I was taking Tylenol and Ibuprofen around the clock;but nothing would help the pain to subside.

Around noon Saturday, my grandmother came into the room and asked, "are you alright?" "This is unlike you to be in bed this long". I said, "no, I'm not feeling well". She said that I may have had a light heat stroke. I concurred, "maybe so". Because of course I wasn't going to say what was really wrong with me. After the following day of still lying around, I knew that I had to get up, otherwise I would become suspicious. I was feeling horrible Sunday but I got up and tried to act normal. I went to band practice the following week, barely going through the motions with the dance routine because I did not have any energy. I continued to line the bed with garbage bags each night to keep from soiling the bed. I wore two sets of shorts with a pad in both sets because I was bleeding heavily through both almost every hour. This continued for almost another week. I suffered in silence and told no one what I was experiencing. I was in pain all day and night every day.

On Thursday, after band practice and after arriving at my grandmother's house, I practically crawled into the bathroom. When I sat on the toilet, I had an unusual feeling, unlike any I had ever felt before. It was a combination of an urge to push and the most horrific pain I've ever felt. Then, I felt like something was coming out. Next, there was a large splash in the toilet. I was afraid to look because I knew what it was. I was so scared to look but I had to see. I finally mustered up the courage to look in the toilet but all I could see was red. So, I grabbed the yellow gloves that my grandma cleans the bathroom with and placed it on one of my hands. I placed my hand down in the bloody toilet water and grabbed what was solid, held it there while I flushed with the other hand. I waited to get clear water to see what was in my hand. I listened as the water ran in the toilet until it stopped. I looked away because I did not know if I was ready to look at what I was about to see. After sitting on the floor for several minutes, in a pool of my blood, I finally turned to the toilet and looked in my hand. It looked nothing like a baby but it was the remnants of my pregnancy. I knew then that my baby was dead. I had walked around for over two weeks with a dead baby in my stomach.

I couldn't hug my baby goodbye. I couldn't tell anyone. Am I supposed to get it out of the toilet? Should I bury it? My heart is torn apart. This is my unrecognizable baby in my hand. What am I supposed to do? I did not cry. I weeped. I placed a towel in my mouth to muffle the sounds of my cry; and I weeped and sobbed. I got down on my knees and held what was left of that pregnancy in my arms and rocked and mourned. I mourned not just the death of my baby but the ideal of what it meant to me. Then I apologized to my baby, "I'm so sorry". "I never met you, but I think I loved you". "You deserve to be put to rest in a better way than this". "I'm so very sorry". Then, I dropped it back in the toilet and flushed. I was so devastated. My spirit was destroyed but I didn't know what else to do.

Friday, my first cousin Lisa, who was a few years older than me, came home from college. No one was home. My grandma and grandfather were gone and my mom allowed me to stay there for days at a time during the summers since it was close in proximity to the school. I was home alone. My cousin had a key to the house and she came into the room where I was lying in the bed. She looked at me in bed and yelled, "Leia, what's wrong with you?" "You look really sick." I was in so much pain, I could no longer keep the secret. I told her right away. "Can you take me to the hospital?" " I was pregnant and I lost my baby". "I've been bleeding for fourteen days now and I'm in really bad pain". "I can't take it anymore, I really need to go to the hospital". Lisa said, " I'll take you now, because you are really pale and you don't look good".

I staggered out of bed and got into her car; she took me to the ER. When we got there, Lisa explained my condition to the clerk. Then she asked how old I was. Lisa said I was fifteen years old. The receptionist said that they would take me back because my condition seemed dire. However, I could not be seen by a doctor without parental consent because I was under the age of eighteen. They would have to wait for my mother to come. My mama was at work and she worked out of town. I begged Lisa, "please don't call my mama, please don't". Lisa said, " I have to call her because I don't want anything bad to happen to you". " You really need to see a doctor". Then, I said okay because I knew she would find out eventually anyway.

    My mother showed up about an hour later. It felt like the longest hour waiting for her to get there. The nurse said, "we want to run a few tests before we say what's going mama". "Can you step out for a moment and we will call you back in, in a few?" I was escorted out to a restroom to take a urine pregnancy test. Next, I went to take a sonogram. The doctor waited until my mother was called back into the room, the nurse, and my cousin then he revealed the results of tests. "The pregnancy test is positive". "The sonogram shows that she has had a spontaneous abortion or miscarriage but there are still part of the pregnancy left inside of her uterus". "She is going to have to have surgery to remove the rest of what did not already pass out". My mama said, "pregnant?" "I know she is not." "You mean I left work for this?" "You ought to be ashamed of yourself; I'm so disappointed in you." "Since, you want to be grown, you're going to get a job and pay for your hospital bill made by you and your baby". The doctor said, " I know you're upset mom but she could have died." " She has lost a lot of blood and what's left in the uterus could have turned necrotic and poisoned her to death." " She got here just in time so take it easy on her." My mama said, " well that's her fault". The doctor gave me a pain shot, scheduled me for surgery on Monday, and released me. My mama said in a very angry voice, "get your stuff and come on". As we were waiting for the release papers, my mother continued to say how much of a disappointment I was. The nurse was standing there taking it all in with a stupid smirk on her face. Then she had the audacity to come up to me and whisper in my ear, "I hope you learned your lesson".

Did anyone even consider that while everyone was beating me down, that I was a mother that lost a baby? It did not matter that I was fifteen. I was still a hurting mother. Nobody consoled me or asked if I was alright. My mama was focused on embarrassing me because she felt I embarrassed her by becoming pregnant. The nurse was focused on getting in all of my business so she could contribute to making a spectacle of me. At that moment, I wished I had died with my baby.

      We rushed in the door at my mama's house when arriving back from the hospital because the phone was ringing. It was my friend Necy. She called to ask how I was doing. She said, "I didn't know you were pregnant." "My mama just told me that my aunt's friend works as a nurse at the hospital; and she called her about an hour ago and said you were at the hospital." "She said you were pregnant and your cousin took you to have an abortion and you got sick from it and had to come to the hospital". "She said that y'all didn't tell your mama and she was at the hospital cutting up with you". I said, "It's typical here for people that work at these places to breach confidentiality;but at least she could have told the truth." "Lisa was just in town and happened to find me sick." "Yes, I was pregnant; I'm sorry I didn't tell you." "I lost the baby by miscarriage not abortion." "The medical term for miscarriage is spontaneous abortion." "And, we just walked in the house; that means she started calling telling people my business before I even left the hospital." " That's so sad". My mama yelled, "Leia, you need to hang up that phone!" " No privileges for you for a while". " You're on punishment". I told Necy, " I gotta go". Then, I hung up the phone.

My mom came back into the living room where I was sitting and told me, "you need to call that little boy that got you pregnant and tell him that y'all have a hospital bill to pay". "My insurance doesn't cover maternity for a minor and I'm not paying no bill for somebody that wants to act like they're grown." I said, "okay". I called Bud. His father answered the phone. "Hello", in a very deep, professional sounding voice. "Hi, Mr. Smith, is Bud home?" "This is Leia." "Hey, young lady." "Yes, he is; hold on a second". "Hello". " This is Leia". "I know you haven't heard from me in a while." " I just called to tell you that I lost the baby and I'm not pregnant anymore." Bud said with excitement, "yes! I'm so glad". There was an awkward silence. Then he said, "I'm sorry". "I didn't mean it like that." I cut him off; speaker louder and over him. "My mama told me to tell you that we need to pay for this hospital bill that we made because her insurance doesn't cover it." "I'll let you know when I get the bill." "Bye". I hung up.

Later that evening around 9:00 while my mother was still gone, the phone rang. I looked at the caller ID and it was Bud. I wonder why he's calling because I hadn't heard much from him over the past few months when I was pregnant. I answered, "hello". He said, "Is this Leia?". I answered, "what do you want with me?". He said, "I just called you back to check on you and explain myself". "How are you doing or how do you feel?" I said, "I'm fine; but I have to have surgery Monday." "But, why are you asking, now? You didn't want to know how I was doing when I was carrying your baby." "You got what you wanted so there's no need for you to be calling me." " You're not about to be a daddy by me." Bud said, "I'm sorry. I never meant to turn my back on you but I'm only sixteen and I was scared." "I didn't know what to do and I wasn't ready to be a father." I said, "Wait a minute. I'm fifteen and wasn't ready to be a mother either." "Furthermore, how scared do you think I was when the changes were happening to my body. A baby was growing inside of me, not you!" "And you left me!". "

The doctor said I could have died." "You were not there for me." "So, you know what, I don't need you to be here for me now; all I need is for you to split this hospital bill." "Don't you call me unless it's about that money." Then I hung up on him.

Early Monday morning, I checked into outpatient surgery at the General Lafayette Hospital. My vital signs were taken. Then, my mother signed some paperwork. Checking in was pretty fast. Then they put me in a room and said someone would be in soon to take me to surgery. When my mother and I were left alone, she said to me, "I hope you learned your lesson; this is just an embarrassment". There was an awkward silence while waiting for the nurse or whomever was supposed to take me back to surgery. They couldn't come get me fast enough.

I was always uncomfortable when alone with my mother. She seemed just as uncomfortable as I did. Even though I have always lived in the same house as my mother, we have no relationship. We seldom had conversations. I remembered when I was about seven years old; and it was Mother's day. I woke up really early in the morning before the sun had come up. I went into the bathroom and locked the door. I got the Comet cleaner and shook it all over the tub and the toilet. I was on my knees scrubbing. Apparently, I made too much noise, my mama heard me, and woke up. I was trying to finish before she woke so that I could surprise her. When she started beating on the door, I kept saying, "wait a minute, wait a minute". She got a fillet knife from the kitchen that she had brought home from the old catfish factory where she used to work. She picked the lock and opened the door. She found me and the bathroom covered in Comet. I had Comet on my hands, arms, shirt, and face. She said, "why would you do something like this?" "You've created a mess!" "That's all you do is make a mess." I was trying to tell her that I was trying to clean up and surprise her for Mother's Day. That was my gift to her. I wanted to make her smile. I wanted to do something to make her happy for a change. Up until I was about eighth grade, I almost always made straight "A's". I participated in things in school like the choir and plays. She never said she was proud of me or that I made her happy. Good grades were an expectation; she said, "that's what you're supposed to do". It was never, "I'm proud of you". I've never heard those words from my mother.

It was no surprise that my mama was unhappy with me. She always seemed unhappy with me, with everyone, and everything. She always seemed to be very emotionally disconnected; actually showed little emotion about anything. Never a woman to raise her voice. She always had a very stern countenance and looked very cold. Her insides matched her face; it was cold and disengaged as well. I know I messed up; a lot of people do. I couldn't mourn the loss of my unborn baby because of it being overshadowed by the disgrace I brought upon my mother. Nobody realized that I was hurting. I would rather have some compassion when I was hurting than to be scolded right now; not now. Not right now. Fuss at me later. I'm okay with being accountable for my rights or my wrongs; but right now, this very moment, I need a mother, I need compassion, and understanding. I need her to understand, I wasn't trying to get pregnant. I only wanted to experience what sex was like without having someone take it from me. All that I had ever experienced was as an eight year old girl having a thirty-nine year old man on top of me, taking from me what I didn't offer to him and what I could never get back. I wasn't a "fast" little girl as my mama calls it. It's a euphemism describing girls that are promiscuous and easy. I wasn't in love with Bud. I wasn't trying to fit in. I was just curious about what it was like for sex to be consensual. I couldn't tell her that though, because she forbade ever talking about what happened to me at eight years old. So, solicitude or empathy was the last thing I can expect from her. However, adults making improper decisions regarding children caused this child to make an improper adult decision; but she could not understand that.

The nurse finally came in to take me back. She could not have come sooner. I had enough of the tension in the room and I was ready to get it over with. The IV had already started in my arm. I was rolled into the ice cold operating room. The tall white male doctor with dark brown hair and a blue scrub began to speak to me about the forthcoming procedure, "the procedure you're about to have is called a D&C and will last approximately thirty to forty-five minutes". He said, "the nurse is going to give me something to make you relax and you may fall asleep". "Then, we will take you down to recover until you wake and discharge you with some instructions." I watched as the young white nurse walked to my bedside with needle in hand. She injected it into the port on the IV and said start at the number ten and begin counting backwards. I said, " ten, nine, eight, seven…."

"Six, five, four", were the numbers I continued to speak as I was awakening. I did not realize that I had even been asleep. I black nurse was in the recovery room with me and asked, "what you say baby?". I said, " they told me to count backwards from ten when I was about to go into surgery". She smiled and said, "oh, you're out of surgery, you've been asleep about an hour". "I need you to go tee-tee in the rest room so then you can be released to go home". I went to the bathroom to pee. When I emerged from the restroom, she was waiting for me and my mama was sitting in the chair near the window. The nurse read the discharge instructions and handed me the paperwork. Then she said, "now, you're a pretty girl, this is your chance for a fresh start". " Don't go back out there laying up with these little boys making a name for yourself; because all they do is talk about you and put all your business in the streets". "They don't care about you; all they care about is what they can get from you." I didn't respond. I didn't even look back at her after the initial shock that this lady had the audacity to counsel me after she assumed that she knew my story. Then, she looked at my mama and said, "I don't mean any disrespect, I'm just trying to help her; but these little boys don't love her". "They don't love you; they just tell you that stuff to get in your pants". Then my mama said, "yes ma'am, you're right". She needs to listen. Oh, I heard her, loud and clear. I also heard the subjective views that crossed the line of professionalism with this lady scrutinizing me.

I really felt like the people that are "putting all my business out in the streets" are folks like her that work in the clinics and hospitals and go home and tell their friends and family everything about your diagnosis. Then, have the nerve to tell me how I'm supposed to handle my business and say things like "these boys don't love you" as if she talked to him or something; and he told her that. Actually, Bud did tell me that he loved me. I'm the one that didn't love him. It was my idea for us to lose our virginity to each other out of curiosity. You know, that's what I hate about being here, people think they know you, pass judgement on you, and offer you advice to try to fix you. When actually, they are the ones with the problem because they don't know how to mind their own business. "Go fix yourself." All she had to do was give me my discharge papers and let me go. I'm so over this hospital and the people that work here.

A week has passed and most of my time is spent at my mama's house. She doesn't let me go to my grandma's house much now because I've been on punishment. In actuality, I didn't go many places before. Homework and projects were the excuse to get to Necy's house so that I could see Bud. I have gotten some of my phone privileges back. Bud has started to gradually call more and more. He keeps pleading for forgiveness, for understanding and pledging his undying love for me. I am unwavered. I do not care. I just go through the motions to stay connected to him to make sure I get the money for the hospital bill. I pay attention to people and I have noticed that once people are no longer cool with you, you can hang up the idea of getting your money or whatever is owed to you unless they are truly honest, accountable people.

The phone just rang. My mama picked up. After a few minutes of small talk, I heard her say, "Leia, come get the phone". When I walked into the kitchen to get the phone from her, she said, "this is your daddy." " You need to tell him what's been going on with you." I covered the phone with my hand so that he could not hear the conversation, "please mama don't make me tell him". " I don't want him to know that." She didn't say anything else so I was glad she left it alone. I went and took the call in the living room and hung up the phone in the kitchen where my mama was washing dishes. I did not have a good relationship with my dad neither was it a bad relationship. It was nonexistent. He only usually showed up if I had an awards program or play or something at school if I invited him. I didn't invite him often because I was always uncomfortable around him. I didn't talk to him much because I thought as a child that the parent should reach out to try and develop a relationship with their non-custodial children. I didn't call him much and he didn't call me much. It was just understood that we don't talk to or see each other often. When I was ever around his friends or family, he would brag on how smart I was and my accomplishments even though he was so aggressive and abrasive to me. Nevertheless, he was still my dad and I did not want to disappoint him . He asked, " when does school start? Do you need anything?" I replied, "no, I'm okay". He said, " I'll send you a couple of hundred dollars anyway." I said, "okay, thank you.". He continued, "your sister has just started working at Parisians in the mall." I said, " oh, that's good". Then, we heard a click on the phone and a voice said, "you need to know what's been going on around here". It was my mama and had picked up the other phone. My dad said, " oh really". My mama continued, " your daughter went and got herself pregnant". He said, " oh, she is about to have a baby?" My mama said, "no, she lost it; she had a miscarriage and she not pregnant no mo'." "She didn't want to tell you. I just felt like you needed to know what's been going on with her around here. I'll get off and let y'all talk." He said to me, " when I get to town, I'm going to beat your mutha fucking ass". "So, you think you are grown now. I knew you were nothing but a whore." "You're just a whore." Then he slammed the phone down in my face.

    I was appalled and humiliated but even more so I was enraged. I almost never talked back to my mama. I just said yes ma'am and accepted whatever she said. The tears began to fall down my cheeks and I felt like a percolator about to burst. I could not contain my rage. I got up from the couch and went into the kitchen and asked her why she would do that. I finally got the courage to speak my peace. "Since you wanted to tell him what's been going on around here, you should have started a long time ago." " You could have started with telling him about you allowing your boyfriend to have sex with me then marrying him after the fact." " I don't even sleep at night in this house with him here." " You were so wrong for telling my daddy that!" " Then you let him call me a whore." " Now, that man is saying he's going to come beat my ass for me allowing a boy to do to me what you let your husband do to me?" "When I turn eighteen, I'm gonna call the police on both of y'all and they're going to take him to jail for what he did to me and they're going to take you for not doing anything about it." "You know what, I don't even want to live here anymore; I don't want to be around either one of y'all." " I never wanted to move in with you, anyway." " Tomorrow, I'm packing my stuff and you can take me to my grandma's house." I stormed out of the kitchen and into my bedroom. When I passed my mama's bedroom, that creep was sitting in the room all ears. I know he heard me and for the first time, I didn't care.

    The next day, she took me and my stuff to move into my

grandma's house. I was so happy to get away from there. There were other things that had been happening that I chose not to tell my mama. If she did nothing about what I told her before, I did not expect anything different about this time and I just spared myself the drama. After we moved in her house, when she would leave me home alone with him, he would tell me, "nobody loves you". "Your daddy doesn't love you, that's why he's not around." Your mama doesn't love you, that's why she believed me over you." When I was thirteen, I was playing basketball on my goal in the backyard and I went to sit in his truck to take a break. I found my dirty panties sticking up between seats. I would help my grandpa do little jobs to earn money. I would save my money in my underwear drawer in my bedroom. My money kept coming up missing. I would ask my mama if she borrowed it. She would say, "maybe Stan borrowed it; I'll make sure he pays it back". Sure enough it was him. But what was alarming should have been that he was in my underwear drawer. Why was he there? Then, one day she brought my panties to my room and said, "I found these in my room". " You must have accidently mixed your underwear with mine when you were folding the laundry." I said in a low mutter, "I may have", when I knew that I didn't put them there. I was just convinced that whatever happened, she believed him over me. So, I did not contest anything. I was just glad to be getting away from them, from that house, and to finally start sleeping at night again. Maybe my tenth grade year of school will be the beginning of a better time in my life.

Chapter Six: Traded the Big Coward for the Little Liar

I have a really busy schedule from school to work, to band practice, and meetings at this social civic club that I'm the president of. Every move that I make Bud is still tagging along. He's talking about marriage now and talking about getting me pregnant again so that he can prove that he will support me next time. Just in case he didn't learn, people don't always get a second chance to do things correctly. His opportunity has passed.

I got a job at the local grocery store, Clover's Food Mart. Almost all kids in high school here that wanted an afterschool job usually worked here or a fast food restaurant. Shortly after I started working, Bud applied and got hired too. He followed me everywhere I went. If I wasn't on the phone with him, he wanted to be at my grandma's house. He picked me up for school in the mornings and picked me up after school and took me to work. He gave me a ride home after work and called when he made it home to talk until he fell asleep. He was my shadow but he graduated from high school a year before me. I told him that wasn't normal. When he proposed to me, I was seventeen and he was eighteen. I told him that I would accept the ring as a promise ring but not as an engagement ring. I said, "to be honest, I'm sure that when you go to college you will find plenty more girls that are way prettier than me". "Why don't you wait until you have experienced some other things or some other people before you decide to settle down with me". " Actually, I think that we are too young; our focus should not be on marriage and relationships". "It should be on creating careers for ourselves." I was over it. I had made up my mind that after the last hospital bill was paid, I was going to let him go because I felt smothered. I really felt like he thought he had some sort of connection to me because he lost his virginity to me. Then, deep down I felt like he stayed and tried so hard to stay with me because of his guilt for abandoning me when I needed him; but the last thing I needed was somebody's pity love.

I know he stayed around for some other reason that I could not figure out because my grandpa really subjected him to some harassing, intimidating behaviour. If I were him I would have left a long time ago. When Bud would visit and my grandpa was drunk, he would not allow him to sit down. He would say, "ole nigga, stand up; you can't sit down in my house". Or he would just pull his gun out on him and chase him out of the house for no reason. When he was drunk, my grandpa would really act real tough, erratic, and verbally and physically abusive to everyone in the family or the people that visited us. However, he was so quiet, almost silent when he was sober. I really hated having Bud or any company over when my grandpa was drunk.

We continued in this relationship as assurance to get the money for the bill but he didn't pay all the time like he was supposed to do. Some weeks he had excuses about stuff that he had to pay for. I would go ahead and pay both of our parts because my mama would call the hospital and check to see if it was paid. I did not want to hear anything from her if we had not paid for it.

This particular Friday after we got paid, he took me to the hospital and we made the last payment. I was glad that stipulation to this relationship was removed; now I could part ways with him. We hung out that day and he took me out to dinner. When we came to my grandma's house to drop me off, we sat in the car and talked before I got out to go in the house. "Bud, I really appreciate dinner tonight and everything you have done for me, but," then I paused with hesitation. I didn't want him, I didn't want to hurt him, but I knew it would hurt more if I drug it on any longer. That's why I was hesitant to break up with him. He said, " But what?" I said, " we can't be together anymore because this is not working for me". He asked, "what's not working? Just tell me what to do and I'll fix it". I told him, " there's nothing you can do; please don't make this harder than it has to be." " My mind is made up." He said, " I feel sick, I think I'm about to throw up. I can't live without you." I interrupted, "wait a minute, just a while ago, you turned your back on me when I was pregnant and now you can't live without me?" "I'm sure you will be fine. I'm really not trying to be mean but that does not make me feel sorry and you shouldn't want me to feel sorry just to stay with you." "I'll check on you later but I'm about to go in the house. Good night". I walked into the house and left him sitting outside in his car on my grandma's carport. I really did feel bad but I knew that if I did not have tough skin, I would be in this same miserable situation for years to come. I had to make a decision and stick to it. I had to be quick, say what I mean and mean what I say. I was that, very short.

    A couple of months later at one of the step shows hosted by our social civic club, I saw this handsome young man. He looked like a younger Nelly. His name was Devonte Williams. After the show, he and his junior frat brothers came up to my group and I and we all started talking. A couple of my friends and a couple of his friends actually hooked up also. We exchanged numbers and it was on from there. We talked everyday. I had quit the job at Clover Food Mart to get some distance between Bud and I; and had started working at Church's Chicken with a couple of my friends. He would drive his mom's car to my job after school with his friends that were dating my friends. I asked him where he had been hiding because I had never seen him before. He said that he transferred to school in Lafayette a couple of years ago and he was put behind because he came from the city and his mom moved around a lot. He was a freshman and I was a senior. I asked how old he was and he said fifteen. I had heard that some transfer students say that they were "put behind" when they transferred to another school. I didn't know how true it was but I didn't believe he had a reason to lie to me. Then, I observed how he would come by my grandma's house late at night driving his mom's car at like 1:00 and 2:00 in the morning to see me. He was always hanging out with his friends at all times of night in his mom's car. I never was allowed to do that. Bud wasn't allowed to do that at a younger age either so I believed that he was about to be sixteen. There was no way a mother would allow her child to be out all times of night if they were that young.

Our relationship moved fast. Eventually, I introduced him to my grandma. When he came over to meet her, he was reluctant to come into the house. I kept insisting, "come on in; why are you so shy?", while pulling his arm. He finally came into the house and refused to make eye contact with my grandma. When she asked him questions, he mumbled under his breath and kept his head down. My grandma asked, "who yo people?" " What's your mama and grandmama nem names". He answered bashfully, "my grandma is Erma Williams and my mama is Dorothy Williams". My grandma replied in a loud voice, " oh yeah, I know all your folks, your grandma goes to the Kingdom Hall with me". " I haven't seen your mama in years though." I noticed his uncomfortableness so I conjured up a reason for him to leave and I escorted him out. My mama was arriving at my grandma's house as he was leaving.

When I walked back in, I asked what my grandma thought of him. She said, "baby, you need to leave that child wherever you found him because something ain't right". " He's too sillified or something." I laughed. My grandma often made up words to describe her perspective. "What's sillified grandma?" She said, "well, silly; you know what I mean". "He wouldn't look up at me and acted like he couldn't talk; something just ain't right." I came to his defense and said, " he was just nervous about meeting you for the first time". Then she said, "and I remember when Dorothy had that boy, he is way younger than you". My mama intervened, "you need to leave that little boy alone". I just rolled my eyes.

I thought when I moved to my grandma's house I wouldn't have to deal with her anymore. She would come over every evening after work trying to dictate things in my life as if I was still in her household. Because my mama said that I needed to leave him alone, I knew that I would keep dating him. I was defiant of everything she told me. If she said to go left, I went right. If she said to go up, I went down. After I left her house, I always did the opposite of what my mother said. She would come to fuss at me about stories of things that I had supposedly done wrong that her husband, Stan told her that I did. He said that I was sleeping with married men, I was sneaking boys in the house, and that I was sneaking out of the house with boys. I did none of that. One day, after I moved out, I saw him at the gas station talking to some of his buddies and I didn't speak. They said, "isn't that your stepdaughter". When I came out of the store he stopped me, pulled me to the side and said, "I want you to know I heard what you said to your mama about calling the police on me". "If you ever try, nobody will believe you." "I'm gonna drag your name through the mud like the whore that you are ". " They'll never believe you." I snatched away and walked off. Sure enough, that's what he was doing. My mama was always accusing me of something. She never asked me if what she heard was true, she just always said, " you need to stop what you doing", whatever it was. My grandma even said one day, "I would have a problem with a man that always has something negative to say about my children but wants me to accept his". "Something is wrong with that. You need to look at why he always has something to say about your daughters."

   Devonte and I are a serious couple now. To escape seeing my mama, if I'm not participating in plenty of extracurricular activities, I'm at his house. On this particular day, his friend comes by and says that he needs to talk to him alone in a very solemn voice. I went into the living room so that I could hear the conversation outside. I heard his friend say, "man Shantella saying that she was sick and throwing up at school and you didn't even care. She's talking about getting both of her brothers to jump on you". Devonte said, " man I ain't worried about that cause that ain't my baby anyway. I don't know why you telling me." When he returned into the house, I asked him what that was about. He told me, "some chick trying to say that I'm her baby daddy but me and some more boys ran a train on her. It could be anybody's baby". I asked, " did you have on a condom". He said, "no". I replied, "well it could be yours". He said, " it could be not too". Then I asked, " is this something that I need to be concerned about?" He said no.

    That "no" didn't last long. Soon after, there was a beef between Shantella, her friends and my friends and I. Shantella stated that my friends and I were coming to their school taking all of their men. She also said that the reason Devonte was not supporting her during her pregnancy was because I wouldn't let him. One day, all my friends and I got called to the gym right before school let out by the principal and questioned about if we had been to the junior high school. We replied, "no". He continued, "well, it was reported that you all have been going over there trying to pick fights with some girls over some young men". " If I find out that it's true, you all will be suspended. Your best bet is to not go over there at all." We were so pissed when we left school because we hadn't been there doing anything. I had only heard descriptions of what Shantella looked like. I had never even seen her before.

    When I arrived at my grandma's house, she met me in the kitchen where I was getting a snack and said, "Do you know uh ruh, Shantella Marshall?" I was thinking oh my goodness, "what now?" I answered, " yes ma'am, what about her?" She continued, " Well her mama called here today and cursed out your granddaddy and said she was gonna kill you if you keep messing with her daughter and that the little girl was pregnant". " Then your Uncle Kent called here and said that little girl's mama and her friend's mama came to his house today talking about you too." " He said the lady said her daughter came home from school crying yesterday and that you and your friends go up to the school every evening picking at her because she's pregnant by your boyfriend." "Her friend's mama said that her daughter said you and your friends are at the school all of the time picking at all of them because all of your little friends have a boyfriend at their school." I said, " none of that is true". "Well, I have been to the school a couple of times to pick up Devonte after school but I have never met her; I don't even know what she looks like." "That girl and her friends are just telling stories on me." I couldn't say the word "lie". It was like using profanity. I assured my grandma that I would never do anything like that and I felt like she believed me; but the rest of this town was who I had the task of convincing.

    I called my friends Arlicia and Erica and told them to come by my grandma's house because I had to tell them what had happened. They arrived with Judy and Ciara, a couple of other friends. As soon as they got out of the car, Arlicia began, "my mama said that Tiffany mama told her that she needs to keep me away from you because you're gonna get yourself in some trouble picking at Shantella." I asked, "what does Tiffany mama have to do with anything?" Arlicia said, "you know Tiffany and Shantella supposed to be best friends that's why her mama said something. My mama knows Tiffany mama, grandma, and aunts. We used to play together when we were smaller. But anyway, she said all Shantella's friends told their mamas because they said that you are eighteen so you're grown and they're going to let their mamas handle you because you're wrong for trying to fight a pregnant girl." I said, "wow!" "Y'all know that when we go to that school, we don't mess with anybody". " I have never even met Shantella. What does she look like?" Erica starts to describe her, "she is light-brown skin, kind of skinny, real long hair". Then Arlicia interrupts, "let's take a ride; I'll do something better and show her to you". We all pile into Arlicia's mom's car and head out. Arlicia said that they grew up on the street together. Before her parents split, their family lived a couple of doors down from her. Arlicia's father still lived there. As we were riding, I started thinking, I don't know if it's a good idea now to ride by her house. She is already accusing us of stuff and we haven't done anything. I don't want to give her any ammunition. She obviously knows who I am. I don't want to be seen with my friends riding by her house. Arlicia says, "you need to know who she is just in case she tries to surprise you and jump you or something". "We can say that we're going by my dad's house." Reluctantly, I agreed but what could I do. We were already in the car and gone anyway.

When we passed this older kind of dilapidated house with a bunch of neighborhood children outside playing, Arlicia said, " that's it". "That's her house and there she is outside in the front yard." I saw a girl; she looked so young with a bulging bellying peeking from underneath a short yellow t-shirt and a pair of denim overalls. She was thin and very fragile looking. She didn't appear at all like a person that would be telling all these lies on my friends and I; but I finally got to put a face with the stories. That face saw us too. She told everyone that we were riding by her house picking at her which wasn't true again; but how can you argue your point when you were actually there. We literally said nothing but I should have followed my first mind and just not gone by there.

The lies and accusations continued for the next few months. It progressed to my principal calling me into meetings again threatening suspension if I got caught intimidating her when I actually steered clear of the girl. Every other day, my grandmother was telling another story of something else, asking of what I had supposedly done, and warning me of what was said could happen to me. However, my mama never asked if I did what I was accused of doing. She always believed the worst about me and believed everything people in the streets said about me. She never asked. Her response was, "you need to stop messing with that little girl before you end up in jail". When I went to work, to the store, games, or school events, I had respected people in the community and some of my former teachers saying things to me like, "you're too old to be messing with that little girl", "you should be ashamed of yourself for picking at that girl", or "I thought you were better than that". Everyone condemned me solely on the words of a girl that I had never met and there was nothing I could do about it.

    I was tired of each day coming home to my mother waiting at my grandma's house with a new accusation and telling me to stop dating Devonte. I actually started spending more and more time at his house. I was cooking for his younger sister and brother. I was helping with their homework. I helped his mother with bills sometimes. Not because she didn't make the money. It was because she didn't manage money well. She made plenty of money. She enjoyed all that life had to offer by partying, drinking, and hanging out with her friends. Her kids were what she sacrificed by being gone a lot. She gave them plenty of money, bought expensive clothes and shoes, but would neglect paying utilities and have to borrow sometimes to keep the lights and water on. I knew she loved her children but she didn't quite know how to show them; I just felt like she was trying to figure out how to love herself. Dorothy became a mother at 13 years old. She missed out on her childhood and spent most of her adulthood partying trying to recapture what she lost. So, I kind of filled in like a big sister and I practically started living there. Then, one day I asked Dorothy if I could move in with them. I told her about my relationship with mama and being molested by her husband when I was a child and I no longer wanted to be around them anymore. She told me yes and let me move in with them.

    Then, she told me that people were coming up to her asking if she condoned the relationship between her son and I. She said, "what's wrong with my son?" "Is he not good enough for you or something?" I said, "yes, he is good enough for me and I am good enough for him". "Maybe people have something to say because I am two years older than him." "But, I don't understand why people are so concerned and so upset by a couple of years and if you are his mother and you like me and we love each other then that's all that matters". She even talked with Devonte and I one day about signing and giving authority for him and I to get married so I know she loves me. Then she says, "wait baby, you said two years?" "How old do you think he is", she said with a smirk. I answered, "he's 16 about to turn 17, right, because I'm 18". She said, "naw baby, he's 14 about to turn 15". My heart sank to my stomach. I told her, I don't believe it and that's not what he told me. She told me to follow her and she went to get his birth certificate and showed me his birth date. I was shocked. I couldn't believe that he had lied to me. My grandma was right. He walked back in that door at just the right moment from going to Burger Hut for his mama. She said while holding back laughter, "why did you lie to Leia about your age?" He said with a stupid looking smile on his face, "I just felt like she wouldn't talk to me if she knew how old I was". I said with anger and disgust, "you are absolutely right". I thought about Shantella and the bad things he said about her. They were probably lies as well. She may have had a good reason to be upset with him also. Now, I'm questioning everything he has ever told me. Dorothy said, "it's too late now, but I think y'all are good together; it doesn't matter to me". I realized she had a problem too if she felt that was acceptable but she was correct in that it was too late now.

    Later that night, his mama was on the phone in her room. When she got off, she called him in to talk to him. Usually when she talked to him, she talked in my presence; this time was different. When he emerged from her room, he told me that Shantella's mother had called her and informed her about the pregnancy and that the baby was due in a month. She also told her that I was picking at her daughter and that he denied her baby. He told me that he told his mother that he didn't care what Shantella or her mother said that it was not his baby and he was going to stay by my side no matter what. Then, I realized that the reason that Shantella hated me so much was because she believed that I was the reason he chose to deny her and her baby.

I had a serious conversation with him. I told him, " I grew up without my father and you grew up without yours". "That baby needs his daddy in his life". Then, I told him, "I don't know if you all really ran a train on her, it's two sides to every story and I know it hurts her for y'all to keep telling people that." "Whatever the situation is, if that's your baby, she needs your support during her pregnancy". "I know it's scary for her going through that alone, I experienced it, too". " If you want to try and be with her to be there for your baby, I understand; it will hurt but I understand". " I always wondered if my life would have been better if I grew up with both my parents." Devonte said, " I don't want her, I never wanted her; that happened before you". I started to cry and I said, "can you please tell the world that y'all's situation was before me". "Everyone blames me for the mess when I had nothing to do with it." But no child should have to experience what we did". "I would never keep you from your baby but she has ruined my life because she thinks I influence your decisions." Then Devonte said, "that's why I don't want anything to do with her because she attacked you for no reason; the only baby I'm claiming is the one that we have together, whenever we have one". Shantella didn't even know that I was secretly rooting for her to have the very thing that she was fighting me about. People can be so preoccupied with their perceived ideas of what they think you're doing that they completely miss out on the help and blessings meant for them. I didn't hate her. I actually understood her position. Truthfully, I didn't really love him. She could have Devonte; but he didn't want her, which had nothing to do with me. I only dated him to spite my mother for the things she allowed to happen to me and because she didn't want me to be with him.

    After the baby was born, his mother went to the hospital, signed his name on the birth certificate and made the child his name sake. Then, she had a baby shower at her house for Shantella. This was exactly what Shantella wanted. She was still spreading rumors about me and painting herself as the victim. Her goal was to get me out of the picture. It worked out for her because her manipulation made Dorothy start to pick arguments with me. It progressed to one day she called my grandmother and told her the reason she allowed me to live at her house was because I told her that I was being molested at home. She said she needed to know if it was the truth or if I lied to get over there with her son; she said I was too old for her son and that it was time for me to come back home. He has a child now and needs to focus on that and finishing school. She never had that conversation with me. My grandma called my cell phone and told me what Dorothy said. I was appalled. So, I immediately packed and left after telling Devonte what she said. I never told Dorothy I was currently being molested. I told her what happened in the past and how that affected my relationship with my mother. I was crushed that she would use something so sensitive and confidential against me for someone so conniving like Shantella. I knew she made that up as an excuse to have a reason to put me out. Next thing I hear, Devonte says his mother suggests that he and Shantella date each other. I understood Dorothy's mistakes as a mother but I admired her efforts to be a good mother even if it was trying to buy her children's love. I didn't even get that effort from my parents. So, I know she was trying to do what she thought was best for her son and grandson. However, I really wanted a relationship with her because I wanted a mother figure in my life more so than I wanted a boyfriend. Now, that idea was gone thanks to Shantella. I never wanted to deal with Dorothy again after she crossed me.

I went back to my grandmother's house, with my broken spirit. She talked to me and told me that a lot of people had been talking about me living there and it didn't look good. My argument was that it was none of anybody's business. My grandma told me that she and his grandma, Mrs. Erma Williams, were at the Kingdom Hall a couple of weeks ago and another witness overheard them talking about us and intervened in the conversation. Sister Alice Peoples was a busy body that often got in the business of others and gave her unsolicited advice. Alice asked my grandma, "oh, Sister Devine, is your granddaughter Leia dating Sister Williams's grandson?" My granda answered, "yes". So, my grandma said, later on it was brought back to her that Alice had made a visit to Dorothy's house and inquired about me dating her son. Alice told Dorothy, " I have sons; if that little woman called herself sleeping around with my sons, I would have her arrested for statory rape". "If I were you, that's what I would do." I couldn't believe it. Sister Peoples used to study the Bible with me when I was 12 years old. I stopped studying with her because she always used to tell me if I didn't come to all of the meetings at the Kingdom Hall or if I missed a Bible study, I was going to die. I asked my grandma, "tell me if I am incorrect, but do you recall this scripture, 1 Timothy 5:13, *"At the same time they will also learn to be idle, going from house to house and being not only idle, but also gossips and busybodies, discussing things they should not mention."* My grandma said yes she knew that scripture. Then I asked, " will she not die for that?" Then, I rolled my eyes. I was pissed that she did that. It was none of her business. Is she exempt from sin and death? Was what she did something God would approve? Every time I see her she is hugging me and telling me how much she misses me from coming to the Hall and how pretty I am. Now, I know it was all fake.

I thought that getting closer to Dorothy, getting the support of Devonte's family, and getting me out of their house would make Shantella leave me alone, but it didn't. She and her friends call my grandma's house playing on the phone all the time threatening to kill me and fight me. Their mothers roll their eyes at me when they see me in public. I just wondered, did anyone take the time to look at the character of either of us. I have never been a trouble maker. I pretty much kept to myself. I was always respectful to teachers and elders, even complete strangers. The exception was that my stepfather was telling people that I was promiscuous and my daddy called me a whore. Even if that were true, that didn't make me an incendiary. I really didn't know much about Shantella but what I heard people say was that she was always in mess. She told a lot of lies and kept up a lot of trouble. So, if that were true, why was this entire town taking her word as the Gospel. Did no one have a mind of their own? Could no one see through it? All the conflict she continued to create for me escalated things with my mother. That combined with my stepfather's incessant stories to my mother about my sexual affairs with married men and boys sneaking in and out of my grandmother's house pushed me to the limit. I moved out.

    I got some of my clothes and put them in my 1988 yellow four door Buick LeSabre and went to Arlicia's house. I would stay with her some nights and Necy's some nights. I never consistently stayed at either's house because I didn't want their parents to know that I didn't have a place to go. In between nights at their houses, late at night I would drive through the back yard and park in the back of my grandmother's house and sleep in my car, if I didn't get a hotel room. I would still go visit Devonte and make sure my cell phone was charged when I left there, so I had an alarm.. I was afraid trying to charge my phone in this raggedy car would prevent it from starting the next day.

    This was not the car I planned to have. My dad initially told me if I worked and saved some money, he would match whatever I saved and buy me a nice car. I really wanted a 1999 two door Mitsubishi Eclipse. I worked hard and saved well. One day, I asked Necy to take me to the bank. I went to the bank and asked for the balance on my account so I could call my dad and tell him what I wanted and how much I had saved. I looked at the printout and it said $3,526. I went back to the teller and said, "this can't be right; I should have over $8,000 in my account". She told me, "well you need to speak with your mother because that is the other person on the account". "She could have made some withdrawals from the account". Then, I asked for a copy of the statements for the past six months. I got the statements from her and walked back to Necy's car. I sat in the car and read the statements. I saw, " withdrawal of $200, $250, $500, $100, $160", several times a month over the past several months. Just as fast as I deposit it, it's taken out. I called my mama and asked, "have you taken money out of my account?" She said no. So, I told her, "somebody has taken over $5,000 out of my bank account and the only names on my account are yours and mine". "I'm looking at the statements now." Then she said, "oh, I let Stan get a couple of hundred out of your account one time. I told Heather at the bank to allow him to make a withdrawal because she knows us". I said, " you did what?" " I can't believe you let that man take all of my money; now how am I supposed to buy myself a car?" My mother said, "I didn't know he took that much and I didn't know Heather continued to give him access to your account." "I'm gonna pay you back and I'm gonna take my name off of your account". I know she is going to take her name off of my account. I'm 18 now and don't need her on it anymore. Heather married into the family but we weren't related. I know she knew better than to let my stepfather take money from my account and the only names on the account were mine and my mama; but it was my money only. Needless to say, I never got my money back; but that was all I had when I called my dad to match my money to buy me a car.

He assured me that he would get me something really nice

and I told him I want the Mitsubishi Eclipse. He told me to just keep my money and he would take care of it. He told me that he would surprise me when he got to town and refused to tell me what kind of car it was. When he drove up to my grandma's house with it on a trailer, I knew it was a red flag because he wasn't even driving it. That car looked like a banana colored piece of crap. I was so disappointed. He tried to make me excited by saying, "hop in it and take a spin". I didn't want to but I got in it and when I pulled out of the driveway, I heard something dragging underneath the car. I continued down the street and I looked in the rear view mirror and saw a trail of orange sparks behind the car. I discovered the muffler was hanging, dragging the ground, and making sparks behind the car. My grandfather fixed it for me. However, I was really sad that my dad would get me something like this. He was very well off. He never paid child support for my sister and I, so that was the least he could have done was get me a dependable car. I learned later how unreliable cars can land women in precarious situations.

  I guess my obvious disappointment in the car made my dad mad. When he left me, he went to visit my Uncle Ken where he voiced his displeasure with me in front of all of the company at my Uncle Kent's house. My grandma told me that my Uncle Kent called her and told her that he asked my dad to leave his house because he was made uncomfortable by the things my dad was saying about me. My dad said,"Leia didn't deserve anything." "She should have gotten those boys she fucking to buy her a car". " I knew she was going to be a whore; I could look at her and tell". My Uncle Kent told him to be quiet, "man, you shouldn't say stuff like that about your daughter especially in front of all of these people". My dad continued, " naw man, she was having sex at15 and we only found out about it after she got pregnant; ain't no telling how long she been doing it before we found it." "Once a whore always a whore; and she's an ungrateful whore". Then, Uncle Kent asked him to leave because he said everyone became so uncomfortable hearing my dad speak about me that way.

My grandma saw the embarrassment smeared all over my face. So, she called my dad. "John, I heard that you were at Kent's house talking about Leia." "Everybody was saying that you called her a whore." My dad said in a sullen voice, "well, yes ma'am, I did say that". "But she went and got herself pregnant at 15 years old; that's the kind of stuff that whores do; so, she was acting like one." Then my grandma said, "but that happened months ago". "Why are you just bringing it up now?" "And let me ask you this, how old were you and her mama when y'all got pregnant with Leia's sister?" My dad answered in an even more somber voice, "she was 15 and I was 16". Then my grandma said, "oh ok, that's what I thought". "So, if Leia is a whore, she got it honest. She learned it from her parents." "But the problem I have with you is that y'all did the same thing she did but none of us parents called y'all names like that; and you had no right to do that to her". Then my dad said, "yes ma'am you're right, I'm sorry". My grandma replied, "yeah, okay, but I'm not the one you need to be telling that to; you need to apologize to Leia". Then, my grandma hung up the phone. Needless to say, I never got that apology. My dad had an issue with pride. He never thought he was wrong for anything even if his wrong slapped him in his face. I believe that the only reason he disrespected me like that was to deflect from the piece of crap of a car that he bought for me. If it just possibly happened to be once in a blue moon that he realized he was wrong, it would be over his dead body before he apologized. It was bad enough that he said that hurtful stuff to me, his daughter; but now that he has told everyone else, I can't escape this reputation that precedes me. I would be perfectly okay with accepting responsibility for things I have done. Having sex with one boy does not make me a whore; but how can I prove my stepdad and now my dad to be wrong. I'm never talking to that sperm donor again.

High school graduation has arrived. I'm excited to reach this milestone but I am also simultaneously apprehensive to what's next for me. I want to attend Johnson State University but my mama doesn't because she says it's a party school. People always assume that HBCU's are party schools and "they say" that girls that attend those colleges and universities get "turned out". I believe that you can get "turned out" anywhere you go to school or even if you stay at home and don't go to college. For some reason, it's more respected to attend a PWI as if it being predominantly white constitutes it being better. I really think that it's just the simple minded people from this small town believing white is right and black is wrong. It really doesn't matter to me if it's a considerably white school or primarily black school, that does not determine the quality of the school. I just want to get away from here and be with my friends; and most of them are going to JSU. Even though I don't have a good relationship with my mother, deep down I still try to do things that I think may please her and make her start to love me. So begrudgingly,I decided to attend the University of Southeastern Mississippi in hopes that it could be a catalyst for change in my relationship with my mother. My cousin graduated from there and everyone was so proud of her. Maybe it can be the same for me.

The parking lot is packed with cars. I hope my family gets a chance to get in the gym and get a seat before the graduation starts. If they are standing, they will not see the graduates march in because my mom and grandma are too short. We march in with our white cap and gowns looking like a fleet of angels. All my friends and I are in the front of the processional with our gold honor sashes because honors students were in the front. I was so proud that I had smart friends. It was always a kind of friendly competitiveness with us to do well in school. It paid off. However, the last couple of years of high school. I could have done better, but I just did enough to get by. Everything going on at home distracted me from focusing on my future. Then, growing up going to the Kingdom Hall, we were always taught that the end of the world is coming any day now so we need not put too much focus on the future, including education. Secular education was frowned upon. No one really encouraged you to get a four year degree. My mama wasn't a Jehovah's Witness but she kind of subliminally supported the teachings in raising us and that was the only place of worship we had ever attended. We never celebrate any holidays or birthdays. So, everything was just traditional religious practices because my grandma was a Jehovah's Witness.

Graduation was so emotional because I am really going to miss my school and what I had known for the past several years. Many of the people that used to bully me when I was younger, suddenly became the people that wanted to associate with me in high school. Guess it was because I dressed a little better after I started to work and buy my own clothes; but I found good in all of them despite what they used to say and do to me. I will miss all of them, too. We marched out in order of the honor students first and we were in alphabetical order; so I was near the front because my last name is Devine. When we reach the foyer to exit the gymnasium, I am greeted by my daddy and loud abrasive language. In front of everyone he says, "why the fuck didn't you tell me that you were graduating today?" " I had to hear it from my best friend because his daughter is graduating with you." " You know you are a real stupid mutha fucka." "I should beat your ass right here." " Then, I was late because I didn't know what time the graduation was so I missed it; me and your step-mama are just getting here and it's over." "You know you are a real stupid knucklehead." Then he grabbed my arm and snatched me. All eyes were on me. It was like he was yelling through a megaphone and everyone was quiet, dead silent. When he stopped talking people were looking at me, anticipating a reply. I didn't say a word. I did not invite him to my graduation. He already embarrassed me a couple of months earlier by calling me a whore in front of a lot of people. Now, he is embarrassing me at my high school graduation in front of the entire town. This is the only public high school here so everyone is here. I am so humiliated. If he didn't grab me, I would have acted like I didn't know who he was and that he wasn't talking to me. I'm good at ignoring people. Then suddenly I get a shove from behind and I look back and everyone is piling up behind me. The other students were yelling, "go, go." "Who is holding up the line?" When they realized it was me, everyone started saying, "Leia move, get out of the way." I walked away from him, went to the raggedy yellow buick he bought me, and cried my heart out. This was supposed to be a day of celebration and he ruined it for me.

Chapter Seven: Your Suffering Don't Mean Nothing to Me

I have found a couple of people at USM from Lafayette that attended high school with me. Two of my childhood friends and classmates also attended. Tasha and Shemeka were actually cousins; we attended school from elementary through high school together. We didn't hang together in high school as much as Necy, Arlicia, Erica, Judy, and I. Actually, Judy, Erica, Arlicia and I were all in the band, the same social civic club, and dated a group of friends. So, we spent more time together than Tasha and Shemeka. Nevertheless, it was good to be around some people that I was cool with. I felt a culture shock being at that school.

Considering that I attended an all black high school and graduated with all black classmates, I felt so out of place being in an environment of about 40% blacks. I had exposure to other races that my friends did not experience. Being in the gifted class in school afforded me the opportunity to mingle with the white gifted kids from the other white elementary school in Lafayette. The district only had one gifted teacher and she was split between our two schools. We had gifted class events and trips together so I got to get to know some of them unlike many of my friends. Even though it was in the 1990's there was still a black elementary school and a white elementary school there. Majority whites lived on the north side of town and almost all blacks lived on the south side of town. The children in the school district attended school closest to their homes. Our town was still unconsciously, habitually segregated. People were conditioned to understand that we did not belong in the white neighborhood or white schools and few tried to comingle. After the 8th grade, those white children left public school and attended private school so that they did not have to attend high school with black children. Of course all white families could not afford to send their children to private school. I learned from a younger co-worker, Haley, that worked with me at Clover's Food Mart, that she, like other white teenagers, worked to earn money for school. Some white owned businesses would allow some children under 16 years old to work there to earn money to pay for a private education to prevent them from having to attend Lafayette High School with us blacks. None of my friends' families were Jehovah's Witnesses either. We had a mixed congregation of blacks and other races of people that attended the Kingdom Hall so I had some exposure there as well; but consistently attending school and living around whites was unusual for me. Not bad, just unusual. I had to get accustomed to it.

Meanwhile, I was dropped off at school with my stuff by my mama and her husband. That Buick my dad bought was in too bad of shape to take to school, so I had no car. Tasha did not have a car either so we depended on Shemeka to take us to Wal-Mart and to run errands. I was so uninterested in school. I was homesick and even though I was not in love with Devonte, I still missed his companionship. I hated the cafeteria food. We had a lot of choices but all of it seemed disgusting to me. I started feeling sick all the time. Certain smells make me nauseous. I talk to Devonte everyday and he wants me to come home every weekend but I can't because I'm over a four hour drive away. My mother never came back to visit or pick me up so I had to catch a ride with others whenever they were coming back home. He assured me that he was being faithful and waiting for me.

    I noticed that my period was late again this month. I was taking birth control inconsistently so I think I made it irregular last month and missed it all together. I was glad to learn to manipulate my period because I hated it. Taking the pills at certain times would delay it or make my period come on when I wanted it. However, this month it felt a little different. I told Shemeka about it and she suggested that I take a pregnancy test. I have not had sex in a month since I've been at school so I know I couldn't be pregnant but I will take a test for argument's sake. Tasha, Shemeka, and I went to Fred's Dollar Store near the University and purchased a test. When we got back to campus, we all went to Shemeka's room to hang out. I went to the restroom and took the test. I placed it back into the box and brought it back into the room with me without reading the results. Tasha pulled the test out and said its two blue lines. Shemeka gasped. I said, "we don't even know what that means so be quiet". I got the instruction insert from the box and read aloud, "two blues means pregnant". I couldn't believe it, again. If it were correct, that would mean that I was pregnant this summer before I left for college. I was happy but nervous. I knew Devonte wouldn't do me the way Bud did me. He would be by my side. I called him and told him immediately. Just like I expected, he was excited for me. I schedule an appointment with the clinic not too far from the university here in Mercy, Mississippi.

    After my appointment that Friday, I returned home with my sonogram results to show Devonte. While I was there, his mother came home from work and we told her that we were expecting. She was not excited like she was about Shantella's baby. Then she said, "you did that purpose because that other girl has a baby with him. You need to take your old ass back to school." I did not get pregnant on purpose. I was not trying to get pregnant but I wasn't trying hard not to get pregnant either. I really was glad to have an opportunity to have someone to love me. I know that my child will love me and I will love it no matter what. I will not be subjected to the things my parents did to me or deny him love like I was. I'm not copying or competing with Shantella. Dorothy has me mistaken; but I couldn't understand why she didn't feel like her son may have gotten me pregnant. Why is the girl always the blame for pregnancy? He actually did want to get me pregnant. As a matter of fact, he said it numerous times; but it's my fault.

    Over the next few months, it was difficult being in school making the long walks across the huge campus to class and being severely ill from morning sickness. I couldn't keep anything down, I hated the food, and I didn't have money to buy anything outside of my meal plan at school. At my last doctor's visit, he said I had lost 30lbs and that I needed to start gaining some weight. To make matters worse, the long pretty black hair I had, had all been shaved off. I dyed my hair blonde and permed it later. It broke off so bad, that I just had to cut it all off and start over. I looked really bad; skinny, bald headed, and pimple faced from the pregnancy. However, Devonte said that he still loved me and our unborn child every weekend I got to come home.

Erica called me one week that I was at school and asked me if he and I were still together. She said that a younger boy that attended high school with us was in a fight in Stevenson, Mississippi about 7 miles north of Lafayette; and Devonte and some of his friends were with him. "Apparently, the boys from our town were fighting with the boys from their town because our boys were dating girls from their school and the boys in Stevenson didn't like that." "Supposedly, Devonte is messing around with a girl from there." "I also heard he was sleeping with Felicia." "You need to check on that story about Felicia because everybody in town be getting on her."

I couldn't hang up the phone fast enough to call him. I didn't come right out and ask him about the women because I knew that if I did he would probably lie. I strategically asked if he had been in a fight first to get him to talking about the situation. "I heard Tony and some guys for Lafayette got to fighting with some guys from Stevenson." " Have you heard about that?" He started singing it all, " yeah, man". "Those niggas thought they were going to jump my boy Tony; I wasn't going." I said, "I'm glad you were there to help him; you're a good friend." "Why did they get into it anyway?" He said, "cause my nigga came and took their girl". I said, "you know I have some family that lives there so I know a few people there, who is his girlfriend?" "He talks to a girl named Rhonda." Then I said, "yeah, I heard; so which one was for you?" There was a long pause. Then when he started to speak I cut him off and said, " before you lie, I already know who she is so please don't lie". I knew nothing but he didn't know I didn't know anything, but I'm about to find out now. Then the excitement in his voice was lost as he said, " well, I'm just friends with her and she is Rhonda's friend." Then I yelled, " who is her!" He said, "Angelic, but it's nothing, we're just friends, that's all". Then I asked, "well, what about Felicia". "I know she's no man's friend; I know what she does and what you are doing talking to her?" His reply was, "she's been trying to have sex with me, I don't want her. I told her that I was in love with you". I went off. "I'm off at school pregnant with your baby and you out here fighting over other chicks and sleeping with another." "When I get back to town, let any of that stuff still be going on, I'm beating everybody's butt." He assured me that he would cut it off.

    I had another doctor's appointment today but I didn't have much money for a cab. It's about a seven mile walk to the clinic from my dorm. I'm going to walk half way, about three and a half miles to the gas station and call a cab from there to take me the rest of the way. The other girls I know are in class that could give me a ride and I'm not dealing with Shemeka anymore. I always gave her gas money when she took us anywhere, but then she started to take advantage of it. I lived in the upperclassmen dorm because I registered late so I had a kitchen in my dorm. Everytime I cooked she came over, ate like a pig, and took a plate to go. I never charged her. I didn't have parents to send me money like her and Tasha did and I didn't have a job. I started talking to the girls whose hair looked really bad at school and told them I knew how to do hair. I did hair in my room and earned money to buy grocery and laundry detergent for myself. Then Shemeka would come and eat all of my food up and never offer a dollar or wash a dish. When I asked her to take me to the store or to the doctor she charged me $10. That was more than the five we initially would give her. If Tasha and I and maybe Tasha's roommate would go or other girls, she would charge us all $10 each. She could make $40 off a ride to Walmart but wanted our homework answers and cooked meals for free. The last time I had to go to the doctor, I didn't have money and she said, "no money, no ride". I was done with her. I walked all the way to the clinic that day at five months pregnant. I would rather walk than have someone belittle me like that or have to owe someone anything. After I finished my appointment and came outside it was raining. Ugh. I should have checked the weather. I walked back to the gas station over three miles in the rain and called my cab to get back to my room. I'm soaking wet.

    I've developed regular customers now, so I'm making pretty decent money. After class on Tuesday nights, Tasha walks with me to the grocery store. She stopped riding with her cousin Shemeka as well for the same reason. Everything we need is pretty much on the street Carter Road where the University of Southeastern Mississippi is located. Restaurants, convenience stores, and pharmacies. My clinic actually is also just much further east down the road. West on Carter Road is where the other things are and where Tasha and I walk. I would keep my knife in my pocket and walk there. The west side is the hood. This particular Tuesday, Tasha can't make it because she has a group project so I walk alone in the dark. I cross the highway where the road intersects and get some Taco Bell to eat. I ate in, alone, because I knew I was going to buy groceries afterwards. Then, I walked to the AGI grocery store to shop. After checking out, I had too much to carry so I wobbled about half a mile back toward the campus and stopped at a Dollar General store to buy something to put all of my grocery bags in. I placed my bags on the sidewalk outside of the door because I didn't want the employees to think I was trying to steal. As I looked up, I saw a couple, a young black girl and her black boyfriend looking at me. I was so happy; I found a garbage can with wheels on it. I'm heading to check out.

    The couple was checking out in line in front of me. I noticed the girl looking at me and whispering to her boyfriend. I wanted to buck my eyes and say, "got an eye problem and roll my eyes". It's so rude to stare at people but I didn't say anything. I sure was thinking it though. After checking out, I took my garbage can outside and picked all of my grocery bags up and placed them inside. It was a perfect idea and perfect fit. Then I was on my way dragging the full garbage can behind me and pushing the big five month pregnant belly in front of me. It was pitch black outside; only the street lights and headlights lit the way. I was about a mile from the campus now and at a stop light I saw the couple, again. The girl rolls her window down and asks if they can give me a ride somewhere and if I attended school at the university since I was walking in that direction. I said, " yes, I attend school at the university but no thank you, I'm almost there; I really appreciate it though". Then she said, "are you sure?" "We saw you at the store, you have a lot of stuff, you're really big and pregnant, it's cold and dark, you're alone, it's not safe out here and you have to cross the highway to get back to campus." "I just want to help you; I felt sorry seeing you struggle like that." I smiled and said, "oh, that's really nice of you but I'm okay, I walk down here and shop all the time; I just bought too much this time." "But I really appreciate your offer and I have some protection in my pocket too but thanks anyway." She reluctantly said, "okay", and they drove away. I don't trust anybody, not even women. If I had gotten in that car I may not have gotten back to campus.

I remember when I was five years old, the lady that worked at the bank that gave my money to my mama's husband, her niece babysat me one day along with the lady from the bank's son. He was six years old. Her niece was called Strawberry. Strawberry asked me if I could do splits first then asked if I put my legs over my head. When I put my legs over my head, she grabbed both of my legs and held them over my head. Then, she had her six year old cousin pull out his penis and rub it between my legs. Then while still holding my legs, told him to lie on top of me and grind on my genital area. Thank goodness I was wearing pants but I know women can be perverted too. Strawberry taught me that. So, I definitely didn't trust that kind speaking helpful girl and her boyfriend. I have fought a lot in my life. I might be able to take one of them out but two of them with this big belly was a losing fight and I wasn't going to take a chance. I'm walking the rest of this dark, cold mile alone.

This weekend I went home and I'm at my grandma's house washing dishes when I hear the doorbell. It's four of the Jehovah's Witnesses out in field service stopping to see my grandmother. They all came in and greeted me while waiting on my grandma to put on her bra. My grandma never wore a bra at home. She was heavy chested and was uncomfortable wearing bras all day. She talked briefly and told them that she would meet them outside, they exited the house, and returned to their car. When she emerged, she went outside to the car to take them something and finish the conversation. Sister Alice Peoples doubled back and came back in the house to talk to me while I was alone. She said in her sweet voice, "hey baby, how are you doing?" "You look so good; give me a hug." "What are you doing here?" I replied, "I'm just home from school for the weekend". Then she said, "let me ask you something, who is your baby daddy?" I was dismayed and unnerved at the nerve of this lady to ask who I was pregnant by. I did not respond to give the opportunity to redeem herself and take it back or get out of my grandma's house. Oh, but she did not. She repeated it. "Did you hear me?" "Who's baby are you carrying?" I responded, " you don't know him". Then she tried to force compliance by offering a name, "is it Dorothy's son?" I responded again, "like I said, you don't know him". I refused to answer. When my grandma came back in the house, I told her what happened. Then she told me that Alice had been visiting Dorothy and discussing my relationship with Devonte. My grandma said that Alice was adamant about finding out the paternity of my unborn child so that she could convince Dorothy to have me arrested. I told my grandma in disbelief, "you meant to tell me that these are christian people?" "This lady used to study the Bible with me, why would she go so far to try to hurt me about something that's not her business?" "I'm not a Jehovah's Witness, Devonte is not a Jehovah's

Witness, and his mama Dorothy is not a Jehovah's Witness so why is Alice in the middle of this?"

    The following month in December, I returned home from school. I don't plan to return to the University of Southeastern Mississippi. Then my baby is due in the Spring, so I won't be returning for that reason either. I'm at Devonte's house most of the time. His mother asked me to come over more but when I'm there she acts like she has some resentment toward me. Shantella comes over all the time. Making up excuses just to try to make me uncomfortable. She tells everyone that I got pregnant on purpose and says that it's not Devonte's baby. Devonte works at Clover's Food Market now. My ex, Bud, still works there also. Now, it's beef with Shantella and I and Bud and Devonte. Everyday, I hear a new story about something Bud has done to Devonte because he still loves me. I never told Devonte but Bud did call me one day and say that he didn't care that I was pregnant and he would fight for my love and to have me back. I told him to leave Devonte alone. I left him because of him, way before Devonte came in the picture and there was nothing he could do to get me back. I told Devonte to ignore Bud and make his money because we have a baby on the way. He did not listen, almost got in a fight and lost his job.

    Necy, Leslie , and their family threw me a baby shower a few months later. Their family treated me as if I was a part of their family. They really went all out. It was the first time in my life that I had people to really show up for me. Devonte was there also. My mother and grandmother showed up with a gift but with the gifts from Necy and Leslie's families, my friends, and members of the social civic club, I was loaded. For once, I did not feel bad about not having the support from Devonte's family. My son was born the next week. Dorothy, Devonte, and my mama were there. I really believe that Dorothy was there just to see what the baby would look like and possibly dispel some of the rumors or get some truth. She looked at my baby and said, "he is mighty light skinned". I just said, "yeah he is".

It was interesting to me that Shantella's baby looked nothing like anyone in their family but she gave her baby his name. Dorothy has known him and me to be together in a relationship but questions my child solely on hearsay. Now, I'm not what they call high yellow but I'm not dark. Dorothy is biracial. My dad is biracial.Devonte took his complexion from his dad but our child could have been light or dark. It doesn't matter, because my son was light skinned did not mean it was not his son. Devonte and his mother fought all the time about her comments about our baby. She had nothing to do with him. She would get Shantella's baby, bring him to her house, keep him over the weekend, and give Shantella money but never acknowledged my son as her grandson. My baby and I would be in the house and she would walk right past us as if we did not exist. Finally, it all came to a head one day when I asked her what it was going to take for her to accept my child. Then she said, "when we get a DNA test." "I heard you were messing around with your ex, George, the superstar football player, and that's his baby." "He is light skinned and tall just like that baby looked when it was born, light and long." I told her, "ma'am, I heard that same allegation from Shantella that George was supposed to be my baby daddy; I can't believe you deny your grandson over something a child says. She can't tell you who I've been sleeping with just like I can't honestly say who she has slept with." "Well, I'm not sure who you thought I was, but first of all, I don't sleep around like that." " Second of all, George is my ex, but everyone I date, I don't sleep with." "He couldn't possibly be my baby's daddy because we never had sex." "I would be glad to give you a DNA test and prove all of you all wrong but I suggest you get one done for Shantella's baby, too." " Can't you see that you are hurting your son, yall fight all the time because you care so much about a child that he doesn't claim and you deny a child that loves so much." "You really need to check who's side you are on."

  I returned to school the following semester at a local university. I attend classes Tuesday and Thursday. I am a substitute teacher in Lafayette school district Monday, Wednesday, and Friday. This particular day, I was called to substitute at the high school, and Shantella attended that school. I was apprehensive about going and I prayed that I was not assigned to any of her classes or her friends' classes. While in class one of her friend's friends started a conversation in the classroom about Shantella and Devonte. I did not say a word. I knew that if I did not say anything it could not be used against me. The girl was really trying to provoke me to say something by stating that Shantella says that I was jealous because Dorothy and their family doesn't accept my child. Then, I asked her to be quiet about people's personal business and their children. School was not the place to discuss things like that.

During the last class period of the day, the principal came over the intercom in my class and asked me to stop at his office before I leave for the day. When I entered his office, he walked me to the conference room where I was confronted by three students, Shantella, and her mother. The principal said, "it was reported to the office that you were discussing this young lady and her child in the classroom; apparently you both share that same baby daddy." Shantella's mother replied, "no they don't because she is a whore and don't know who her baby daddy is." Shantella and her friends started laughing and Shantella told her mama to calm down. I responded, "I did not say anything about her or her child." Then her friend Demetruis said, "yes you did I was in the classroom and I heard you." The other girls concurred and said, "we heard her too". None of those girls took not one of my classes that day. Before I could respond again, the principal said, "you must have said something because her teachers for other class periods called the office and said that she was in their classes crying and was sent to the office". "She wouldn't be crying for nothing." I replied, "but sir, there was one little girl in the class that brought up Shantella and I did not respond; I asked her to quiet. You can ask the class, don't take my word for it." "That was it." He said, "well why would these kids do that far to be crying and lying on you if you didn't do anything." Shantella's mama said, "Leia needs to be fired because she doesn't need to work at a school with kids and she is messy like that; I want her fired." The principal dismissed everyone except me. As they exited the door Shantella looked back at me and smiled and her friends looked at each other and laughed. The principal talked to me. He said, "he wasn't going to fire but he had already talked to the superintendent because the mother had called the superintendent prior to meeting with him and I needed to go talk to him for him to render a decision about the situation."

When I went over to talk to the superintendent, he listened a little more than the principal. After all it was my high school principal that had several meetings with me during my senior year about the same stuff. The superintendent said that after hearing the situation, to make the parent happy of Shantella, he would recommend that I was not called anymore to substitute at the high school. He was not firing me but banning me from the high school. I was never called for another substitute job that year at any school in the district. When people heard of that, they didn't want to call me because they wanted to avoid trouble. I just cried. That cut into my money. I broke down, went to the Office of Human Services and got on Food Stamps. This girl was trying to destroy my life.

I did not dislike her at first because I understood that she felt like I was the reason Devonte wasn't there for her, but now is a couple of years later. Her baby is here, his family loves her and loves her baby, she should have just left me alone. Now that she is relentless in trying to destroy me, I really don't like her. I'm fed up. That was the last straw for me. Erica called me this particular day and said that her and her boyfriend were at Devonte's house. Her boyfriend was Devonte's friend. She said Shantella came in the house and said in front of them, "Leia's ugly baby ain't Devonte's, that's why none of his family claim her baby". Even though Shantella had said that same thing plenty of times before, I knew she said it in front of Erica so that she would come back and tell me. That was it for me. I drove right over to Devonte's house and caught her walking out of the house. I said, "what did you say about my baby?" Before she could get it out, I punched her in the mouth. I kept punching until I had her on the ground. My hair had grown back long so she pulled my hair, but I kept punching. I was not angry about that immature comment. It was the culmination of all the lies on me, the destroying of my reputation, and now costing me my job and my ability to provide for my child when she had Devonte's family. I had no one. We fought until the police arrived and arrested me. People just stood around and watched. Devonte forbade his mama from stopping me because he said Shantella deserved it and she had it coming.

I knew this town had nothing but trouble to offer me so I called my best friend Necy, who was at Johnson State University and told her that I was coming to school there. I researched what I needed to do to lease an apartment in University City, if I wasn't 21, and it was to become emancipated. With the money I saved, I hired an attorney, scheduled a court date with the judge and asked my mama to meet me there. My mama showed up with my grandma and relinquished her rights to me. I became emancipated at 19 years old. I got my income tax return and Necy and I got an apartment together.

Devonte said he wanted to come with me. I told

him that he had to work or go to school. Everyday, I went to school full time and worked full time at a department store. Necy and I worked at the same place, so we made our schedules alternating so that one of us could be available to take care of my son when the other was at work or in class. It worked out perfectly. Each night I got home from a long day of work and school he would be lying around waiting for me to cook and have sex with him. When I refused, he started accusing me of cheating. I wasn't cheating. A person that does nothing and had nothing to contribute, could not understand that I would never have the energy to sleep with someone that does nothing for me. I told him, "I'm not sleeping with anyone else but how do you expect me to be attracted to someone that is wearing the same gray sweatpants when I leave in the morning and when I get back at night". "All you do is watch my tv, play my PlayStation, and eat my food." "You're not babysitting because that is your son." "You can't babysit a child that belongs to you; but I pay for the baby to go to daycare everyday and Necy and I take turns picking him up." " What do I need you for?" "I'm not sleeping with anybody else, if I was you would not be here because you serve me no purpose?" "You have one more week to go looking for a job or try to get into somebody's school." "If not, I'm going to take you back to Lafayette to drop you off with your mama because I am only raising one child and I don't need anybody to watch my tv for me, I can watch it for myself. Goodnight."

The following morning, I guess the conversation front the previous night troubled him. He said, "I see how you're dressed when you leave here, I know it's somebody". I said, "no it's not and I'm not about to get into this before I go to work". "I ordered you some pizza and here is the money to pay the delivery man when he gets here; I'm gone." Devonte took the money from my hand and threw it back in my face. It angered me so bad, I punched him in the jaw. Then he punched me in the jaw. We went blow for blow as if we were in a boxing match. Then, I charged into him like a football player and we fell into my glass end tables and broke the glass. I kept punching him in the face and he kept punching me everywhere. Then he grabbed me in a bearhug really tightly and said, "stop, I don't want to do this" " I love you." I got up, wrapped my broken bleeding finger nail in a paper towel and got my purse. Then I said to him, " guess you thought I was a punk." "Did you think you would throw money in my face and that's it?" " I will fight your ass every time; don't ever try me again." "Don't ever even look at me like you want to put your hand on me." I was tired of people in my life taking advantage of me. I was tired of being a victim. I was going to fight for myself for a change. At the end of the week, I dropped his butt back off at his mama's house with his stuff and those gray sweatpants.

  Over the next several months all I got was phone calls and voicemails of him threatening to kill me one moment, then professions of his undying love the next. Then, he used visitation with our son as an opportunity to see me and fight with me more and more. Almost every time we met to exchange the baby, I got a push, a slap, punch in the face; but he was met with a push, a slap, and a punch in the face right back. I even started to carry a pocket knife. I called it my pocket machete because of how large and sharp the blade was. I definitely would give him a run for his money with every fight. However, I knew that despite how good of a fight I gave him back, men are naturally stronger than women and if he ever got the best of me, I would fillet him like a Delta Pride catfish. I had always been a person to never go down without a fight. I never started trouble with others but I subliminally welcomed the fight because it allowed me the opportunity to release the anger, aggression, and resent from the afflictions of what other people had done to me that I could not defend. The whipping I gave to a person today was just pent-up punches, kicks, stomps, and bites meant for someone else that probably did me worse.

    One day, he went to the extent of following Necy and I on our way back to University City and tried to run us off the road, with our son in the car. When we stopped by to pick up my son, I was dressed in a red short sleeve blouse, fitted jeans, and red stiletto shoes. Apparently, I looked good to him because he immediately started rambling about I better not have his son around any other guys. Reading between the lines, I felt like he assumed that because of how I was dressed, I was going to be with a guy when I returned. Because of my lack of response, that incited fury in him. We pulled off with Necy driving and he hopped in his mother's car and followed closely behind. He followed us for about 10 miles down the highway. We stopped because Necy had to stop by her house to pick up something from her parents before I returned. I asked her, "do we have to stop?" " You see he's behind us and I really don't feel like fighting today." She said, "I don't think he is going to try to fight you at my house."

I said okay. When we pulled up in her driveway, I noticed that he slowed down and stopped along the street in front of her house. As she got out to go in the house, simultaneously, he was walking up to the passenger side of the car by me. At that moment, I thought about locking the door.

When I went to reach for the lock, he pulled the latch and opened the door with one hand and grabbed a handful of my hair with the other hand. He drug me from the car by my hair with what seemed to be supernatural strength and speed. I didn't even have the opportunity to grab a hold of anything. I landed on the ground. My back met the hard, bumpy concrete driveway and his fists repeatedly met the top of my head. While I was falling out of the car, one of my red stiletto heels came off. It was only attached by the strap hanging around my ankle. I almost didn't feel the blows to my head because my focus was on diligently getting that shoe from around my ankle. I got it. I'm ducking and covering my head to block the licks with my left arm as I scramble to get up from the ground. Then, I turn around and charge into him like a bull, unfazed and numb to the punches that are now to my face. I lit into his face and head with the heel of that red stiletto shoe like a hammer on a nail.

Now, he's the one trying to block my blows because the tables have turned. By this time Necy's cousins that were playing nearby, have spotted us and run over to separate us. One of them went in to get Necy. She eventually comes out of the house and gets in the car. She said, "I'm so sorry", as I got in the car. Her cousins let him go when I got in the car. I thought I was over. Then, I felt the wind blow against my cheek as the door swung open again. I'm so disappointed at myself for forgetting to lock the door again but I thought it was over. I grabbed the side of the door only to be met with him slamming my hand in the door. The door bounced back open and as he was running alongside the car backing up, he slammed it on my hand again. Necy turned and the door shut. We continued to drive but he did not follow. Her mom called her cell phone to check on us and to deliver the news that he was still at their house. Apparently, his mother's car ran out of gas just as he approached Necy's parents' house. As their conversation continued, I drifted into my own mind. I finally started to inspect my body for wounds from this altercation. I have a few knots and bruises on my face. I looked down and noticed a hematoma lump emerging on my hand from being slammed in the door. He seemed to be trying to physically destroy me.

My reputation he tried to destroy as well, just like some of the others in my life. He told people in our hometown that I was a stripper and a prostitute in University City. He said that I was sleeping with everyone and that he would take custody of our son from me. After that last fight, I did not see him or talk to him. I ignored his calls. Three months later, he calls and I finally answer. He says he finally got a good job and he has gotten himself together. He said, "this is what you told me I had to do for us to be together and I did it now can we work things out?" I responded, " I'm sorry, time waits on no one." "If you knew I was waiting, you would have never made a move; I have moved on." "But I am glad you're doing something with yourself and now maybe you can set a good example for our son." I guess he forgot about the last fight or maybe he expected me to forget. Either way, I didn't care because I didn't want him back. I never loved him anyway.

About a month after that I put him on child support. He consented to the child support without contesting anything but his mother decided that before he should pay child support, we needed a DNA test. It's so interesting to me that these mothers are not present when their sons are having sex with women and making these babies, yet they have so much to say about paternity. I really wish she would learn to mind her business. That's precisely why this boy still behaves as a boy because his mama won't allow him to take responsibility and accountability for his actions or lack thereof. The next time I dropped off my child at her house, I told her a piece of my mind,"you want the DNA test, not the daddy." "But I will give you what you ask for so that you can finally accept my child."

When we were in court, the bailiff disseminated three pieces of paper to Devonte. He passed them to Dorothy and she opened them up and read each. Then she looked at me and said, "I'm surprised, the test said that he is the father". "I thought he wasn't my grandson." Then I saw Shantella and Felicia together and Dorothy said to Felicia, "I'm sorry for how I treated your baby, he's the father too." Shantella was smiling. Like she was so happy to know that our children had been deprived of their paternal family. I just walked away. I did not care what was on the third piece of paper.

Back about a year ago when I was living in University City, I got a phone call from Shemeka. I had not talked to her since college, so I wondered what she wanted. She called to tell me that she needed me to talk to Devonte and convince him to talk to her friend Felicia because he got her pregnant. Shemeka said, "I know you're a good person and Devonte won't listen to anybody but you". "He got Felicia pregnant now she completely ignores her. She said that he told her when they were sleeping together that you and him were still together but y'all were having problems because he had to get himself together." "He said after he got a job that y'all were going to get back together, so Felicia had to keep them a secret so she wouldn't ruin his chances of y'all getting back together." I said, "First of all, he and I were not together and I was not planning on getting back together with him." "Second, you mean to tell me you are calling on behalf of girl that thought she was creeping with my boyfriend but he wasn't actually with boyfriend, having unprotected sex with somebody else's alleged boyfriend, gets pregnant, then wants my help to convince him to be supportive to her when she thought he was still my man?" "Girl, you gotta be kidding me?" "Please get off of my phone?" " She messed around with someone else's man, got pregnant, and now wants the alleged girlfriend's help?" "She got what she was asking for. I could understand if he lied to her like he was not with anyone and he was." "But he lied to her like he was with someone but my feelings were not the same." " I actually heard about her a few years ago when he and I were together, I was pregnant, and at school." "She was trying him then, if they were not already messing around." "I don't feel sorry for

Felicia, I can't help her, and don't you call me anymore." I hung up the phone.

I got my butt back to University City as fast as possible. I was reminded of why I left Lafayette, too much drama. I had moved on with my life and was now pursuing my dreams. I finally had a purpose and a focus. I failed at Southeastern Mississippi and I failed at the college back home; but I was making a change in my academics here. I learned that the success of students in college is not solely based on academic abilities. I reflected on my life and realized that all the social, emotional, mental, and financial conditions bestowed upon me affected my ability to be successful. I was now ready to face them, overcome them, and complete my degree program. I loved living in University City. The friends that I hung out with the most my senior year, also attended school here too. So, I enjoyed being here with them. The next thing on my bucket list was to try out for a dancer in the band.

I practiced and exercised to prepare for tryouts. Then, the cold weather coupled with exercising outside without a coat, caused me to get a sinus infection. I had a fever, chills, and sweating. A few days after my fever went away, I felt better, but my legs started to get sore. I was so disappointed because I knew what was happening. After a fever, I almost always developed sore, swollen painful lower extremities, limited mobility and dark urine. This has been happening to me since I was 10 years old. The children at school used to call me hemorrhoid, when I had a flare up because they said that I walked like I had hemorrhoids. I would take a pillow to school to sit on because the desks would hurt my butt. My condition had progressed over the next few days and I could no longer drive; but I did not miss a day from class. I just moved a little slower and it took me longer because I was on crutches by then. I borrowed my friend's girlfriend's crutches. I had Necy to drive me to the clinic. They ran some tests on me, drew some blood, prescribed 800 milligram ibuprofen and sent me home to rest.

    Meanwhile, for some reason, it was on my mind to call my dad and make amends with him. I hadn't talked to him in a couple of years. I told him what my mama's husband did to me and that was why I had sex. I was just curious. I was not fast or promiscuous. My dad cried and apologized to me. He said, "why did you never tell me that?" " I never knew; I feel like it's my fault because if I was in your life none of that would have happened." "I'm coming to Mississippi and I'm going to kill'em." I told my dad no and that was not the answer now. I quoted Romans 12:19 to my dad *"Beloved, never avenge yourselves, but leave it to the wrath of God, for it is written, "Vengeance is mine, I will repay, says the Lord."* " This happened 13 years ago and there is no need to come here and try to avenge my honor. As of today, I have finally forgiven him." " I have forgiven him for myself, so that I can find closure, healing, and happiness in my life." "Daddy no more tragedy needs to happen, let God have his way." I really didn't know where those words came from because I never forgave him before this very moment. I hated him but now I actually felt sorry for him because I knew that he had to deal with someone far more powerful than me, God. My dad said, " you're right, and I'm so sorry. I want you to know that I will be here to protect you from now on." He said the infamous, "daddy love you". I said, "I love you, too" and actually meant it this time.

    The next day Necy and I are in the Union at Johnson State and I get a call from an unfamiliar University City number. I answered and it was the clinic asking me to come back for test results. Anytime the doctor calls you in for test results, it isn't good. We left right away and went to the clinic. They let me bypass all of the patients in the waiting area to go straight back to the doctor. The doctor asked had I been exposed to Hepatitis? I said no. She said that I had really abnormal labs to be so young and asked had I overdosed on Tylenol, taken any recreational drugs, or drank excessive alcohol. I said no to all of them. Then she said that the explanation she thought was that there was an error with their test and we were going to repeat them. Meanwhile, after the tests are complete here, I want you to go straight to the hospital's ER to be examined just in case they are correct. I have already sent your records over there and they will be expecting you. Then the doctor walked out. A few seconds later she ran back in and said, "Leia, please tell me that you did not take those 800 milligram Ibuprofen?" I replied, "no ma'am, I didn't take any". "Thank goodness!", she exclaimed. "Your liver enzyme count is way too high for you to have taken that Ibuprofen." "Your liver enzyme count and your CPK count are extremely high." "You could have died if you took them." " May I ask, I know you are in a lot of pain, but why didn't you take it or did you take some other pain reliever?." I responded, " I just got a feeling that I shouldn't take it this time." "I actually usually do take some pain meds."

"But for some strange reason, something told me not to take it this time and I didn't." " I just bear with the pain." The doctor said, "that strange reason you had just may have saved your life."

Necy and I left and went directly to the hospital. I told the receptionist my name was Leia Devine and she said, "we have been expecting you". They took me straight back. The nurse asked me to undress, put the gown on, and give her a urine sample. I had been in the restroom for a while when Necy knocked on the door and peeked her head in. "Hey, you alright?" " Why is it taking so long for you to pee in the cup?" I replied, "I know right, but I keep pushing and nothing is coming out." "Will you bring me some water to drink?" She returned with some ice water from the nurse in a University City Baptist Hospital cup. I drank as much as possible to try to induce some urine. It still didn't work immediately. Necy came up with the bright idea to turn on the faucet in the restroom. That worked! I yelled, "I gotta pee, now get out." She ran out in a hurry, waited a few minutes, and said from beyond the door, "pass it to me so I can give it to the nurse". She stuck her hand in through a crack in the door and reached for the cup of urine. When she got it, she immediately came back into the restroom and interrogated me, "what is this?" Then a white male nurse came in right behind her and asked, " is that your urine?" With a bewildered look on my face, I answered them both, "yes, that is my urine". Necy said, " man, it looks like coke or coffee; I've never seen pee that color before." " You're scaring me!" I said, "shoot, I'm scared too". The nurse came over and explained, " from her urine, it looks like her kidneys are starting to fail; that's why it took so long for her pee". Then, he held my urine sample up to the light and said, "I can see pieces of matter, protein and/or particles that could not be broken down floating around in the urine." " We need to start an IV and get her on some fluids asap!"

 I was admitted into the hospital. Necy picked my son up from daycare and took him back to Lafayette for my mother and grandmother to care for him. My friend Arlicia, Necy, Frankie, and Leslie came to visit me. A couple of girls from classes came to check on me, too. Surprisingly, a guy that Arlicia was dating came almost everyday to visit me as well. I remember us having a party at our house for the Southern Magnolia Bowl Classic game; and he got wasted. I took his keys and wouldn't let him drive home. We let him sleep on the floor with a blanket and pillow but we knew he was safe with us. I guess that meant enough to him for him to consider me a friend and be concerned about me. We only knew him from Johnson State and dating Arlicia; but the people I considered friends that Necy and I let move into our apartment periodically, did not come to check on me much at all. I learned a very valuable lesson then. When you're down sick, don't expect the people that you have been there for, to be there for you. On the contrary, the people that you may think you did the least for, just may be the people that support you the most.

 After Necy told my mom and grandmother, they came down to the hospital the next day. By the time they made it, my condition had deteriorated to paralysis and I was in extreme pain, constantly. I was swollen with fluid all over my body and no longer looked like myself. The doctor asked me if I had taken drugs, exercised excessively, or binge drank. I answered no to all of his questions because I hadn't. Then the doctor asked, "are you sure?" I responded, "yes, I'm sure; you can run all of the tests you need to confirm my answer. I have no reason to lie." He said, " I already have and we can't find anything". He took my mother and grandmother in the hallway outside of my hospital room and talked to them about my condition. He didn't want me to hear him but I did. "We have run many tests on Leia and they have all come back inconclusive." "She has liver inflammation, high CPK count, and renal failure. Right now, she is getting worse before she will get better." "I can't say if she will die or not; we're just going to treat her symptoms and keep her as stable and comfortable as possible." My grandma had the look of despair written all over her face. Even if I didn't hear what the doctor said, the look on my grandma's face said it wasn't good. Then, for the first time I could remember in my life, my mama told me she loved me. At 21 years old, it was so awkward and uncomfortable because she never said it to me. She was never affectionate, no hugs, or cuddling, which inadvertently made me the same way, hard. I was a hard, cold woman. I didn't want to be hard but I didn't know how not to be.

My mom left and came back to visit me once more. She called and checked on me but didn't visit anymore. My grandma couldn't drive, so she took a Greyhound bus and then a cab from the bus station to the hospital to stay at the hospital with me. She stayed almost my entire stay at the hospital. A month has passed now and I got a phone call from my younger sister and she was upset. She said she had an argument with her dad about a conversation she overheard between him and our mom. Apparently my mom was planning to come visit me and bring my child to visit me when he forbade her to come. He said, " you don't need to keep putting your new car on the road, putting all those miles on your car to see her". "If she's gonna die, she's gonna die. There's nothing you can do about that." "Don't mess your car up running down there every weekend; you have a new BMW." My sister said that my mama complied with his advice and didn't return to visit me. She got upset and confronted our mama, "that's your daughter, you can get another car, not another daughter." "Are you really going to listen to that mess that my dad is saying?" I believe that if my younger sister's twin brother was still living, they would be a force to be reckoned with. He was hit by a car and killed at 10 years old. She definitely has always stood up for me. She stands up for whatever she thinks is right regardless who it is. I actually wasn't really upset though because I had grown accustomed to my mama not choosing me. I was numb to the hurt.

    Now, it is month two that I have been in the hospital. I am getting shots in my stomach to prevent blood clots because I'm lying in bed all day everyday. It burns my stomach so bad. Then, I'm getting injections to get rid of this fluid retention. The medicine to reduce fluid retention is stripping my body of potassium, so I have to drink that nasty super sweet potassium. I can feel my heart skipping beats and palpitations; and my muscles are so tired that I can't even raise my hand or arm to brush my teeth or wash my face. I just lie there day after day. I'm getting so many fluids in the IV that every three days I have to get a new IV because I'm getting blown veins. My arms, hands, and wrists are sore and painted purple and blue from bruises of needles drawing blood every morning at 4:30 a.m. and old IV's. My grandma brushes my hair and she tries to hide the large balls of what used to be my long beautiful hair that are falling out but I can see it. Every few hours the nurse comes in and changes my bedpan and my urine drainage bag hooked to my catheter, checks my blood pressure, and temperature, gives me a bath and changes my hospital gown. The things that I once took for granted, I value so much now. Having the very private, intimate things that I used to do for myself like going to the restroom, taking a shower, and putting on my clothes taken away at 21 years old is so humbling and embarrassing. I never would have imagined that complete strangers would be wiping me. Everytime the nurse left I cried.

  Month three, still not no answers about my condition. It's 3:33 am and my grandma wakes up and sees me wide awake. She asks, "Leia, what are you doing awake?" " Are you having problems sleeping?" I answered, " No, I can't sleep. I'm tired." She asked, "tired, how? You're not doing anything." I said, "I'm tired of living. I have made peace with it now." "God, must have known that I was about to die because I made peace with my dad too, right before I was admitted into the hospital." "I'm ready to die; I'm tired and I can't do this anymore." " I want to die now." My grandma got upset. She said, "no Leia, you have to live for your child". "Do you want me to call Necy for you?" "Do you need someone to talk to?" I told her, "I already talked to God." "You don't understand, Necy

can't understand, I'm a young woman and I no long have a quality of life." "I'm lying here suffering as if I haven't suffered enough already in my life." " I just can't take anymore." "Then if I had cancer or something at least I would know what I have and some idea of how to treat it. You can't treat what you don't know. The doctors don't know what's wrong with me so they can't fix me." "I give up." My grandma called Necy anyway. I didn't say much more to her because my mind was made up.
I didn't sleep for a few more days. I had been refusing the pain medicine. I just lied there in pain, eating very little, waiting to die until my grandma told the doctor and he ordered the pain medicine which forced me to fall asleep. I slept so hard, I did not notice the nurses coming in to take my vitals and draw my blood. I slept through it all.

     When I did wake, the doctor was in my room to give me an update on daily blood work. "Your liver enzyme count and your CPK have gone down a lot but you still have a long way to go." " I'm gonna start you on physical therapy to gain back some mobility". "It will be simple things like learning to use your arms, learning to sit up, and learning to stand again." I ran track; who would've thought I would be learning to merely stand up. Life has a way of humbling you. Even though I had not become a Jehovah's Witness or lived primarily as a Christian, I wasn't a bad person either but the Bible teachings were embedded in me. I could recall scriptures relevant to almost any situation. What came to mind was when I would hear people say that "God was testing you" or " God was trying you to see if you were going to trust him". One of the nurses and the chaplain at the hospital told me that I was experiencing this because God wanted to see how I would act in this situation, would I rely on him. I didn't say anything in objection or disrespect, I just listened; but I remembered James 1:13 " *Let no one say when he is tempted, "I am being tempted by God," for God cannot be tempted with evil, and He himself tempts no one.* And I wondered, if God loved me, why would he do something so bad to me. God did not do this. If he didn't love me, he would have let me die when I prayed for it. Instead, He woke me each day and now He's helping my condition to improve.

    It's month four since I've been in the hospital and now I've progressed to going down to the therapist rather than them coming up to my room. That's the only time I can leave this room. I'm on a walker now. The therapist told me that I may be on a cane or walker for the rest of my life. I told him, "I'm gonna walk out of here in my heels just like I was before I came here; I will not be on a walker." My grandma is still here with me in this prison. I really hate being in this hospital. Not because it's a hospital but because I just love being outside so much more. If I had my way and the world was safe enough, I would sleep outside if I could. That's how much I love the outside. I feel like I'm locked up. As I stared out of the window and watched the cars pass by I noticed the stores across the street. I told my grandma, "I'm gonna walk over to Fred's and buy myself some shorts and a t-shirt." "I'm tired of wearing this hospital gown." She snickered and said, "Girl, you must be losing your mind, too." " You can't leave the hospital and come back; and you have the IV in your arm." "They're not going to take that out for you to go shopping and come back." I laughed along with her and said, " oh, you're right." "I didn't even think about that; I'm just ready to leave this place."

I've been gaining more and more strength each day. My counts are still high but the doctor says that they are low enough for me to go home. Necy picks me up in my car from the hospital and takes me back to our apartment. I haven't seen this place in a while, but I'm so glad to be home. Necy and I split the rent. Neither one of us have worked in a while but I pay my portion of the rent from my refund check from school. Necy gets help from her parents.

I still have a little money left so I'm going to call Chula Vista Motors, where I got my car and let them know what's been going on, that I've been in the hospital, and I'm going to send my payment tomorrow. Chula Vista is a little town about 5 miles east of Lafayette and it has a little mom and pop car dealership owned by this white man from there. I've heard that he likes to sleep with black girls and will give them a car with no down payment.

I remember when he propositioned me when I first bought my car, but I turned him down. Mr. Bob Hawkthorne, the owner, told me, "Leia you are a very pretty girl, if you do something for me, I can work something out for you to avoid a down payment". I tried to turn him down in a respectful way because he was old enough to be my daddy, "umm, no thank you sir, Mr. Hawkthorne", in a very timid voice. Then, he was very persistent, insisting that he could give me a really good deal. I continued, "I don't think that's a good idea sir; I appreciate the compliment and the offer, but I'll pass." He was relentless with his advances and even put his large pale hairy hand on my back and rubbed down to my butt. I stepped back and distanced myself from him.

    Finally, I was fed up with the back and forth and I put my foot down. I raised my voice very loudly and sternly, "Bob, all that you're going to get from me is this down payment, nothing more." "Don't you put your hand on me anymore." "I know what you must be used to but it ain't me." " I need a car and I have worked to save this money to get one." "I don't have any credit and I don't have any other options but I would rather leave here walking with my money in my pocket and my dignity in my pants, than to leave here giving you something I can't get back, a part of me." "I can't get me back if I give it to you but I can make some more money." "Now, are you gonna take this money or what?" " Cause that's all you're going to get." Bob looked at me with a face the color of red Hot Tamale cinnamon candy. Looked like his reddish blonde hair stood up on his head. I know as a young girl and black girl that I was way out of line for speaking to him like that. He sat down, filled out my paperwork, took my money, handed me the keys and told me, "you better not be a day late or dollar short, now get your car out."

    Now, that I have to call him to tell him I'm several days and several dollars short, I hope he forgot that conversation we had a couple of years ago. I called though. He was very polite. I explained that I had been in the hospital and would make a payment tomorrow; I would like to set up payment arrangements. He agreed. He said, "after we get your payment tomorrow we can discuss arrangements." I was relieved. Maybe I can start to rebuild my life and get back on track now. Since he is going to work with me, I'll just get my money order today and go ahead and drop it in the mail today.

I had Necy to call the university for me so that I could talk to my teachers while I was in the hospital. I need to maintain my grades so that I can get another refund check to pay my bills until I'm able to work again. Necy gave me a letter when I got home from the hospital. I opened my mail from Johnson State; it was a letter with my grades. Only one teacher gave me a "D". The others all gave me "F's". I was already on probation the prior semester because I wasn't doing well nor was I focused because of my own personal issues. They did not accept my doctor's excuses. I didn't understand how teachers couldn't believe I was hospitalized for over four months. Now, I've been suspended from school. I won't be able to get a refund check now. So I'll have to get well soon so I can get a job. I cannot go back to Lafayette. There's nothing but trouble back there for me.

The next morning, I had Necy to get up with me to take me in my car to fill out some job applications. I'm still not driving well yet because I'm not healed or strong enough yet. Necy takes me places in my car when I need to run errands. By the time someone hires me though, I should be getting around better and able to drive myself. When we go outside to get in my car, we can't find it anywhere. I called the University City Police Department to report it stolen because I just sent my payment and talked to Bob yesterday. This is a high crime area so I wouldn't be surprised if it's stolen. When I gave my address, name, and vehicle description, the police officer on the phone said, "ma'am, your car has not been stolen". "It's on our repo list, your car has been repo'ed." I said, "thank you sir", and hung up. I couldn't believe it! That man lied to me! I called Bob right away. When he answered, I said, "why did you repo my car?" "You told me that you would work with me because I had been in the hospital but you lied." I was frantic and crying. Then he answered in a calm voice, " "I know what you must be used to but it ain't me." Then he laughed. He used my own words against me, from when I refused to sleep with him. He continued, "Now you need something from me but you remember I told you little sassy girl, you better not be a day late or dollar short" . "So you can take your dignity and find yourself another car." Then, he hung up on me. I just broke down. I felt like there was one catastrophe after another. I flunked out of school, I have very little money left, I have no car, no job, and I can't go back home. I don't know what I'm going to do.

    I called my mama and asked to use one of her vehicles. She had a BMW and a Toyota Corolla; and her husband had his work truck and a Cadillac Escalade. So, four vehicles between the two of them. She told me that she had to ask her husband first to see what he said. Then, she reported back to me that her husband said that I was bad on cars and he didn't think it was a good idea to loan me one of theirs. Reluctantly, she loaned me the oldest car which was the Corolla. I was okay with that because I was just glad to have a ride again until I can get back on my feet.

    After a couple of more weeks, I was feeling better and able to drive myself around again. Then my mom dropped the car off to me. I drove around applying for jobs and leaving my resume in several places, hoping to secure a job soon. After I paid my portion of the rent and bills this month, I only have $53 left. I thank God that I have food stamps so that my child and I can eat. I no longer get child support because my baby daddy has gotten fired from his job again. I can't look forward to that support anymore. I heard that his mother helps take care of his namesake. I expected that, though. Devonte has even gotten with or gotten back with Shantella, never know what the truth is with his lying self; and they live with his mama. I heard she was pregnant again, too. It's not my business, I don't care either way but I do feel like if the grandma helps take care of one grandchild she should do the same for the other grandchild. For now, I'm going to stretch this money by only buying necessities to get me by each day. I'll drive only to necessary places to save gas. I don't know what I'll do next month if something doesn't come through for me soon. Then,I recalled a scripture, Matthew 6:34 *"Therefore do not worry about tomorrow, for tomorrow will worry about itself. Each day has enough trouble of its own."* That gave me some solace in knowing that as long as I focused on this day only and we can make it this day, then I have done as God has instructed me. I am learning that by following God's instruction, I am reducing undue stress and anxiety by trying to figure everything out on my own. Now, I will no longer try to figure out how I will manage next week or next month; just plan out the most resourceful way to use or not use what little money I do have.

      The next day, my mama called me and told me to go get the oil changed in her car. It cost me $24. While driving back to my apartment, when I stopped at the light, it looked like smoke was coming from underneath the hood. I needed to get it to my place so that I could look at it and diagnose from where it was coming. I had to push it and try to make it home because I did not want my son and I to be stranded on the side of the road. Thank goodness I made it back to the apartments but the car was smoking bad by then. Then I noticed the temperature hand was in the red so I knew it was the radiator. I didn't initially notice that. I asked Necy if she would take me back to the store to get some antifreeze to put in the car to fix the problem. When I got to the store, I got the cheapest one I could find. It was $8.68 cents. I scraped up some change to cover the cents so that I wouldn't have to break a dollar and it left me with $21. I put the antifreeze in the car to fix it but I did not move it again for another week. I moved it when I had to go to the store to buy my son some pampers. I got the smallest pack of the off brand pampers which were $5. Now, I'm down to $16 dollars. I'm starting to worry now because the week after next will be time to pay rent again and I have nothing.

      Necy has already started talking indirectly about my ability to pay my portion of the bills. I know what I have to do, I thought about it before she did. I did not need the sly comments about, "I'm not gonna pay everything by myself next month". People that never had to struggle or want for anything do not understand people that have to do everything on their own with no support. Necy hadn't worked in several months. Her parents paid her portion of everything for her necessities and she had her school refund to cover her wants. She couldn't empathize with my struggle and was so not understanding.

Chapter Eight: Old Bats and Young Cows Don't Give
    You a Break

When I least expected it, I got a call from a lady named Mrs. Strongfellow that owned a daycare center called We All Care located not too far from our apartment. She hired me as a teacher for the baby room. She called me to come in for orientation the following day. That job was right on time.

At orientation, she explained that I would have to wear scrubs to work, discussed the salary, explained that the daycare was a christian based organization, and that they upheld christian principles and values. I felt like this was another sign for me to draw closer to God. He had given me the gift of recalling scriptures at the right time and spared my life. Now, I've been blessed with a christian based job just when I needed it.

She continued with her discussion saying that we got paid every two weeks, payday was the following Friday and I would start on Monday which meant that I would only get paid for one week on that upcoming Friday. Then she handed me a form that outlined the christian principles and asked me to sign it in acknowledgement of them. I asked her if she had any vacancies for my son and she said yes and that she would deduct tuition from my check. He could start when I started. God had worked it all out for me.

My son attended her other center which was about a mile from the location that I worked. After dropping him off, she called me into the office on my first day and told me that her husband was often at the other location. She said, "just so you know, my husband and my daughter are off limits". "He has nothing. I own everything so if you think you're going to take him, you won't get anything." Then she asked when my birthday was. I said November 11th. Then she said, "oh, a Scorpio; I knew I liked you". "So am I; we will get along fine." I thought that was weird but I did not question anything because I was just glad to be working.

    I got paid and it was just enough to cover my portion of the rent with about $40 left to last me until the next two weeks. I made it to the next pay period though. After bills and gas, broke about even each pay period. I lived from check to check with nothing extra. I was okay at the moment because before that job, I had nothing. At least now, I did not have to worry about paying my bills. I started to hang around campus with Necy a little bit. I met a guy there named William and we started dating casually. My life had started to somewhat get back to normal.

    One day, while going to drop my son off at daycare before I went to work, the car started smoking a whole lot. I knew that I put some antifreeze in it so it shouldn't be running hot again. I got it to work but this time adding antifreeze didn't work. I left it there after work and got Necy to pick me up. We found a mechanic to come to the job and look at it for me. He said the hose in the radiator had busted and that the head gaskets were whopped from it running hot. That all equated to an expenditure that I could not afford. I finally called my mama and told her I had problems with the car. She got angry with me and said, "Stan warned me to not let you borrow one of our cars." " I should have known you would tear it up." I didn't say anything. She had a tow truck to pull her car back to Lafayette.

Then I called my grandma and asked her if I could borrow her car. She couldn't drive but when my granddad died two years ago he left her with two cars. I explained to her what happened to my mama's car. "Grandma, I can't burst a radiator hose; what did she think I did?" "Pull the hose out or cut it myself?" "That was bound to happen in an older car and my mama was just being unreasonable." My grandma said, "I know you didn't burst the hose; I understand". "You know how your mama is; she never wants anyone to touch her stuff." I'll let you borrow one of my cars. My grandfather died two years before and left my grandmother with a black Oldsmobile and a black pick-up truck. She let me borrow the Oldsmobile. She said, "since I can't drive, the cars are just sitting here anyway". "Somebody needs to drive them." She just told me to make sure I service it. Necy brought me back to Lafayette to pick up the car. My grandma always comes through for me.

Everything is going well for me over the next couple of months. For the first time in my life, I really like a guy. Chandler has made a profound impression on me. He is unlike any other guy I have ever dated. He is the first college educated man that I have dated and comes from a family of prestige. He works as a Public Relations Manager at his dad's law firm. His mother is also an attorney but his father is now a state representative and does not practice law very much anymore. Dating Chandler has motivated me to want to go back to school and pursue my dreams. Being with him makes me want to be better. My schedule consists of work, my son, and Chandler.

We mostly just go out to the clubs, he comes to my apartment and I to his, and I cook for him and we spend a lot of time together. Sex isn't great but I'm okay with it because I really like him. I'm actually not a very sexual person anyway. I've gone months without it and it's not a problem. I've often been at conflict with myself about fornication anyway. Despite all of the poor choices I've made in my life, my conscience always seems to convict me whenever I've done wrong. I know this is from a foundation built on God's principles by reading and hearing the scriptures. Knowing what's right and having the strength and discipline to do what's right is the battle though. Having the foundation means nothing without continuing to feed yourself spiritually and building upon what you have already learned. Another scripture resonated with me, Hebrews 5:13-14 *"Anyone who lives on milk, being still an infant, is not acquainted with the teaching about righteousness. But solid food is for the mature, who by constant use have trained themselves to distinguish good from evil"*. My foundation was just the milk and I had not matured and trained my conscience enough in God's word for it to bother me to the extent of doing right. That's why it was so easy to give into what a man wanted from me. I gave him what he wanted so that I could eventually get what I needed from him, love.

He wasn't as stellar as what I had heard his father was but he was very charismatic and professional and knew how to work a room. However, I started to notice a few subtleties that seemed familiar to men from my past. He had a few money issues sometimes, not offering to take me out on dates, never buying me anything, and showing up at the club when it was free to avoid paying to get in. Before long, I was borrowing money to help make ends meet for him but he appeared to have it all together. He never missed a social event, dressed to impress in a fifteen piece suit shaking the hands of mayors and councilmen and kissing babies. Nevertheless, I thought it was a temporary setback for him and I just wanted to be there for him to show my support. I wanted to show him that I was a good woman.

Then one day, the Oldsmoblie breaks down on my way to work. I called Chandler to come get me because I had always been there for him and it was now his opportunity to be there for me. Unfortunately, he didn't have gas money to leave work, pick me up, and get back to work himself. I called Necy again. She always comes through. However, this time she seemed reluctant to come. I always give her gas money or repay her by doing things for her as well like her hair but I guess she is getting tired of me now. She took me the following day as well. Later that night, I heard her on the phone with her cousin. She said she was tired of helping me and that I always needed something. I really appreciated her and she was right that I needed her a lot; but she also said that she had never seen a family like mine before that did not support me. She always called her family "my real family" because they were there for me more than mine was. Despite what I heard her say, I understood her perspective so I guessed that she and her family were finally tired of me.

Each day from then on, I would leave early for work and walk about two miles to my baby's daycare and drop him off. Then, I would walk another mile to the other daycare location and start my day at work. I just didn't want to be a burden to anyone any longer. So, I stopped asking Necy for rides to work. The walk wasn't very far anyway and considering what I had just overcome, I was glad to have the ability to walk. I sometimes got a ride offered to me by my coworker. A girl, nicknamed Smurf, who was a little person, worked with me as a teacher at the daycare. She was small in stature but had a big personality and a big mouth to match it.

On this particular Thursday, just like all other sunny afternoons, we were sitting on the playground watching the children play while we awaited their parents to pick them up. Mrs. Strongfellow's 12 year old daughter, Alana, was on the playground as well. I was sitting at the picnic table reading the newspaper when Smurf and Alana walked over and sat at the table to join me. Then Smurf said, "Leia is pretty, isn't she?" Alana said yes. Smurf continued, "this will be your new step mama", and started to laugh. I abruptly looked up from the paper and said, "oh no, don't play like that". "I would never even look at your dad like that." Alana got really upset. She started crying. Smurf was very nonchalant about Alana's reactions and continued facetiously pushing her idea of me being Alana's stepmother. I did not say another word. I just kept reading the newspaper because I wanted no parts in that conversation.

The child ran off. Then I told Alana, "you should not have said that to Mrs. Strongfellow's daughter; it makes me nervous". Smurf reassured me that she and Alana talk and joke all of the time. She said that she likes to get under the girl's skin because she is a spoiled brat. In my mind, I could agree that the girl was a spoiled, obnoxious kid but again I kept my opinion to myself. Alana went in and did not return. Smurf said, "maybe she is mad at me for saying that". "I just thought about it; I heard that Mr. Stringfellow cheated on his wife before with a teacher at the other center that your baby attends." Then I said, "well the child has good reason to be upset; I would be upset at the ideas of my dad cheating with my mama's employee again." "Can you please go tell her you were just playing, that I wouldn't do anything like that, and that I have my own boyfriend?" "Please fix it." "I don't want the little girl mad at me." Smurf went into the building to find Alana and tell her that she was just joking but could not find her. She had already left with someone. After all of our children were gone. Smurf gave my son and I a ride home.

The following morning, like usual, I walked my son to school then I walked to work. When I came in to sign in, Mrs. Strongfellow said, "good morning with your real pretty self". It was peculiar to say that but I just said good morning, thank you with a smile, and went on to my classroom. I didn't know what was so pretty about me. We wore scrubs to work. I wore mine two sizes too big because I did not want to give the impression that I was trying to tempt any of the fathers that picked up their children or Mr. Strongfellow. I am a curvy woman and I have experienced when men look at me, their women give me dirty looks and a hard time. So, I cover everything up. My hair is long but I wear it in a bun and I don't wear make-up to work. I'm just trying to get back on my feet and was not looking to give anyone a reason for confrontation with me. All of this is precisely why I could not understand the, "good morning with your real pretty self" comment.

At lunch time, the assistant director told me that she would take my classroom and to stop by the office to see Mrs. Strongfellow. As I walked down the hall, I got this real sick feeling that something bad was about to happen. When I walked into the office, sitting at the table was Smurf, Alana, Mrs. Strongfellow, and Mr. Strongfellow. Mrs. Strongfellow invited me to have a seat. She slid me a piece of paper and asked, "will you read that aloud if you know how, pretty girl?" I started reading, "This childcare facility operates on Christian morals and principles and any employee that violates these principles will be subject to suspension and/or termination" "Please adhere to the following Christian rules". I stopped reading and asked, "what is this about?" Mrs. Strongfellow said, "it's about what you two said to my daughter on the playground yesterday". I said, "I didn't say anything". Then she said, "oh, yes you did, just shut up." She directed her attention toward her daughter,"Alana tell us what happened." Alana started speaking and immediately crying, " Smurf said that Ms. Leia was going to be my new stepmother and that my dad was going to leave you for her". Alana sounded like a whining 5 year old in her proper voice. She attended a private school with 95% white children and did not seem to have a bit of color in her pesky voice. Alana just stretched the story out and added things to it that were not said. She continued, "and Leia said that she was going to come to our house when you were out of town at your other job and sleep in you and dad's bed".

Before I could respond, Mr. Strongfellow interrupted and said to me, "little girl, I would never date you, and how dare you say those things to my daughter". "I am happily married to my wife and would never even entertain the idea of someone like you; you are beneath me." Mrs. Strongfellow then said, "so from what I gathered you put your little friend, Smurf, up to trying to set you up with my husband through my daughter." " Well let me tell you something, my husband doesn't want you." "And just so you know, even if he did leave me for you, you wouldn't have anything, because these are my businesses, I am the breadwinner, and this is my money." "He works for me."

Then Mrs. Strongfellow slid Smurf a piece of paper identical to mine. Smurf read the paper to herself as she spoke up about the situation. She said, "I am the one that said that stuff and I was just playing with Alana." "Leia didn't have anything to do with it; she didn't say anything" " Alana is just lying and stretching the truth." "Mrs. Strongfellow you told me yourself that your daughter lies a lot and she is lying now." "I'm the one that was talking, not Leia and I was just playing." Then Mrs. Strongfellow said, "y'all had no business having a discussion like that and". Smurf cut her off as she continued to read the paper and said, "oh is this supposed to be a termination letter?" Mrs. Strongfellow said, " yes it is for the both of y'all, you can't work for me and behave like". Smurf cut her off again and threw the paper across the table and said, "y'all ain't no Christians but if I'm fired, bitch I'm not about to sit here and let you chastise me." "Since I am fired, I ain't gotta listen to this." "I told you Leia had nothing to do with it so you ain't gotta fire her but you just insecure cause this nigga cheated on your ugly ass before and you just use your money to try to keep him." "You and your ugly lying daughter can't take a joke." "I'm out of here; come on Leia".

    I did not look at Smurf and let her walk on out. Then I said in a soft voice trying to hold back my tears, "can I go back to work because as you heard, I had nothing to do with that conversation on the playground and I need my job." Mrs. Strongfellow said, "sign the termination papers and leave the premises now. Unconsciously, I did what she asked by signing the letter and hoping that if I showed an attitude of compliance, different from that of Smurf, then she would rescind the termination and let me keep my job. Then she yelled at me, "get out". While her daughter sat there and smiled at me. I walked out of the room slowly and they all followed me. Before I knew it, I did something so uncharacteristic of me. I turned around and fell down on my knees and grabbed the skirt of her dress. I could not hold back my tears and literally started to beg, "please Mrs. Strongfellow, I didn't do anything wrong". "I didn't say anything to your child." "I need my job, I just got out of the hospital, I have nothing, this job is all that I have." " I have no car, I have no help." "It's just me and my baby and I live paycheck to paycheck." " I have nothing to fall back on." " I have nothing." " Please, please let me keep my job." "Smurf told you, she told you it wasn't me." I cried and sobbed on the floor, pleading and begging for my job. Her and her husband stood over me and looked at me in disgust and pity, yet delight. It was as if they found satisfaction in my suffering and begging. Then the assistant director was prompted by my crying to come into the hallway. She picked me up from the floor and told me to go to the bathroom and get myself together. I went into the bathroom but I couldn't stop crying. I did nothing wrong. I went over in my mind how I could have changed the situation or what I could have done differently.

Then I heard loud banging on the bathroom door. It was Mrs. Strongfellow and the assistant director. I opened the door to Mrs. Strongfellow yelling again, " get your ass out of my business right now." She told the assistant director, "call the police on her, I want her gone now". I kept saying in a low voice through my tears, "I didn't do anything or say anything". Then she said, "Oh yeah, and if you think you're going to try and get me back by reporting that I'm out of compliance with my teacher to student ratio, or reporting me for anything, I have friends there and nobody can stop me." " They call me and warn me everytime y'all little bitches try to report me". "Get out!"

I went outside and sat on the curb. I was devastated. I just broke down and sobbed. Then she came outside and said, "I hope you know, the police are on their way because you're still on my property". "Leave the premises now." I finally left then. It was the longest walk home ever. I walked the mile to pick up my son from the other daycare location, before walking the additional two miles home. As we walked home, it started to rain. I saw her husband pass by me as I was carrying my son with a coat over his head trying to shield him from the rain. These people are the furthest things from christians. My walk home allowed me to think about all that had transpired. I started to feel so humiliated and ashamed of myself for not having any backbone. I couldn't believe that I groveled at this woman's feet for a job. I really needed a job; but more important to me was that I wanted to prove my innocence.

  Once again, in my life I have been misjudged solely on how I look. I know that was the case because she mentioned numerous times, "with your real pretty self". I know it was because of her perception of me that made me guilty. How I look does not mean I was interested in her man. It only means that how I look makes her uncomfortable when her man is around me because she is insecure. Truthfully, her man is old enough to be my daddy and he can't even be my sugar daddy because she's the one that makes the money, not him. Now, I have lost my job because this insecure woman can't pay her man enough to remain faithful; and every halfway decent looking woman in their vicinity is punished for it. What she should have done was divorce him if she can't trust him and set herself free; or forgive him and deal with her own personal troubles instead of destroying the lives of women that work with her. There will always be a threat and you can't fire us all, honey. This was just an opportunity for her to eliminate any competition. Only to her dismay, I was not in competition. All I was trying to do is eat and keep a roof over my child and my head each day. I wasn't even thinking about her man. She doesn't know what I've just overcome. Now, I don't know what I'm going to do. I don't know how I'm going to make it. I have to figure out how to eat because she can't figure out how to keep a man that doesn't want to be kept.

It's been about a month now since I have been unemployed. Necy is mad with me because I didn't have the money to pay my part of the rent this month. She says she's moving out soon because she finished college a few months ago, her parents were paying all of her portion of the bills, and it's time for her to pursue a career.. She's moving back home to Lafayette this summer to find a job in her degree. I didn't feel like she should have been mad with me for something out of my control. I didn't fire myself. She didn't understand the struggle because she never experienced struggle. Having a few broke days and not wanting to ask her parents for more money was not the same as not having and not having any help or support. I have no one to loan or give to me. I had to figure it out on my own. However, I did use the last of my check to pay my portion of the utilities. This is the first time we have ever missed paying rent and we won't be evicted before she decides to move out.

After about 3 more weeks, Erica hooked me up with a guy from Lafayette that lived here in University City who was the director of a daycare and he gave Erica and I a job there. William would take me to work some days and I would ride with Erica some days. Eventually, I had saved enough money to get my grandma's car fixed. So, I am back riding again. When

I'm off work I am spending more and more time with Chandler. I don't tell him that many days I spend my last few dollars to put in my gas tank to come see him. Seeing the caliber of man that he is and the status of his family, I felt like I needed to hide my struggles from him and act as if I was accustomed to association with people like them. Chandler never raised his voice at me and rarely cursed. It was the first time I experienced a real gentleman. For the first time, I dated someone that I desired to have a future with. He and his cousin, Greg, were roommates. I got the opportunity to meet his cousin's girlfriend and we became cool. It started to feel like I was becoming a part of the family.

Greg was a new attorney that worked at Chandler's dad's firm as well. They both would leave for work at the same time in the mornings. So when my son was back in Lafayette with his dad, I would stay some nights with Chandler. Today, I didn't have to work and coincidently, Greg's girlfriend Catherine stayed the night as well. When they left for work, we both were left there together. I hear a knock at the bedroom door as I just finished getting dressed and it's Catherine. "Girl, I just looked out of the window and they're gone." I said, "yeah I know". Then she said, "don't you want to look through his room and his stuff." I said, "no, I'm okay." "I don't go looking for stuff because I might find something and get upset and it may not be what I think." "If I'm meant to see something, I won't have to go looking for it." Catherine said, "well, I go through everything, everytime he leaves me here". "I'll look through Chandler's room for you if you want me to." I said, "no that's okay". Then she asked for my phone number and reluctantly I gave it to her. She started calling me after that telling me about her visits to the firm and outings with Chandler's family and asking why I wasn't there. I would make up a lie like I was busy or something but in actuality, he didn't invite me. I began to realize that the relationship I thought Chandler and I had did not exist. It was not a relationship. It was a situationship. I was convenient for him for whatever situation he needed, sex when other women weren't available, cook for him and his friends, dance partner in the club, or a ride when he had car trouble. Catherine started calling me to tell me about the other women she saw him go to lunch with, the women stayed the night when I wasn't there, and the women that came to their house parties which I was never invited to.

    I felt he could somehow sense that I was damaged or not good enough. However, not just for him though, I needed to validate that I was worthy and that my step father was wrong about me. Because Chandler was so different from the guys I had dated, I really wanted it to work. That would have been proof to myself that I am worthy of someone good, someone like him. I ignored what Catherine would tell me and eventually stopped answering her phone calls so that I did not have to hear about his escapades. I told myself that if I didn't see it with my own eyes, it wasn't true. Then, I began trying my best to prove to him that I was a good woman, a faithful woman. I knew I was smart but I had to show him that. I knew that when he saw how I could support him, cook for him, clean his house, and give good sex, he would eventually committ to me. I gave him all of me. Not because I was in love with him but I was in love with the idea of what we could be together. The opportunity to create a future for myself that was so different from my past. I just needed to have a partner and belong to a family that shared my same desire for success. I wanted to belong to a family that was a staple in the community, the opposite of what I had come from. A family that appeared to be the epitome of a successful black family. I thought that I just needed to show him who I was and who I wanted to be.

    Meanwhile, I'm driving to work today, my car starts stalling as I'm driving down the interstate. I took the nearest exit so that I'm not on the busy interstate with a disabled car with my baby in the car. He attends the same daycare at which I work so he travels with me each day. I'm on one of the streets on the south side of downtown with a bunch of dilapidated buildings, prostitutes and homeless people. It's a high crime area and I'm so scared out here alone. I have my pocket knife and some mace but I don't have a cell phone. I couldn't afford to keep paying my cell phone and my other bills. There are very few cars passing by. Then, I finally see a gray Charger with dark tinted windows and big shiny rims passing by. I knew I recognized that car from my apartment complex. Then it slowed down near me and the passenger window slid down with a cloud of marijuana smoke emerging before I could see the face of who was inside. It was a guy named Mike that hit on me several times before that used to live in our apartments. He said, " hey, Leia". "You good?" I asked, "can I use your phone to call my roommate, my car broke down?" He said, "yeah baby, no problem". I called Sophia and she said she was on her way in her cousin's car. Then I called AAA because my grandma paid for it for me because she knew that the car was old and may have some problems. I told Mike thank you and he could leave because my friend and AAA were on their way. He insisted, "naw I'm a gentleman and I'm going to wait here with you until they arrive to make sure that you and your son are safe; this is a bad area". I told him, "I'm sure we'll be fine and know she'll be here soon. I don't want to keep you from wherever you were going." He refused to leave. Then he told me that his step father was a mechanic that lived in Marion and I should get my car towed there. He would make sure that my car was fixed.

    I had a gut feeling that I should not but I didn't know any mechanics and I did not want to be without a vehicle again. So, I rode with Mike and the tow truck and Sophia along with my son followed us about twenty miles to Marion to his step dad's shop. As we were riding, I paid close attention to street names and landmarks because this place was in the backwoods of Marion, Mississippi. I had never been there ever before. It looked like a deserted place where someone might go to dump a body that would never be found. All the while riding, Mike never stopped talking, "I finally got a chance to get you alone". "I've been trying to holla at you for a while now." "I would see you and your friends going out to the clubs and stuff and you be looking so good." "I sent you some gifts to your apartment but you sent them back…... the bottles of wine." I said very sternly, "I don't drink". He said, "flowers". I said, "I'm allergic". He said, "the shoes". I said, "I never got any shoes. My roommate got the shoes." "Your messenger didn't specify who they were for and she got them." He said, "they were for you". I told him, "I don't take money and gifts from men that I'm not dating because eventually they will want something in return and I ain't got nothing to give". He said, "I don't want nothing but for you to give me a chance". I didn't say anything else. Before I got out of his car, I reluctantly agreed to go out to dinner with him Friday as a thank you for him helping me when I was stranded. I was not interested in him at all but I knew he wouldn't give up.

    I tried to be slick by scheduling dinner at 6:00 pm. It's summertime and gets dark around 9:00 so it should be plenty of time to eat and get me back before dark. He picked me up from our apartment. Mike took me to a chinese buffet. I really didn't have an appetite because I didn't want to be there. I just thought that would make us even for him helping me. I tried eating but the appearance of his gold and diamond grill shining at me from across the table spoiled my appetite even more. I forced down one plate of food then just sat there and watched him eat. I never saw anyone eat that slowly. I knew he was deliberately trying to waste time. He kept alluding to needing to stop by his hotel room because he no longer lived in University City. He said that he just happened to be in town when he found me stranded. He had moved to Texas since he moved out of the apartments that we currently live in. I told him, " you can drop me back off at my apartment before you go to your hotel room". He drug dinner along until it got dark. I just sat there watching him keep feeding his fat face. Finally, we left.

    When we got in the car, I told him to take me home first. He did not listen to anything I said. He went to the extended stay to his room instead. He said, "I just have to pick up something it won't take long". I said okay and I'll wait in the car. He said, " you ain't gotta be like that". "You been acting funny all evening and I helped you; I didn't have to do that." I said, "I appreciate your help but I have to get back to my baby". "I have been gone long enough." He insisted that I come up for a moment. I was afraid to say no and upset him because I knew he was a thug. My heart started beating so fast and my skin got flushed because I got this eerie feeling that I shouldn't go up to that room. Against my better judgement I followed him up to the room. I could feel my heart beating in my throat as he opened the door and escorted me in. He said, "have a seat, I have to use the restroom and I'll be right back out". He patted the bed signaling for me to sit on it. I opted to sit in the chair instead but it was further away from the door and I didn't want to go that far just in case I had to make a run for it. I sat on the very corner of the bed and looked at the door in anticipation of trying to run but he was using the restroom and left the door crack. The bathroom was adjacent to the exit door so I know he would see me if I tried to leave. I just sat there waiting for him to get whatever he came to get so I could go home.

    I was focused on all the thoughts going through my head and clutching my purse ready to sprint out the door when he came out the restroom and said, "let's go". When he emerged from the restroom, I gasped in shock. He was not ready to leave. He was butt naked and erect. I thought I was going to faint. I immediately got sick and nauseous at the sight of his naked body. He was fat from the waist up and skinny from the waist down with the largest penis I had ever seen in my life. I yelled, " why are you naked?", while shielding my eyes as if the sun was shining. Then I immediately started pleading with him. "I just want to go home, please just let me go home." He walked past me to the chair in the far corner of the room and picked up a bag. He returned to me and threw a stack of money on the bed and told me to take my clothes off. I said, "I don't want your money". Then he got another stack from the bag and threw it on the bed and said in a louder, more demanding voice, "take your clothes off and give me some head". I did not move and did not say another word. Then, he kept taking more and more stacks of money out of that bag, now throwing them at me. He then became irate and started yelling, "do you know how much money this is?" "You stupid if you don't take this money." "The other hoes I've dealt with would've done it for the first stack." Then he started to masturbate in front of me and say, "you know you want this big ole thang". "That's all y'all women want and talk about, a man with a big thang." "You better come get this." Then he yelled, "look at me, look at this". I was so disgusted and sick at the mere sight of him.

I was still clenching my purse because I had what I called my pocket machete, which was my big pocket knife and my mace in my purse. I was thinking, "if I mace him, then he might get so mad that he kills me". "If I cut him, then I'm going to have to kill him because I know he's going to kill me." I'm scared that there just has to be a gun at the bottom of that bag, because I know he has one with that kind of money. Then he pushes me down on the bed and we wrestle over my pants. He pulls them down and climbs on top of me. I was frantic; my mind was all over the place trying to figure out how I was going to get out of this situation. I felt like if he raped me, he was probably going to kill me or something so I wouldn't tell. I started praying, "God please give me the weapon to defeat this man". "Please God let me get out of this alive without having to give myself to him." "I don't want him."

  Then God answered my prayer by helping me recall the scripture of Proverbs 3:21-23, *"My son, do not lose sight of them. Safeguard practical wisdom and thinking ability; 22 They will give you life, And be an adornment for your neck; 23 Then you will walk on your way in safety, And your foot will never stumble."* That scripture meant to me that I had to use my mind to get out of this alive. My ability to be a critical thinker was my gift and my weapon from God. So, as he tried to penetrate me, I crossed my legs and asked him, "wait?" I said, "you said the other women would have done it on the first stack of money which means that you do this all the time." "So, what makes you think I want to have sex with you unprotected?" "Then, you know I have a child so you know I've had unprotected sex too." "I have a man now, anyway." "I've been with plenty of men unprotected before him." "I could have AIDS or you could too; we don't know." "I'm not saying that we do, I'm just saying that we might, you never know." "We don't want to do this without a condom." "I really like you but we have to use protection." "Do you have a condom?" I actually remembered seeing them in the car when he got his wallet out of the glove compartment, before we went into the restaurant. I'm so glad that I pay attention to everything.

He said, "yeah but it's in the car; stay right here and i'll be right back." "I'm gonna run down and get it." I said, "okay, baby I'll be waiting right here for you, naked when you get back." He threw on his robe and some slippers and hurried out the door. I pulled my pants up and grabbed my purse and ran to the window. I looked out the window and watched for him to get into that car. When I saw him get in, I took off as fast as I could, out the door of the room, running the opposite way from the elevator, to the stairs because I knew he wouldn't come that way. I only had one flight to go down because we were on the second floor. When I got to the exit door I stepped out and stood there. Waiting for a moment, in fear that he may still be in the car and may see me outside. Then, I took a deep breath and ran. I ran and ran for my life. I ran across the parking lot until I reached Frontage Rd. I continued to run until I reached Interstate 59. I ran across dodging cars and I climbed over the median. After crossing both sides of the highway, I ran between the residential areas going through backyards and avoiding streets trying not to be seen. I hoped that he did not come looking for me. My adrenaline and fear helped me run all the way back to my apartment and I fell upon the door in exhaustion when I arrived. Necy and Sophia opened the door and I told them everything that had happened. I didn't call the police because I was scared. I didn't even know his full name. All I knew was Mike.

The next dilemma was that I had my grandma's car towed to his step dad's shop out in the middle of nowhere. The following day, I had to call him. I had to call him to get the car back. I called from Sophia's phone because mine was still out of service. I was so scared to call, as if he could do something to me through the phone. I was so nervous but my friends assured me that they had my back. When I dialed the number it said, "this number is out of service." I called back thinking that maybe I dialed the wrong number. I got the same message again. Then I realized, he probably blocked Sophia's number because he knew it was me. So, I tried calling from Necy's number. I got the same message again. With all of that money he had just last night, I knew that he could have paid the bill. He purposely disconnected his service. The girls and I got into Necy's car with the motive to go get my car. We took knives, baseball bats, hammers, and mace. Whatever got our way, were not going down without a fight. Then we set out to the backcountry of Marion. I directed Necy through what appeared to be forests, around curves, and behind hills to a remote location where we found my car. I thank God he gave me sense enough to pay attention and blessed me recall it. We all got out to go talk to the step dad about giving up my car.

    I said, "hi sir, Mike, your step son, had me get my car towed here". "Is it fixed yet because I want to take my car?" He laughed and said, "that nigga ain't no kin to me but here is your key". "He's always telling women that." I said, "oh wow he was lying!" He said, "that's all he does, is lie". I went to crank my car and it started right up. I asked the mechanic, "how much do I owe you?' He said, "nothing because I didn't fix it". I was shocked. I asked him, "well how is it starting right now but it wasn't before?" He said, "maybe the spark plugs were loose or something". I did check those but I haven't fixed anything." I felt like that was only God because I really had no money to get it fixed anyway. I would have been sacrificing paying a necessary bill to get the car fixed. We left and drove home and I never saw Mike again. If that was even his name.

    Later that evening, I hung out with Chandler again. I did not tell him of my experience because I didn't want him to be upset with me for going out with that guy in the first place. Chandler I had started to slack off seeing each other as much because he seemed to be so busy all of the time now. After Chandler left, my friends, my son, and I walked to the park around the corner from our apartment so my son could play and we could just get out of the house. I was sitting on the bench minding my business and a brown skinned older woman walked over and sat beside me. She said, "how are y'all doing"; but there was only me sitting there. I replied, "hi, I'm fine", with emphasis on I'm. She said, "no, I meant y'all because you are pregnant with twin girls and congratulations." I said, "no ma'am, I'm not". Maybe you have mistaken me for someone else. She said, "no, I have the right one." "I came here today just for you to give you this message." "Your mama is going to hit the fan but she will be there to support you with those babies." "Don't you worry about that man anymore because he is not what you think." "He will not be there for your entire pregnancy but you will be fine." I did not believe her because she was a total stranger.

    Coincidentally, my cycle was late that week. Two weeks later I took a pregnancy test, and it was positive. I had not been intimate with Chandler in a few weeks so I was freaked out knowing that the stranger was correct about my pregnancy. Chandler came from a great, upstanding family so I knew the other part of she would not be true. When I told him I was pregnant, he told me to get an aborotion. I was so hurt. He said, "I don't want any more children, I already have one",and "I can't take a woman home that already has a child; my family would not approve of a woman like you." "It's best you get an abortion because I don't want and we're not together". I asked, "when were we not together?" He said, "we never were together". Then I reminded him of when we were in the club and I was dancing with a guy and he said, "you belong to me so don't be dancing with all these other guys". "You said I belong to you." "So what does that mean?' He said, "it doesn't mean that we are in a relationship". I said wow! "You have played me." His response was, "no you played yourself".

I went to the clinic the following week for my first appointment. My ultrasound revealed that I was indeed pregnant with twins and I was seven weeks pregnant. I didn't speak to Chandler very much for a while because I was hurt by his response. I really wanted it to work between us because I wanted my children to have a two parent household, unlike myself. I now knew that it wasn't going to happen with him. To help me cope with this realization, I decided to go back home to Lafayette for the weekend and I went to the Kingdom Hall for Sunday service. I reflected on the things God had delivered me from and I started being conscious of my spiritual relationships not just when I needed God for something anymore but all the time. I realized that had I been obedient and lived according to God's standards, I could have avoided a lot of unnecessary pitfalls.

Service was good for the first time since I was child. As a child, I took for granted my relationship with God. I listened to the lessons and teachings but I did not apply them because I didn't understand the difference in practicing religion and having a relationship with God. I now valued the service and the congregation of like minded people. As I was leaving, I did what we were accustomed to doing and that was standing around talking to the Jehovah's Witnesses inside and outside as we exited. While standing outside with a group of younger witnesses, I was approached by Sister Blackmon. She was an elderly lady in the congregation that had been there for many years. She said, "Hey Leia, look at you." "You were sent off to school to get an education not to go get another baby." "Make this your last one." I was appalled that she said that and that said it in front of everyone. Then, she had the audacity to just say that anyway.

She was not "friends" with my mama or grandma and she never even really talked to me more than a superficial conversation. What right did she have to give an opinion on my life? It was already a difficult situation to have conceived children with a person that didn't want the children or me. I had to accept my choice not to abort and it was a simultaneous and embarrassing choice to be a single mother again. The very people that explained, "come as you are ", meaning your emotional and spiritual capacity, had the nerve to judge my spiritual and emotional state of being by addressing my pregnancy. I was there in an effort to ignite a personal relationship with God and correct my inability to make sound decisions. The devil must have known and sent Sister Blackmon to derail me. Another characteristic of the people from the Mississippi Delta was that they felt entitled to give their unwarranted opinions on your life because they saw you grow up as a child or knew your parents. In some twisted logic in their heads, they all felt okay with telling you how they felt about your personal choices. I wanted to tell that old bat, you don't know me, so don't speak on me; but I remained silent and respectful. I just got in my car and left.

    I stopped by my old job at Clover Market before I left town to get a few fruits for snack. I ran into a girl, Janet, that used to attend Johnson State University in University City with us the semester before last. We also attended high school together so she was from Lafayette but she was younger than me. I remembered seeing her on campus but she only attended her first semester. We didn't run in the same circles in high school nor college but we knew of each other. I always spoke to her and she always spoke to me so I thought she was okay. I didn't know she withdrew and was back home but it wasn't my business anyway. She was working as a cashier. When she was ringing up my items she said, "aww you look so cute pregnant, what are you having?" I said, "I'm not sure yet, I just know twins". Then she said, "well I hope it's not ghetto triplets because Chandler used to hit up my roommate when he was messing with you, too." "Hope she is not pregnant, too." "I told her to be careful cause he ain't wrapping nothing up." "I used to sleep with him too and he never wore a condom with me either."

My mouth dropped. I could not fathom why someone would tell me, a pregnant girl something like that about her children's father. As if that wouldn't hurt my feelings. I didn't even know that cow like that so I couldn't comprehend why she would want to hurt me so bad. I soon learned a valuable, repetitive lesson. People don't have to know you to hate you. They can hate the idea of you from their own distorted perceptions. From my experiences, black women, especially, seem to hate each other. These two women, the old bat and the young cow are the reasons why I'm ready to get out of Lafayette and why I can't move back here.

I returned to University City that afternoon to find out that I did not have to go to work the following day or anyday afterwards. Erica said that the daycare lost its licensure and we no longer had jobs. We were still a couple of months behind on our rent so in another one month, we would probably be evicted. Necy decided to move out at the end of the month instead of waiting for me again this time. I put my pride aside, called Chandler, told him about my situation, and asked if I could come stay with him until I figured things out. He reluctantly said, "I gotta ask Greg and see how he feels about you being here." Chandler continued, "and where are you and your son going to go during the day when we leave for work?" "Y'all not going to be able to stay in our apartment when we're gone, everyday." "Then you probably gonna have to help with a bill or two." I said, "you know what, that's okay". "We will figure something out." All of his and's and but's were indicative of him not wanting us there despite me being pregnant with his babies. I was not going to beg anyone anymore. I went back to my apartment and went to sleep hoping that I would wake up from this nightmare. What else bad could happen?

Necy had her parents and brother to move all her stuff out at the end of the month. She told me that I needed to get our stuff out so she could try to get her portion of the security deposit back. I told her that we forfeited our deposit by not paying the rent the last couple of months. We were just lucky that evictions had not happened yet. She was so angry and was ready for me to leave so she could try anyway; but I couldn't go because I had nowhere to go. She left my son and I and she moved back to Lafayette. We continued to sleep in the apartments without paying rent for three more weeks. During the third week, we left the apartment for me to drop off some job applications. It was even more difficult to find a job now because no one wanted to hire a pregnant woman. They didn't blatantly say that but it was obvious from the looks I got when I went in a place to return an application.

This time when my son and I returned, I went to unlock the door with my key but it didn't work. I could see the shiny new gold locks and knobs on the door. They had finally come and changed the locks. For the next few days, my son and I ate and slept in my grandma's car and parked in the parking lot of our old apartment complex. Then the back pain became so unbearable for my pregnant body I had to find somewhere to lie down and sleep. I asked the neighbor that lived across from us could my son and I stay a night or two with her. She said, "yes that's fine, I'll enjoy the company." I was so grateful for a comfortable bed to sleep in. I had a little money but it was just enough for gas and food. I couldn't afford a hotel room. After day two, I went to my car and discovered the window had been busted out. It was busted just enough to gain entry to the car.

    The culprit was trying to steal the car and had disconnected the steering wheel and pulled all of the wires out from underneath the steering wheel. The efforts to hotwire the car were unsuccessful but my car was undrivable. Now, I literally had nothing. I had no job, nowhere to live, and no ride. I fell to my knees in the parking lot as tears ran down my face and my two year old son patted my back to console me. He said, "it's going to be okay mama; don't cry", as he wiped my tears from my cheeks. I had to face the inevitable and return back to Lafayette because I could not make it here anymore. My grandma sent one of her friends to get me and my son and bring us back home. I just couldn't catch a break.

Chapter Ninet: Don't Insult the Comeback Queen

I'm seven and a half months along with the twins. I go to work everyday as a call center operator. I've only talked to Chandler once since I left University City. I called and told him that I was having twin girls. He said, "they don't make girls in his family and twins don't run in his family". "I need to be sure that they're his babies because he doesn't believe it." I had nothing more to say to him until the day of delivery. The lady from the park was correct when she said he would not be there for me during my pregnancy. I never heard from him.

I was at work and was told that I could leave early because it was slow. I was so excited to get off early that I took the stairs instead of the elevator to get to my car really quickly. When I made the first step, I tripped and fell down two flights of stairs. I held my stomach to try and shield my babies from the impact, but I bumped my head on the fire extinguisher when I finally tumbled to a halt. I hurried up to make sure no one saw me but I had to laugh at myself because I had always been a klutz. I felt fine with the exception of my head. I had to put ice on it because I had a knot on my head. However, later that night I had a few pains but I attributed it to Braxton Hicks contractions.

Like usual the following day, I went to work but still had some pain. My past experiences taught me to be grateful to have a job so I often sucked up my pain and worked through it without complaints. At my last fifteen minute break, I used the restroom and sat back down in my cubicle. Then my water burst. I told my supervisor and everyone got all excited and offered to call the ambulance. I went to the local hospital but my doctor was still in University City which was an hour and a half away. After checking in, I got the OBGYN that was on call there. He was a tall handsome white male doctor with dark brown hair. He came into my room and did not even touch me. He said he spoke with my doctor and the options I had were that since my babies were premature, he could deliver them and have them transported to University City to the NICU because that hospital did not have a NICU; or he could release me and I could go with my doctor on my own. I asked if they could transport me. He responded, "I'm not requesting for you to be transported". "I told you your options." I asked, "well sir can you examine me to see the status of my babies and if it would be feasible to travel there on my own?" "Sir I can't have my babies here and then they be taken away from here; we need to stay together." The doctor replied, "well that's your problem and your choice." "You Medicaid recipients have too many demands." Immediately, I snatched the IV from my arm, with blood dripping down my fingers, I put on my clothes and walked out. I went home, packed a bag, ate, shaved and showered and I drove myself the hour and a half to my doctor.

I let Chandler know and he and Greg surprisingly showed up for the delivery. Him remaining there the entire delivery witnessing the pain and labor I endured, I guess made him sympathetic to me. After seeing his daughters and the tiny faces looking exactly like his, he finally dropped the hard exterior. It didn't last long though because he was right back to turning his back on me, rather, on us now. He never wanted to come to Lafayette to visit his daughters. I almost always had to pack up and go there when he wanted to see the twins. I did it because I was glad to have a man finally in my children's lives that halfway wanted to be there. I wanted that for my children even if it was at the expense of me exhausting myself or sleeping with him sometimes even though I was over him. I was already tired because I had to drive them there three times a week to the doctor to check their bilirubin levels because they were premature. Then I would come home, cook, and take care of my son. By now, his dad and Shantella had gotten back together and lived together with another baby on the way. Because I did not choose Devonte, he chose not to have anything to do with my son anymore and his mom Dorothy did not acknowledge my son either. I took care of everyone on my own.

  Everytime I asked Chandler for money to help buy something there was an excuse or I had to wait until the next paycheck. When the girls were two and a half years old, I asked for some money to buy pampers. I often asked no one for anything, not because of my pride; but because I was told no so much, I just opted to figure it out on my own. I was tired of needing help and never getting it or being criticized because I asked. I almost never got any help. Chandler told me to wait until he got paid. I was exhausted from a couple of hours of sleep, I had a crying baby in my arm, my son patting on my other leg asking for something to eat, I had just spent my last few dollars on formula because I didn't have time to pump breast milk at work. I was broke and tired and just needed him to buy pampers. I just snapped. "Sooooo you want me to tell these babies to hold their pee and poop until you get paid and buy some pampers because I ain't got it?" "Pampers are a necessity, it can't wait." Then he says, "well you can figure it out; you always do". I was like "wow"! I just hung up the phone. He soon learned that, when you do something that adversely affects my children, I'm not going to let it ride. You better know I got something brewing. I went and filed for child support.

    About three weeks later, he called enraged after he received the letter in the mail from Child Support Enforcement. "Why would you put me on child support?" "That's for men that don't take care of their kids, that's not me." "My mama said you're just trying to get in my pockets." "My family said that you're just money hungry." I knew that with both of his parents as prominent attorneys, they knew that it was his side, my side and the truth. However we sometimes can get blinded from the realities when it comes to ourselves and our families. I knew that I didn't come from a family of much and I did aspire to have money and success but I wanted my own. I don't know what he told them about me but I always sensed that his mother did not care for me. She never really said much to me. So, it wasn't surprising that she would say that. She treated me as if I was beneath her.

    I told Chandler, "I've paid for daycare alone for almost three years for three children." "I buy food, formula when my breasts are empty, clothes, shoes, and I'm taking off work for check-ups and sick babies on limited sleep." "I only ask for something when I have spent all that I have and all that you have is an excuse for me." "So you can tell your family, I'm not money hungry." "I was not just trying to get in your pockets or get a baby with somebody with money." "If that were the case I would have slept with your daddy not you because he has the money." "That's not the kind of woman I am." "I have worked for everything I have and never looked for a handout." "Just so you know, I give my children's fathers a grace period and if you haven't proven that you can voluntarily take care of your children in that allotted time, then I will take measures to help you involuntarily take care of them." "Your time has run out." "Nobody has to ask me to provide a roof over their heads, cook a meal for them, change their pampers, take them to school, take them to the doctor, or spend time with them." "Why do I have to ask you?" "Then you give me what you have left of your little money and your little time and call yourself somebody's daddy." "Nigga, please; spare me the humor." "Then y'all have the nerve to judge how and where I live." "I can't afford to live any better because while you "daddies" give your children your last, this mother gives her first and all." "Maybe I could live better and do better if you split half of the parenting responsibilities with me; free up my money and free up my time." "And for the record, if you really wanted me to get an abortion, you could have at least offered to split the price." "Next time, you better think twice about insulting the Comeback Queen." Then, I hung up in his face.

    I was so tired of people making my life difficult. I was so tired of people misjudging me. I was so tired of these grown boys making me the scapegoat for their denied shortcomings and their mamas having their backs. I'm playing the game of life with the cards I've been dealt. I really hated that I respected his parents and wanted them to respect me, because that bothered me that they thought ill of me. I wished he hadn't tainted my image. Chandler portrayed me as some gold digger that was so in love with him and that I did this to trap him. Not the case.

History was repeating itself. I finally got my child support, but he didn't see the twins anymore for over 4 years; just like my son's dad. Of course he told everyone it was my fault, but I was over it now. They called me all types of things. However, I had been called worse by better and didn't care what they had to say about me anymore. His relationship with his daughters was his responsibility and I no longer felt guilty about absent sperm donors. I couldn't force visitation but he was definitely going to give me my money. I refused to sleep in another car with another child of mine while their daddies turned a blind eye to my cries for help.

Chapter Ten:: The First To Tell a Story Is Not Always the Truth

My grandma has me going into the post office for her. While walking down the street, I noticed a police car almost slamming into the back of the car in front of it. When I came out of the post office, the police car was now waiting in front of the entrance. The officer on the passenger side said, "hey my partner thinks you're beautiful". I said, "does your partner have a mouth?" Then he laughed and introduced himself in a deep professional voice. He reached out to shake my hand and said, "hello, my name is William but everyone calls me Will and yours?" I said, "I'm Leia, Leia Devine." He asked if I was from here and I said, "yes, I've been gone a while but I just moved back." He continued, "you are so beautiful, I almost ran into the car in front of me, looking at you." I said, "Oh yeah, I saw a police car almost in an accident". He asked for my number and reluctantly, we exchanged numbers. I was not attracted to him at all but my friend told me that I should date the guys I'm not attracted to because one of them might be my future husband. I thought that maybe men know men better than women do. So, I took his advice and gave this one a chance.

After talking on the phone for a few weeks, I learned that he had been married twice before. Well technically, he was still married to the second wife but they were separated and he lived with his mom until the divorce was final. He asked me out on a date but I declined. I told him that separated was not divorced and I refused to go out with him until he had closed the door to that chapter of his life. We continued to talk on the phone for a couple of months. He continued to reassure me that he was getting divorced and kept asking me out. I kept saying no. Then one day, I agreed, "the day you get your divorce decree, I will go out on our first date with you".

The following Friday, he told me to get dressed and be ready by 7:00 pm. I did as he requested and was ready promptly at seven. When he arrived at my grandmother's house to pick me up, he came to the door, introduced himself to my grandma, and presented me with a piece of folded up paper. I was so impressed by his courteousness and chivalry. When we got in his car, I opened the folded paper and it was the signed divorce decree between William Blake and Emma Blake. He was a man of his word. We went out to eat and to a hole in the wall for dancing. He was a real gentleman.

Chandler was a real gentleman also. That is until I had children by him. So, my guards are still up with Will. Oftentimes when we are talking on the phone I hear his children say, "dad let me in" or "open the door". He says that they live with him at his mother's house the majority of the time and he closes himself in his room so that he can have privacy to talk to me. When I hear them ask that, they're trying to get into his room. I really can empathize because my three children keep up so much noise in the background that it is embarrassing. I let him know that I really loved seeing a man so present in his children's lives and that was attractive to me. Paying child support alone, does not make you a father. I told him that he no longer had to lock them out when we conversed on the phone because I understand.

Our relationship progressed really quickly and

we were seeing each other almost everyday and going out on dates almost every weekend. One day, after leaving my grandma's house to visit me, my grandma said, "you need to leave him wherever you found him because he is a snake". I asked, "why would you say?" "He is good to me." "I have not slept with him, he did not pressure me to go out with him when I refused, and he pays my kid's daycare tuition." "Which is over $600 a month". "That's more than my own daddy has done for me". Then she says, "something just ain't right about him and I feel like he's a liar". "You need to be careful."

I continued to see him because I felt like my grandma didn't really know him. She wasn't being fair to him and didn't give him a chance. He had done all the right things when courting me. In time, I believe he will win her over as well. After a few months of dating, we started to become intimate. Because he lived with his mother and I with my grandmother, he always got a hotel room for us. I thought that was more respectful than trying to lay up with me at my grandma's house. My grandma couldn't see it but he was doing all of the right things.

This past Sunday, when we were at the bar, this brown skinned older lady came up to us with a smirk on her face pointed at me as she hugged Will. She said, "I see you playa". He said, "naw naw that ain't me." Then, she looked me up and down and walked away. I asked Will, "what was that all about". He said, "nothing she just be joking around; I've known her for years." I brushed it off because he hadn't given me a reason to doubt anything he said thus far.

The following day, my old friend Erica called me and asked, "are you back in Lafayette?" She had moved back when Necy moved back after graduation from Johnson State University. I said, "yea I've moved back; what's up?" Then she asked, "are you dating someone here?" I said, "yes, an older guy named William Blake". Erica said, "I know, that's why I called you". His wife knows our family very well and came by my mom's house and told her that you were dating her husband. I said, "wow, this is the first that I am hearing of that, but I can assure you that we did not date when they were married". Then she said, "well do you know where he lives". "Of course I do, he has lived with his mom since they divorced". Erica replied, "are you sure, have you been over there to see it for yourself?". I told her that was what he told me. She continued, "I believe he's lying to you". " I really think they are still together because that woman came up to my job and acted a clown about him because she knew we were friends and I would get the message to you." "She said that they had been having some problems but were back together and you need to leave her husband alone." I told Erica, "when we met, he approached me and in conversation said that he was in the process of a divorce," "I refused to date him until his divorce was final." "He showed me the divorce decree." She advised me, "well you better check into that because she ain't doing all of this for nothing."

Before I could make it home from picking up my children, it was my mama calling me asking when I would arrive at my grandma's house because he needed to talk to me. I said, "I'm on my way now". When I got there, they both had a serious look on their faces. I put the twins down and said, "what's going on, it looks bad?" My mama started with, "you need to leave that woman's husband alone". My eyes got big from disbelief. I thought we were beyond accusing me of things before inquiring of innocence. My grandma intervened with, "Will's wife is a nurse at the clinic and one of the friends from the Kingdom Hall, Katherine, works with her at the clinic". "Katherine said that the director was talking about filing charges against you for calling up there playing on the phone and harassing Emma." I said, "I don't call up there and harass that lady". "I didn't even know she worked there." "And mama that is not his wife; he showed me the divorce papers." "Y'all know me, I don't keep up mess like that." "I would not be picking at a woman about a man that is already mine." "He is with me, they are divorced, I already got him." "So why would I want to pick at her." My mama said, "I don't know why you would but you need to stop before you get arrested again". Again, my mama tries to showcase my mistakes. My rebuttal was, "again, Shantella was picking at me and I got fed up". "I don't start anything with anybody, but I will finish it". Then my grandma tells me that he cannot come visit me at her house anymore. I just said okay until I could talk to Will and get to the bottom of what was going on.

Later that night, he called me during his shift at the Lafayette Police Department. I immediately told him what was going on in addition to now receiving a lot of blocked calls. He said he preferred to talk to me in person and asked me to meet him at the police lodge where the officers took breaks sometimes. I met him there. It was like a house on the inside with a few bedrooms, kitchen and living room in the back. He asked me to come to one of the bedrooms. When I sat down, he put his arm around me, kissed my cheek and said, "you know I love you right". I said yes, "then he said, my ex-wife just can't handle the divorce and is trying to run off in hopes of getting me back." "She is just lying on me". "She knows that it is over and I've moved on to someone better." "She's mad." Then he says, "now I need to ask you something". "When I went up to the clinic to pick up my kids from her, she yelled out that I was with this young girl that's sick and dying." "She said she read your medical records and you have some kind of disease." "Did you give me something?" I asked, "where were you when she said this and were other people around?" He said, "in the waiting room and there were some people in there." I said, "wow, I can't believe that lady went in my medical records." "And first of all before you start interrogating me about something she said, why is she upset if that is your ex-wife?" "Do you still have something going on?" "I don't care who my ex's are with after me." He said, "of course not, but what's this about you being sick?" I finally addressed it.

"I have a kidney disease." "Not something communicable that can be passed on to you". "She should have researched it before she said I was dying." "I'm fine." "I don't have problems from it all of the time." Then he said oh ok. At the same time, we heard beating and yelling at the door. "Will, I know you are in there with that whore. Open the door and let your family see her." He tells me, "I'm about to go outside, don't open the door." He goes outside and I could hear him and her talking. "Why would you bring my mama and my kids up here?" "You need to go home and keep my kids out of your mess." Then I hear her say, "I'm your wife, why do you keep doing this to me?" My heart dropped to my stomach. Why was she calling herself his wife when he showed me the divorce papers. They are divorced. Then his mama says, "this is a good woman, you need to keep your family together and stay out of the streets with these whores." I heard him say, "nobody is in here with me, y'all need to go home". Emma said, "I see her car outside." Will says he doesn't know who it belongs to.

Will comes back in, goes to another room and makes a phone call. Then he comes back and says my captain is my shift commander tonight and he is going to come get you out of her. I said, "if you're not with that woman why can't I just walk out of here or why can't he make her leave since y'all are not together?" The light came on for me then. I realized, my grandma was right, he's not to be trusted but I haven't gotten the truth yet.

Captain Easley knocked at the back door while he had another officer in the front distracting Emma and Will's mama Rosie Mae. Captain told me to come out and get into the back of the police car. I got in and he said, "lie down on the floor." I did. I couldn't see where we were going but while we were riding, he told me to call somebody, preferably a male, to come get my car. He said, "tell them to park at the gas station, QuickTri, which was near the police lodge, and walk to the police lodge and get your car." "Then we will meet them somewhere so you can get in and get your car back." My cousin's fiance came, met us on a back road, I gave him my car keys and he did as the captain instructed while we waited there for him. I asked the captain, "why am I being snuck out and sneaking around like I'm doing something wrong." "If I'm his girlfriend and she's his ex-wife why didn't you just make her leave?" He replied with a peculiar look on his face, "young lady, are you sure this is his ex-wife?" When I got my car, I sat there for a minute before pulling off. I heard the captain on the phone with Will, "she's good, but you can't keep doing this." "I'm tired of bailing you out." So, I started wondering who else had he been caught with at the police lodge.

  I went home and I really didn't want to talk to him that night. He didn't call me either. That was a first. It was a Thursday night and my grandma came home from the Kingdom Hall shortly after I arrived back. My grandma came into my room and said, you're not going to believe what was said to me tonight. Sister Blackmon came up to me and said, "you need to tell your granddaughter that she needs to leave that woman's husband alone." "We stopped by Emma's house when we were out in field service to check on her." "Sister Katherine was friends with Emma and told us that she had been having a hard time at work cause your granddaughter was picking at her and messing around with her husband." "We offered her some scriptures and words of encouragement." My grandma said, "I told her, Will came to my house and told me that he was divorced and showed me his divorce papers." "That woman is lying, they are not still married and as far as I am concerned, him and my granddaughter are grown so they are free to do whatever they want." Then Sister Blackmon says, "well they might want to get back together and your granddaughter is in the way." I was shocked. This lady is eighty years old. Furthermore, I was not even a Jehovah's Witness. Emma nor Will had ever set a foot in a Kingdom Hall. So why were they all in my business and siding with this lady? Then we were taught that we were not supposed to associate with people that were not Jehovah's Witnesses, so how was Sister Katherine friends with Emma? I appreciated my grandma for having my back on this one but that Janus-faced implementation of the scriptures was just the reason why I had yet to become a Jehovah's Witness.

It's been two days now, since I spoke with Will. So, I decided to call him and give him the news that we were expecting a child. He said, "I'm so happy and I'm not going to you like your other kids dads; I will always be by your side." "I knew you were upset by what happened at the lodge so I just gave you a couple of days to cool down." I didn't tell him that I heard the conversation between Emma and Rosie Mae and him. I usually wait until I have all the evidence before I accuse anyone of anything.

Meanwhile, to make and save money for the new baby, I started substitute teaching again some days in Lafayette in the day time and working at night as a communications officer in University City. There is a new superintendent so I have a clean slate from the rumors and lies Shantella and her friends told on me. I would drive an hour to work in University City so I was only home at night two nights a week. I would put my children to bed and my grandma watched them until I got home in the mornings. I would usually sleep most of the day until it was time to pick my children up from daycare.

The blocked calls that used to just hang up developed a voice. She even started calling my grandmother's house cursing at my grandma. I started getting calls from 6 am in the morning until 2 and 3 in the morning. I knew who it was even though she never identified herself. Emma called when I arrived at work and would say, "if it's your man why is he in my bed right now", or "come get your man from my house." If I was with him, she would call and say, "he is with you now but he just left from sleeping with me". He witnessed her calling me but never said anything but, "I can't stop her because she will keep me from seeing my kids so I don't want to upset her". One thing I loved about him was that he seemed to be a good father so I didn't want to hinder him from seeing his children. I didn't say anything about him not checking her. However, I took it upon myself to go press charges on her for telephone harassment. That should stop it. It didn't; she started calling me from payphones so that her number couldn't be traced. That's when I knew she was crazy.

One day at my substitute teaching job, I was placed at the school that Emma and Will's daughter and son attended. I thanked God that I was not placed in one of their classes. However, I did see the children at dismissal when Emma picked them up and they all looked at me. I left that school and went to Lafayette High School to pick up my sister and cousin. I saw Emma there again. She was picking up her oldest daughter. When we were parked and awaiting dismissal, Emma rolled down her window and started yelling at me, "whore, he will never be your man!" "This is his family, right here." Everyday I picked up my sister and her cousin, Emma would yell obscenities at me, even throwing up her middle finger and licking her tongue out like a five year old. I always turned my head and ignored her.

A couple of weeks later I was called by the principal to come to the office. I'm usually called by the secretary for substitute jobs but it didn't cause alarm because I knew the principal. When I sat down in the office, he said, "I just wanted to warn you of what may be coming". "Emma came here crying and said you had been in the classroom talking about her husband and picking at her son and daughter." "She wants me to fire you because she said that whores should not work around kids." "I already knew that you were not assigned to any class with her children." "I also asked the children in your classes if you talked to any of them and the nature of the conversations." "They said nothing bad about you." I tried to hold my tears back because this was a repeat of what Shantella did to me. The women around here get angry about men and try to destroy other women. The men are the problem but we would rather hurt each other than try and find the truth and address him. The principal continued, "I told her, you can wipe those crocodile tears because I know you and your husband." "Y'all business is all in the streets; and he's always cheating." "Then you're all around town fighting these women that he cheats with and takes him back." "I never had a problem with Leia and I'm not going to fire her." "Then Emma told me that if I didn't fire you she would go to the superintendent." I thanked the principal. "You are one of the few people that took the time to look into the validity of this lady's story." "Everyone else just believes the worst about me without consideration." "Thank you so much."

A week has passed and I have not heard from the superintendent but I did hear from my mama again. She called me and said, "my step-daughter, Loretta, came by our house." "She said Emma is her classmate and came by her job to talk to her about you and y'all sister." Loretta was a cashier at the convenience store. Loretta said Emma told her that when you pick up your sister and cousin from school, you come by her job and you, your sister, and her cousin pick at Emma at her job. Loretta told my mama and step dad that she was just looking out for her little sister, even though that was my sister also. She said, "I love my little sister and I just don't think it's right for Leia to involve a minor in grown folks business." Of course my mother agreed and that was just the ammunition my step dad needed to find something else wrong with me. Stan said, "my daughter needs to stay away from Leia; she has always been trouble and she is a bad influence on her little sister." My mama said, "you're right", as if I was not her daughter. I told my mama, "isn't it kind of funny that Loretta wants to come by and look out for her little sister when she never cared much to visit her or talk to her before". "Then, ask your child if I did that; ask her cousin if I did that." "They have cameras at the clinic, tell them to roll the cameras back and show us coming up there." "Why won't you ask instead of believing the worst about me?" "That's my sister, I wouldn't do that."

Later that night my sister called me upset. She said that she wanted to run away. I asked what happened? My sister Kimberly said, "my dad told me to stay away from you and walk home from school from now on". He said, "I needed to stay in a child's place and not get involved in your business and stop picking at Emma". "I told my dad that Emma was lying on you and me and that he and mama could ask Bryan what we do when you pick us up from school." "I told them that I had witnessed her messing with you and never said anything." "Then he said I was lying and taking up for you." "So I told him you must be taking up for Emma because y'all messing around?" "My classmate that lives across the street told me that he saw Emma coming to our house a few times after mama leaves for work." "What is she doing over here in our house when my mama is gone?" "Then he slapped me in my face and told me I was too fast and grown and needed to shut my mouth and mama didn't say anything." Kimberly said, "I never said anything but the next time I see her, we got beef now because she has put me in it and I wasn't." Then I asked mama, "So you just gonna let him hit me in my face about that woman that's lying on both of your daughters and do nothing?" "And you know what mama said?" I said, "what?" "She said, you should not have gotten smart with him." "Girl I'm so mad." I told her that I was sorry she got pulled into my mess.

Today, my aunt stopped by my grandma's house after I got off work and had dropped the kids off at work. She told me that she wanted to tell me something before she told my mom. She said, "I was off of work for a doctor's appointment last week and passed by your mama's house." "I saw Emma coming out of her house." "I heard a lady at work say that she was supposed to be messing around with your step daddy." I said, "Kimberly said it and he slapped her in the face". "So it's probably true." "Maybe my mama will believe it coming from you." My aunt didn't tell her right away. She was off work another day for her follow-up appointment and rode by my mama's house out of curiosity. She saw Emma's car there again. This time my aunt went and knocked on the door. Emma answered my mama's door. My aunt said, "where is Stan?" As they were standing there waiting, he emerged from the bedroom. Then my aunt asked, "what is she doing at my sister's house?" "If she doesn't like my niece, then she should not be at her mama's house." "Then why are you all up in my sister's house and she is not home?" "You need to leave!" Emma left with her head dropped as if she was embarrassed. My aunt came back to the house that afternoon after my mama got off work and told her in front of Stan. My mama asked Stan why Emma was there. He said, "you know I have diabetes and she is my nurse". My aunt said, "she works at the clinic; when did she start making house calls?" He said, "her doctor lets her leave when she wants to leave". "I can let anybody take care of me that I want." My aunt asks, "oh so you paying her?" He replies, "she voluntarily nurses me." My mama said, "she better not be in my house again when I'm not home." Despite all of that, she still didn't believe I was innocent.

Saturday morning, I woke up and my grandma told me I had some mail. It was something from a pharmaceutical company but the address was to Will and Emma's house. I know that I did not have anything going to their house so why would mail have my name and their address? There was also writing on it that said "needs COA". I went up to the post office before closing and asked what that meant. The clerk said. "the mailman wrote that on it because she knew where you lived and brought it to the correct address and was just letting you know that it "needs a change of address." I told the clerk, "I never lived at that address and should not have mail going there". I went home, opened it and read it. It said, "thank you for your telephone order and your prescriptions will be delivered in 14 business days". So I called the company and found out that Emma had been in my medical records again, got my medicaid number and was writing prescriptions in the doctor's name, using my medicaid number and having them sent to her house.

 I told Will about it. He said, "she wouldn't do anything like that, she could lose her job." As if I would be lying. "But I will talk to her and tell her to leave you alone because you're having my baby." Then he asks me to go drop the charges against her for telephone harassment. He would pay for it and assured me that he would get her in check. He was so charismatic and had a way of making me believe he was doing the right things. I did it. I dropped the charges. Later on Saturday night, my grandma got a call from Will's mother and she told my grandma that she was going to kill me. Then I got a call on my cell phone from a blocked number again, it was Emma and his mama Rosie Mae. Emma said, "yeah, I see he made you drop those charges, he ain't going nowhere." "I'm his wife and he's staying with his family." Then his mama Rosie Mae said, "and as far as I am concerned, the baby you caring ain't my son's child." "It's a bastard just like your other children and I hope it dies." I hung up on both of them. I couldn't believe an old lady would do that.

    Monday, I sat down an defiled a complaint with the U. S. Department of Health and Human Services Office for Civil Rights about her going in my medical records. I was going to put a stop to her myself since I see Will was not. Meanwhile, I finally got that call from the superintendent and I went to see him. He apparently believed her and he told me that I was fired. I was not upset about not being able to make the extra money. I was angry that this lady had defeated me again. I walked out to my car and just sat there crying. I looked at my stomach and started to talk to my baby. "I'm so sorry that I chose another family that hates my and my child and they haven't even met you." Then my cell phone rings as I'm sitting there. It was an unfamiliar number but I answered. "Hello." "Yeah bitch, you won't work in this town if I have anything to do with it." "I see you sitting there crying; cry baby." It was Emma. She was sitting in the parking lot beside the superintendent's office watching me. I just hung up and drove away. I didn't tell Will because he had already proven that he had her back.

    I remembered my friend telling me that divorces and stuff like that was public record so I decided to go to the courthouse and see. I just couldn't believe that this woman was acting like this about a man that she was divorced from. When I looked in the public records, I discovered that he lied to me. The only record of a divorce was from his first wife, not the second one, Emma. I asked him to meet me and let me see the divorce papers again. I looked at them and smiled at him. I just stood there in silence smiling at him. He asked, "what's up?" I said, "my grandma told me you were a snake and I gave you a chance." " Look at your divorce decree, you forgot to change the signatures." "You changed the name in print from your first wife to your second wife's name but you forgot to change the signatures." "Why are you such a liar?" Something I didn't initially notice the first time I saw it, was his birthdate. I said, "and your age, you said you were forty." "This says you're forty-five!" "What haven't you lied about?" "You're still married and you're twenty years older than me!" "I hate you for bringing your wife and mama into my life!" "I hate you!" He said, "I had already left her and filed for a divorce when I met you but I knew you wouldn't date me if I told you she wouldn't sign the divorce papers and that I was twenty years older than you." "I really liked you and didn't want to say anything that would run you off.""I promise I'm going to make it up to you; I'm going to show you that my love is real." "I want to marry you." Against my better judgement, I said, "I'll give you the opportunity to make it up to me". I really didn't love him either but he seemed to be a good father and I didn't want to raise another child without his or her dad so I gave him another chance.

Chapter Eleven: Welcome to the Mud

When I got off work Tuesday morning, I got a phone call from the police captain. He said call him when I got to town. I thought that was weird but I did it. He asked me to meet him at the same spot that he took me that night to meet my cousin's fiance when he rescued me from the police lodge. He handed me an envelope and said, "Will told me to give this to you". I asked, "what is it?" He said, "I don't know but you will find out when you open it". I went home and opened the envelope outside before going into the house. It was a letter, a key, and $1,000 dollars. The letter read, "baby, I'm sorry. I had to leave to go and put myself in a better position to make a life for us and our family. I'm gone to Iraq to work as a civilian contractor and I'll be back in a year. Go to the airport and pick up my truck and park it at your house. Then everyone will know when I come back who I will be with. I only want to be with you. I love you and my son. Talk to you soon." I was in disbelief, like this is a joke. I called his phone and did not get an answer . I called my friend Maria to ride with me to pick up his truck from the airport. I dropped my kids off at daycare and picked up Maria. We went to Lake Platte's airport about 45 minutes away from Lafayette. Then I drove to Jackson and rode all around that airport but couldn't find a truck with a Lafayette County tag. I just assumed he got a new truck because he has always been in a car. When I got back to town it was almost time to pick up my kids so I called the captain back and asked did he tell him what airport he wanted me to pick up his truck from because I couldn't find it. I was so tired. I had worked all night, been driving around all day, and hadn't been to sleep in addition to being five and a half months pregnant. The captain said, "baby, go home and rest; stop looking for that truck because it's not lost". I said, "well where is it because he asked me to pick it up and left the key". He said, "I'm sorry to tell you, but take that money and take care of yourself. Let him go because he ain't no good." "His wife is riding around town in his truck." "Go home, baby."

I was so devastated. I could not eat or sleep for a couple of days. Then I got a call from his number. He had some explaining to do. I said, "hello". "Bitch I bet you thought it was Will." "I read your text messages." "Me and his kids dropped him off at the airport." "And that truck is staying with me". I hung up on her then blocked the number. Then I got a call from an out of state number; I reluctantly answered. It was Will. He said, "baby I wouldn't do you like that". I left my other spare key with my mama. She must have given it to Emma." "I'm gonna make her come park it at your house." Then I asked, "and when did you get a truck?" "You always visited me in a car." He said, "it's my friend's car." "When he's creeping I switch cars with him and I just come visit you in his car so his wife won't think he's at my house." I said, "oh ok." Didn't sound right but I'll let him tell that lie because the truth eventually comes out. He said he left that way because he didn't want to see me cry. I was over this conversation. He had hurt me and allowed me to be hurt and embarrassed so many times.

Wednesday, I got a letter in the mail from the U. S. Department of Health and Human Services Office for Civil Rights. It said that they found no breach of confidentiality. The director of the clinic had conducted an internal audit and the computer system did not show where she had accessed my medical records. The complaint was dismissed. My grandma told me that Sister Katherine told some people at the Kingdom Hall that everyone at the clinic disliked me because I caused the federal government to come in and investigate them. Some people got in trouble for having other people to clock them in and taking extended lunch breaks. That had nothing to do with Emma and my situation. Really, they all took up for Emma because they were angry that they got in trouble for other things. Emma accessed my paper records, not the computer records, but I couldn't prove it. I was just fed up. Emma has succeeded at turning this town against me and I can't win.

  Thursday when I got off work, I did not feel like myself. I felt like I was about to have a nervous breakdown. I dressed my children and went to drop them off at daycare. When I reached a fork in the road to turn towards the daycare, it was like a fork in my life and I had a decision to make. I turned around, packed a bin of clothes for each one of my children and myself . Then I packed my Bible and about 50 of my grandma's WatchTower magazines from the Kingdom Hall. Then I sat down and wrote my family a letter. I told them, "My life is over. This man that I loved invited a woman and his mother into my life that wanted me dead. Emma was falsely accusing me of things and everyone believed her just like they did Shantella. My own mama believed that woman over me. I can't leave home and go in public without people looking at me like I was a homewrecker. Then he left me to deal with it all alone and left me looking like a fool. I did nothing wrong but

love a man that lied to me; but nobody has my back. I
have to leave this place and don't come looking for me
because I will be nowhere to be found. I'm going where
I can have some peace and where nobody knows me
and nobody will judge me. Love Leia."

    I got in my car with my children, went to the
bank, and closed out my bank account. Then I left town
before anybody read that letter and could come looking
for me. I drove 16 hours until I was tired and ended up
in Richland, Virginia. I was stopping, crying, and
praying all along the way. God was the only one that
could fix this situation. We lived in an extended stay for
about a month. I didn't answer any phone calls from
anyone. If they didn't listen to me when I was there,
they wouldn't value what I had to say now that I'm
gone. Then I went to the store and bought a map. I
found the library and went online to find the
Department of Social Services. I used the map to find
my way to the Department of Social Services. I applied
for Medicaid and food stamps because I knew that I
needed to get to the doctor. I was almost seven months
pregnant now and I needed to save the rest of my
money because I was not working.

    My case worker was Charlene. She asked what
brought me to Richland, Virginia all the way from
Mississippi. I broke down and told her everything. Then
she said, "I understand; I left a similar situation and
moved here." "I will help you in any way that I can."
"You can't get food stamps without an address; I can't
send it to a hotel." "I'll send it to my address then when
the card arrives, I'll call you and you can come pick it
up from me." "I told her thank you so much, I haven't

had help and understanding in a long time. " Then she asked, "if you don't have a place by Friday come back and meet me here at 5:00." I said okay. Friday, my kids and I packed up and met her there. She told me to follow her. We arrived at a townhouse on the outskirts of the city. I got out and she said, "y'all come in". We went in and she said, "this is my house". "You and the kids are welcome to stay here as long as you need and we will figure something out when it's time for you to have the baby." She said, "you don't need to go back to that." "Don't pay me a dollar just work on you and take care of those kids." "My daughter is gone with my mom for the summer so y'all can have the spare bedroom." I started crying again but tears of joy. I told her, "you must be sent by God." "He answered my prayers." Then I looked down and saw a "No Blood" VHS tape. That prompted me to continue to look round the room. I noticed other publications from the Kingdom Hall so I asked, "are you a Jehovah's witness?" She said, "well I grew up as one but I haven't been there in a while." I said, "so did I!" I grew up going to the Kingdom Hall but I never got baptized; but that's all I know. "Maybe this is Jehovah telling me that I need to give my life to him." "What are the odds that I would be so far from home, know nobody, and the person that helps me would be a Jehovah's witness?" Charlene said, "well I haven't been in a long time either." Reluctantly she said, "I kinda separated myself, but maybe this is a sign for the both of us that I need to go back also."

After another two weeks of being away from Mississippi, I finally answered the phone for one person, Necy's sister Mesha. She told me that word on the street was that I found out that Will had gone back to his wife and I tried to killed my children and commit suicide. I asked, "where did that come from?" She said her boyfriend's cousin worked at the sheriff's department. She said, "your mama and grandma took the letter you wrote to the police department and tried to file a missing person's report." "They told them that you were an adult and left on your own with your children and there was nothing wrong with that; you didn't have to tell them where you went." "The police department wouldn't let them file a missing person's report."But the chief's secretary made a copy of your letter and made more copies and gave it to Emma and the sheriff's department." "Then I heard Emma made copies and gave it out to people and told them you lost your mind because she took her husband back." I told her, "thank you for telling me." "But I don't want that negativeness in my spirit." "I wasn't saying I was going to kill myself." "You know what, I don't even want to explain myself." "You can tell them I'm alive and my children are fine."

    I finally answered one of those long distance calls too. I knew it was Will. He had left plenty of voicemails. He told me to check my email. He sent it a long time ago but I wouldn't answer him to know that. It was the final divorce decree between him and Emma. He finally got a divorce and wanted me to come back home. I had Mesha go to the courthouse to check this time. She called me back a day later and verified it was true. They were finally divorced. Then Mesha told me that his truck was at his mama's house and no longer at Emma's house. After talking to him and considering what burden I would be on Charlene for her to be babysitting my children while I was in the hospital giving birth, and I had no job yet, I decided to go back to Mississippi.

When I returned, my grandma was glad to see me. She said, "I prayed that you were okay". I told her that a Jehovah's witness opened her home to me and I knew that God had sent his angel to protect me. She told me that was a good reason for me to give my life to Jehovah. I agreed.

It was close to my due date, and Will asked me to have my doctor write a letter to his chief saying that I had complications with my pregnancy so that he could return home and be here for the delivery of our baby. My doctor had sympathy for my situation and he did it. Will told me that he got the letter but he wasn't sure if he would make it in time because an army convoy would have to take through the war zone to get to the airport to fly home. He said, "I won't have access to a phone either until I get back; but I will call you as soon as I get to the states."
I went to the doctor for a check-up because I had reached my due date. The doctor told me that water was broken and I was dilated two centimeters. He sent me straight to the hospital. I tried calling Will in hopes that he had made and gotten his phone back, but no answer. I gave birth alone. I figured he had not made it back to the country yet but I just hoped he was safe. My aunt brought my mama to pick me up from the hospital and she drove me home in my car.

I didn't try to call Will anymore because I really didn't have a number to call him on. I just waited for him. The second night home from the hospital, I heard the house phone ring but I didn't get up. Then my grandma came into the room and said, "Emma has started again." "She just called and said you left a letter on her car Saturday night and if you come to her house again, she would call the police on you." She said you were mad because Will came back to her. My grandma said, "I told her, I don't know and don't care what or where Will is but I know Leia didn't put a letter on your car because she was in the hospital Saturday night." "You can stop calling my house with your lies. It was probably some other woman that he is messing around with."

The next day, I got a call from Will. I was very short with him. Erica, Necy, and Leslie had come by to see our son the day before and Erica said she saw him and Emma together. He asked how I was doing, I said, "fine". He asked, "how is our son?" I said, "fine". Then the baby started crying and he asked who's baby is that, I said, "mine". He asked, "when did you have the baby, why didn't you tell you had the baby?" I responded with a real stank attitude, "maybe because you were at home with your wife and other kids so you couldn't answer the phone for me anyway." Then he said, "baby, I just got back to town when I called you." I interrupted, "you can keep your lie, I saw you with my own eyes". "I saw you at her house, excuse me, y'all's house." Even though I didn't see him, Erica actually told me, I would never reveal my source. I knew to never tell who feeds you information. So, I acted like I saw him myself.

Despite actually being divorced, he and Emma

were still seeing each other. I learned something valuable about that situation, most of the time if the ex still gives you problems, they are probably still dealing with each other. He said, "I had to go straight there to get my truck and my cell phone because she got it back from my mama house without my permission." I told him, "at this point, the way you left, humilitated me." "The way you came back was embarrassing to me." "I really don't believe anything you say." "You can stay over there because obviously you both like that crazy, messy stuff, I want no parts of it." "How do you think it makes me look to everybody?" "It looks like everything Emma says is true, like I'm messing with her husband, and like I'm picking with her." "Don't call me anymore." Then like usual when I was angry, I hung up on him.

A couple of days had passed and I had been ignoring his calls. Around 2:30 in the afternoon, I heard a knock at the door, I answered and it was him. I opened the wooden door but talked to him through the storm door. I said, "what do you want?" He said, "I want to see my son". I said, "you got one over there with your wife. Let your mama tell it, I don't who my baby daddy is". He responds, "baby let me in and let's sit down and talk." I refused to open the door and stood there gazing at him with a blank face and no emotion. He continued, "I do have a son with my future wife", and pulled a box out of his pocket with a ring. He got on one knee and said, "will you be my wife?" "I want to prove to you that I'm serious about us and I'm going to do right by you." I finally opened the storm door and reached for the ring. Then I tossed it out in the yard and said, "you can take your ring, your proposal, and all your drama and get away from me." He ran up to the door to catch the knob before it closed. I watched the doorknob slip from his hand and it closed. He tried to open it but it was locked. I had it set to automatically lock from the outside. He said, "baby wait, I understand how you feel, just let me prove that I am the man you fell in love with." "Let me make things right."I went back to the couch and sat down rocking my baby as if he wasn't standing in the door pleading. Then I turned the tv up to drown out his talking. Eventually, he drove away.

    The following week, my grandma tells me that Stan is down sick. She said my mama told her that he had some complications with his diabetes. Apparently, he had some sores on his testicles that he tried to treat himself and it got worse. He didn't want to tell my mama or go to the doctor because he was scared it may be an STD and that would be indicative that he cheated. So, he just kept it secret. The doctor said he developed Fournier's Gangrene in his testicles and it had spread to his abdominal wall. There was no chance of recovery.

    Ever since I was eight years old, I had been experiencing depression. People didn't understand that even though people may be functional while in public, there was always sadness behind the smile. I often stayed to myself and was not very sociable when I was at home. When I was home, it allowed me to take off the mask. I often did not bathe or comb my hair. I would transition from eating a lot to not having an appetite at all. Since all the drama with Emma, Rosie Mae, and Will I had been experiencing chronic depression. I did not want to leave the house unless it was absolutely necessary. I felt paranoid that everyone was judging me because of the lies Emma told on me and seemed like everyone was whispering about me. I stopped going out for anything. I wouldn't even check the mail.

My family had obviously been talking about me like I was crazy or something. During this time, Kimberly called me and said that her dad wanted her to tell me that my problem was that I just needed some "TLC" and I would feel better; he invited me to come to their house. She also said he told her, "if I ever did anything to you, I apologize." "I'm sick and you and those kids need to come see me." I told her to put me on speaker so he could hear me. "Kim told me you said I just need to come over for some TLC and that you apologize if you ever did anything to me." "Well I don't want any TLC from you and if that is your half-assed apology for molesting me, you can keep it." "If you want forgiveness so you can die in peace, I'm not giving it to you." "I hope you suffer beyond death."

He died about two weeks later. My grandma told me to go support my mama in the death of her husband. I told her, "that would be fake of me to act like I care, because I don't." "I can't sympathize with someone that is mourning over the death of someone that beat her, cheated on her, spent her money, and abused her child." "I'm good." I did not attend the funeral.

My son's dad keeps showing up at my house, leaving flowers, and sending gifts. I finally gave in and started answering his calls. It had actually been quiet for a while too. No calls from his mama or Emma. So maybe he did finally leave her. Erica called me anyway and told me that Emma told people that he used my child's birth as a reason to return to the states because he heard she was dating someone else and he was jealous. I knew it was true and maybe now that he has gotten his ego whipped, he will notice that I was a better woman and do right by me.

    I finally accepted his proposal. I still didn't trust him, I wasn't in love with him, I wasn't attracted to him, but he seemed to be a really good father. I always heard people talking about him and his children. I wanted my children to have what I didn't have growing up, a two parent household. So, I'm marrying him.

    I made amends with my dad so that he would walk me down the aisle. My dad and the entire bridal party came together to decorate the day before the wedding after rehearsal. Well, everyone was there for decorating except my fiance. He disappeared right after rehearsals and he would not answer the phone. I did not let anyone know that I was concerned about not being able to reach him. I had it good at hiding my feelings.

    The morning of the wedding, he called and said that his friends took him out to celebrate, he was drunk, fell asleep, and did not hear his phone. I asked, "where did you fall asleep?" Because he still lived with his mother, I know she wouldn't have welcomed him into her house after celebrating his soon to be marriage to me. He said, "I went home". I didn't believe it but I had no proof so I accepted the story. I always told him, "I'll let you lie to me today because the truth will come out tomorrow."

Chapter Twelve: At the Crossroads with the Delta Devil
 and God

It's my wedding day and everyone is on standby for the ex-wife at the wedding. They know to keep her out. She's been too quiet so I just figure she has something up her sleeve. Nothing is going as planned. I got an amatuer wedding planner to decorate and it looks horrible. We're running late and the wedding is starting an hour behind. I'm ready. Some of the bridesmaids are having problems with their dresses. I heard people are getting up leaving. I am so unhappy.

Finally, I walk out and my dad and my one year old son escort me down the aisle. The preacher begins. "We are joining her today for the union in the marriage of William Blake and Leia Devine." "Anyone object to these two joining marriage, speak now or forever hold your peace." I was relieved that Emma had not come to disturb anything. Then I heard, "I got something to say". "This whore is not good enough for my son." "Nobody in his family supports this marriage and as far as I'm concerned if you marry her, you are no longer my son." Then she grabs her purse and leaves her seat. I had no idea that his mama had made it in. Everyone was on alert for his wife. Nobody was expecting his mama. This was supposed to be one of the happiest days of my life. Yet it has become the most humiliating. I could feel the warm tears start to roll down my cheeks. I did not turn around. I did not want the audience to see me cry. I couldn't believe this was happening. It was surreal. I could hear everything behind me. I heard Rosie Mae walking out. The wedding planner ran up to me at the altar and said, "I'm sorry, I'm going to make sure she leaves." It didn't matter at this point because the damage was done. My cousin approached me on the other side and said,

"Don't worry about it, I'm headed to my car to get my gun; I'm gonna shoot her ass for this." I didn't utter a word to anyone. I just stood there silent with tears running down my face.

    Rosie Mae threw the door open really wide and the wedding planner caught it to prevent hitting the wall. Then she said to Rosie Mae, "Leave and don't come back". Rosie Mae said to her, "who are you talking to? Bitch you must n't know who I am?" Then my dad said, "ma'am it didn't take all of that." "You didn't have to come here and ruin my daughter's day." "If you didn't want to bless this marriage, you didn't have to show up." "I didn't agree with my daughter marrying him because he is 20 years older than her but I still supported her." Then Rosie Mae said, "get out of my face before I kick your ass." "I do what I want to do, you son a bitch you." Then my dad lost it, snatched her wig off, and grabbed her in the collar. He said, "lady I will drag you across this parking lot." They had tussled until they made it outside but we could hear everything like it was center stage. Some guys rushed him to get him off her, Will's friends grabbed Rosie Mae and made her get into her car and leave, and my mama called the sheriff. I wiped my tears and finally looked back. People were grabbing their gifts and walking out.

    The preacher continues, "now if no one else has anything to say, we will continue." "She is entitled to her opinion but that does not stop anything." "What God has put together let no man tear apart." "A man is to leave his mother and cling to his wife." "You are doing a wonderful thing in the eyes of God and he will bless this marriage". I had heard that phrase so many times, "what God has put together let no man tear apart." At that moment, I reflected on all that I experienced with this man thus far and I knew that God did not put this together. We often make poor choices in a mate, "put this stuff together", then we want God to bless it or fix it.

After the wedding, he picked me up and said he was about to take me on our honeymoon. While riding I asked, "where are we going?" He said, "just shut up and ride". He never talked to me like that before so I was surprised. He was always a gentleman even though he was a big liar. Then he pulled over on the side of the highway and told me to get out. I said, "why? What's going on?" He said, "don't you ever question me about where I am anymore." I said, " what are you talking about?" He said, "you asked me where I was last night". "So get out and walk back home, you're going to learn." Then he opened the door, pushed me out of the truck, and drove off. He left me walking at around 9:00 at night in the dark on the side of the highway in Arkdale, Mississippi. It was about thirty miles from Lafayette. I walked for about 15 minutes until I saw a vehicle approaching slowly. It was him, he had returned. He rolled down the window and said, "get in". I got in because I had no cell phone or way to call anyone because it was left in his truck. Then he took me to a motel in Arkdale. I said, "I thought we were going on a honeymoon?" He replied, "this is your honeymoon; this is all that you are worth". "I'm not spending any more money, this wedding cost enough." After getting into the room, I showered and just wanted to get in bed and start fresh from this unbelievably horrific day. From the wedding to being put out on the side of the road. I felt like this was a nightmare and I would wake up tomorrow and my real wedding would occur.

When I got in bed he pulled off my gown, kissed my cheek, my chest, my stomach, and then put his face near my gential. Then stopped and looked up at me. "You thought I was about to put my mouth down there?" "Don't even think about it." "I've married you now so I ain't gotta do that anymore." I said, "I never asked you to do that." "I just want to go to sleep anyway." He said, "oh no, you're going to do your wifely duty." I was disgusted but I just laid there and let him finish.

The next morning, when we got in the truck and he was taking me to my grandma's house, he looked at me with a fresh face and said, "look at you, you're so ugly." "Look at all those spots in your face; you look like you have leprosy." "I guess I have to deal with it now 'cause I married you." I replied, "a pen got you in it and a pen will get you out of it." "You're not stuck." My skin wasn't bad but for years after that, I never allowed him or anyone else to see me without makeup.

Two weeks later, I was at my grandma's house and he called and said that his truck had quit at the gas station. He asked me to come and bring him some booster cables. When I arrived, he got his truck started, then he went into the store to wash his hands. I waited outside for him to return. Then I saw, gray Dodge Challenger with dark tinted windows pull up as he was walking around in the store. A short dark skinned lady exited the vehicle, looked at me with her nose turned up and walked into the store. She didn't purchase anything. I saw her talking to my husband in the store and he acted like he was trying to avoid her. She followed him out of the store and I heard her say, "oh, so you gonna act like you don't know me now huh?" Then he got in his truck and drove away as if I wasn't standing there. He literally did not acknowledge my presence. That silence said a lot. The neutrality told me that he didn't want her to know who I was and didn't want me to know who she was. By ignoring us both he could get us alone and give different accounts of a lie to us both. Then I noticed as he drove off really fast, the woman followed him, so I followed them both. He sped up and it became a chase. I let them go because I didn't chase anyone. I went back home to my grandma's house and was going to call him for an explanation. When I got on grandma's street, I met the same gray Dodge Challenger heading towards me. I noticed at the store that her tag was from Smith County and my grandma's street was a cul-de-sac. So I knew she wasn't there by accident. I had actually seen the car come down there before and turn around. This woman had the audacity to come to my grandma's house looking for my husband.

  She flashed the headlights at me. I pulled over and rolled my window down. She asked, "where is Will?" I responded, "who's asking?" She said, "you don't know who I am?" I said, "I can't say that I do but you obviously know who I am since you are coming by my house looking for my husband." She replied, "husband?" "He married you?" I said, "yes he sure did and again who are you?" She said, "I'm Tamra and can I see your ring?" I held out my hand and wiggled my ring finger. She raised her eyebrows and said, "hmp". "Well he was lying in my bed April 3rd and said he wasn't about to get married to anybody." What she said was indicative that she knew that we got married because that was the day before our wedding. Then she said, "he's not answering my phone call; you need to tell him to call me.". I told that woman, "I'm not telling my husband anything." I was trying to keep my cool because I was angry that she came to my grandma's house looking for him and I got my pistol right here in the arm rest if she wants to jump stupid. Then she answers her phone, "you're not going to believe this!" "I'm standing here with his so called wife, mannn I'm so glad I did not have that baby by him." I didn't say a word because I knew she wanted me to say something; but I was disgusted that he had been having unprotected sex with more than just me. Then she again addressed me, "I can't believe you don't know who I am, I've been laying low with him since he was with his last wife." I responded, "Well I'm his wife now and don't come to my house looking for him again." Then, I rolled my window up and drove the remaining way home.

He called me and asked me to meet him at the cemetery to talk. I said, "Why would I want to do that?" "Apparently you know something that makes you not want to come to my house?" "Do you want to enlighten me?" He said, "I used to deal with her a longtime ago and Tamra mess around with my homeboy Demarcus now." "You can call Demarcus and he will tell you." I responded, " the same married friend Demarcus, that I discovered you were switching cars with so you could keep up your lies to me and Emma?" "He's going to have your back and say he messes with her to save you and I know he has a wife too." "Y'all are just alike." "Then you and he sleep with the same women and y'all are okay with that?" "I know you're lying, but I can't prove it yet." "She was probably the person that put my tires on flat a couple of days before the wedding." "You better tell her to stay away from me before I pop a cap in her." "Stay away from my house tonight; I don't want to see you."

We finally moved in together. Things got worse after that. He was always leaving and staying gone for hours at a time unexplained and returning home to treat me and my children so ugly. He was really mean to my oldest son but I always took up for my son. He was a lot easier on the twins, but I sensed that my son did not like him either.

The bathroom door wouldn't lock so every time I got in the shower, he would come into the bathroom. He would grab my stomach or touch my butt and say, "you disgust me, your body looks so bad with those stretch marks." "No man will ever want that body in the light." I often heard how nobody would want me with four children, how I turned him off, or how disgusting I looked naked. What was even more interesting was when we were out in public he would always accuse me of sleeping with someone that spoke to me like old classmates or coworkers. He even accused me of one of my cousins. When he would invite his friends over, I was not allowed in the room or if they were outside, I couldn't walk past them. My car was parked on the street one night when I was about to go to work. He and his friends were sitting in the driveway drinking and grilling. I walked past to get in my car and Will called me to come back. He grabbed me by the throat and said, "you just want to switch your butt through here so somebody will look at you". "You always want other men to look at you." I asked, "how else was I supposed to get to my car? You all were sitting in the driveway?" He said, "you should have walked around the house and through the neighbor's yard." I began wearing really baggy clothes, my hair mostly in a ponytail, and always walked with my head down. I didn't want to make eye contact with any men because I tried to avoid being interrogated. I wasn't able to visit my family anymore because I always got questioned and accused. "What were you doing over here so long?" "You must have been talking to another man when you went over there because I'll catch you talking to him if you were at home." So I stopped visiting family to avoid problems. My friends stopped coming to visit me as well. He didn't tell them they couldn't come but he made us so uncomfortable that they didn't want to come back when he was there. He isolated me.

All I had left was what I loved to do, watch movies with my children and he took that from me too. I used to watch *Madea's Family Reunion* over and over again. Then he joined us one day and started pointing out how the light-skinned woman was so beautiful. "You see her, now that's fine and beautiful." "That's not you." "She's lighter than you and prettier than you." "Look at her body, you look the opposite of that". "I should have married somebody that looks like her instead of you." This became the norm for almost every show or movie that came on television. He would point out what beauty was and demonstrate how I did not fit the definition of beauty. I stopped watching television when he was around. I could not watch *Madea's Family Reunion* at all without crying.

I started working at the police department in Lafayette as a dispatcher. Because the town was so small, the fire department and ambulance department had all their calls dispatched there as well. James was the assistant fire chief in Lafayette and he often came to the police station to pick up reports. Each day he would tell me how beautiful I was. He would notice and compliment me when I changed my hair. One day he bought all the ladies in the office gift set that included a candle. Mine was orange. He said that he noticed that I wore a soft orange eyeshadow and I always polished my nails a shade of orange. So that's why he bought me an orange gift set. He became a really good friend in a short amount of time. James didn't know it but he was giving me everything I wasn't getting at home. Sometimes all a woman needs is attention from her husband; and what her husband lacks, there are others waiting to pick up the slack. James was just my friend but he definitely supplied that slack. James confided in me and I confided in him. It was like we had known each other for years.

The ladies that I worked with in dispatch acted like I had joined a sorority and thought it would be a good idea to haze me. Shemeka and Tequilla are two dispatchers on my shift and they are a tag team of trouble for no good reason. I only really talked to James whenever he came by and not to them very much because I noticed that they seemed pretty messy among themselves. Because I was new, I remained fairly quiet at work. So each day, they would ask questions about my personal business and how my marriage was going. I was always pretty superficial and always answered, "things are well." I overheard Shemeka say, "I know her marriage is not that good and I'm gonna find out".

During the busiest time of the shift, I had calls coming in left and right. They left me on the radio alone during training. I took my job very seriously because dispatch is the lifeline of the officers and the voice of help and hope in a time of despair for 911 callers. I did not want to mess up. Then I got a phone call on the business line. The woman said, "this Emma, where is your man now, bitch". I got so angry because in the middle of my most stressful time, this lady calls my job and starts harassing me again. Then Tequilla walks back in and asks, "you look stressed and upset, do you need a break?" I said yes and Tequilla took my seat. Then oddly, Tequilla and Shemeka burst out in laughter. Shemeka said, "That was me that called you blocked." "I knew it wasn't all good in paradise." "Your husband must be back with her again." I said, "she's not a problem." "Y'all are the problems". "Why would you do that to me?" Tequilla said, "we were just playing", but I knew they weren't. They were just evil and unhappy. I would often hear them venting about their cheating husbands. I just didn't want to discuss my cheating husband with them. I learned that messy people mind everybody else's business because they can't handle dealing with their own mess.

Friday night, I had to wash and style my grandma's hair and I forgot my curlers in Will's truck. I stopped by the house and got in his truck to get them off of the floor and saw a receipt from the night before. He told me he was in Natchitoches with Demarcus last night. The receipt was from the QuickTrip gas station in Coneville about 40 miles north of Lafayette. You don't have to pass through Natchitoches to get to Coneville. So he lied again. He didn't know that I had done my own investigation and I knew Tamra was from Coneville. He knew he couldn't hang around Lafayette without me knowing so I guess he went to her hometown to see her. I didn't say a word because I knew the opportunity would present itself for me to say something.

    The opportunity presented itself sooner than expected. The following week, I took my grandma shopping in University City over an hour and a half away. So, it was dark when I returned. Will called me when I was about 20 minutes away and said he was dropping his kids off at the game and would be coming to my grandma's house immediately after. When I arrived at my grandma's house, he was not there. We got the shopping bags out of the car and I waited a few minutes. I knew it didn't take that long for him to make it to my grandma's house. Everything in this town was no more than ten minutes away from each other. I started getting this eerie feeling and I just couldn't sit still. I became restless in my spirit. Nobody has to tell you that your spouse is being unfaithful. If you are in tune to yourself and listen to your spirit it will tell you all you need to know. I knew it; I just didn't know who. I told my grandma I would be right back. I accidentally left my cell phone but my mind was occupied by the spirit leading me to where I knew my husband was. I always paid attention yet I often did not say anything until the right time. I saw the house where Tamra's car was parked each time I went by my mother's house. It was right down the street from my mama. I knew she wasn't from her but I knew she worked in this town from the smock she was wearing the first time I saw her. I assumed she rented that house because Coneville was a pretty good distance to drive each day to work in Lafayette. So I went straight to that house.

    When I pulled up to the dark house and saw the gray Dodge Charger parked underneath the porch and Rosie Mae's orange rust colored car parked right behind it as if it usually parked there. I pulled crossways behind Rosie Mae's car. I blocked them in; nobody is leaving until I leave. I got out and knocked on the door. I heard Tamra say, " your wife is knocking on my door". I kept knocking but he would not come to the door. Then, I walked around the house knocking on all the windows yelling. "Will I know you're in there and you need to come on out." I got around to the bedroom window and the blinds were open with the television on. I could see my husband standing over this woman's bed and I could hear her on the phone calling the police. "Y'all need to hurry up and get somebody over here cause his wife at my house, beating on my window." I was enraged seeing him standing in that woman's bedroom. I thought about all that I experienced at my wedding, the harassment I was subjected to by his mama and last wife, and the humiliation he has put me through. We had only been married two months and he was with another woman! My knocks turned into punches and I unconsciously punched straight through the window. I bust the glass out and broke the pane. They both ran out of the room. I walked to the neighbor's house and asked to use the phone. I called my mama and told her to come down the street. "You'll see my car." " Just come down the street because I think I'm about to go to jail again." She asked, "what's going on?" I said, "I can't talk right now, just come on." I really didn't have the mental capacity to explain. My adrenaline was through the roof.

By the time I walked to the front, two police had pulled up, my mama and sister Kim, Will and Tamra were all standing in the front yard. As the last person emerging from the back, all eyes were on me. Will said, "baby just listen to what she has to say". My eyes got really big then and I looked at her in anticipation of what she could possibly have to say to me. "He just came over here to get on my ass about calling his phone private, and told me don't call him anymore he's married now." After a moment of silence with everybody awaiting my response to that crap, I looked around at everyone including the police and asked in the softest, calmest voice, "do I look like a fool to you?" "Do I look like a fool to you?" "She's going to say whatever you want her to say to keep y'all's situation the way it is." "Like she told me, she has laid low since your last wife." "I ain't got time for this, but like you say, if I didn't put my hand on you, you weren't here or it wasn't you." " Well, I put my hand on you buddy, now you can have her 'cause I don't want you anymore." I start to walk to my car. Then Tamra has the nerve to address me, "you knew what you married when you was the side hoe, you got what you expected." I could hear my sister Kim in the background saying, "Sus, she don't want none, she don't want none; but go'on give it to her. "; and my mama saying "nooo Leia, nooo Leia." They knew that once someone provoked me, it was like poking a sleeping bear. I corrected Tamra, "it's when you were not was and I never was a side hoe I dated a liar." "And woman, my problem is with my husband not with you." "That is who I was talking to." "I would appreciate it if you would continue to lay low and be quiet like you have with his second wife and now his third wife." "You have been his side hoe through two wives and he still didn't think enough of you to marry you, I would be quiet if I were you."

Then she ran up to me and I clocked her so hard in her left jaw that it knocked her off her feet. The police grabbed me, but I didn't resist. I was my usual cool self. Tamra started yelling, "I want to press charges and she busted my window out." Then Will says, "baby I love you, I don't love this hoe." Now that set me off and made me lose my cool. I have had enough of false I love you's in my life. I latched onto him like a spider monkey. I jumped up on him, wrapped my legs around his waist, and punched him in his mouth and face until the police pulled us apart. The officer said, "ma'am, I'm going to have to arrest you if you keep putting your hands on people." There was blood everywhere and all over his white t-shirt. It actually wasn't from his face; it was from the glass cutting my hand when I punched through the window. I overheard the officer asking him, "do you want to press charges, you're bleeding." He said no, that's my wife. Tamra was yelling I want to press charges for my window. Will said no, "I'll pay for the window; no one's pressing charges on my wife." It was stupid of me but at this point I was so furious I kept talking crap until the police made me leave. I said to Tamra, "you need to press charges for your face because I knocked your ass out." Then I got in my car, as I was driving off and I yelled out of the window, "Will you better beat me home."

    We didn't talk about it that night. I slept on the couch because I didn't want to be near him. The next morning I woke up, he was sitting beside me on the couch. He started the conversation, "you need to grow up." "Only a little girl calls her mama when she has a problem; you need to learn to keep your mama and family out of our business." I said, "your mama has been in our relationship and marriage from the very beginning and your last wife, your side women, and the entire community." "For a change, I called someone to support me and to see that I wasn't to blame; but none of it would have happened if it wasn't for you." He said, "It was all your fault because you shouldn't have come looking for me." I tried to defuse the situation and offer a resolution. I actually felt kind of guilty of acting a fool in front of everyone. I said, "Look, it's not my fault but we have been through alot already and I think we should go to counseling if we want this marriage to work." Will replied, "I don't need no stranger trying to tell me about my business". "You need to go to counseling to learn how to keep your mama out of our marriage." I couldn't believe that he blamed this on me.

    Over the next couple of weeks Will continued to leave for unaccounted, extended amounts of time. Then I noticed that he often took lunch breaks at this B&W's

Burger Spot. When he was off work and the kids and I ordered food from there, he never wanted anything and even said he didn't really like the food. I put two and two together and knew that he was seeing somebody there. I got food from there one day and noticed how nasty this lady looked at me. I didn't know her but it was enough for me not to want to go back again.

  This Sunday, he left home in the morning and did not return until around 8:30 at night. I had been calling his phone all day and he did not answer. His daughter from his first marriage had been at our house for the weekend. She told me, "Leia don't call him anymore". "He's probably gone with Olivia." "He's been talking to her since before y'all got married and I think she is married too." "He talks to lots of women on the phone." "I really love you, and I want the best for you." "The best for you is not my daddy; you deserve better." "I saw all the conversations with the different women on his phone when he lets me use his phone because you know I don't have one." I told her, "thank you Laquandra." "I really needed to hear that." "I will not tell him that you let me know anything." Then her mama arrived to pick her up just as he pulled into the driveway. When he walked in the house, I noticed that he wasn't wearing his wedding band. I looked at him but I didn't say a word. He started with me. "Why did you cook that crap and you know I don't eat it?" I didn't say anything and just kept fixing my children's plates. He just kept talking. "You don't know how to cook." "You don't know how to be a good wife." "I should have stayed with my last wife." Now that provoked me to say something. I said in the most calm voice, "I'm hip to the game." "You ain't gotta come in here trying to pick a fight with me so that you can leave again." "If you want to go back out there with your whores, you don't need an excuse." "That door will let you out just like it let you in without picking an argument with me." "You can go."

He said something and I didn't hear him and I said, "what did you say?" As I turned with one of the twin's plates, I felt like I had a long blink and the left side of my head and ear hurt really. I was dazed. Will had punched me on the left side of my face and said, "what did I tell you about saying what to me?" He punched me in my face again, this time knocking out. I woke up from gasping for air from a kick to my ribcage. He continued to stomp me in my stomach and chest until it kicked him in his groin. As he hurled over grabbing his groin, I grabbed a chair from the table and beat him over the back with it until the legs broke off in my hands. He finally went into the living room and sat down but he kept talking. "You're not a good wife." "I never should have married you." "You're not a real woman and you are not a good mama." I was ignoring everything, cleaning the chilli from the floor, and consoling my children that were upset at watching us fight. However, that "not a good mama" part set me off. I said, "Maybe I am a bad mama and not a good woman, as your wife, I am a reflection of you." "So you are nothing either, boy." He grabbed me by the throat, picked me up from the floor and threw me onto the leather white couch. He sat on my chest, choking me the left hand and punching me in my jaw with the right hand. It felt like he punched me over twenty times in the same place. I knew my jaw bone was broken. I couldn't breathe with him sitting on my chest, holding my throat, and pushing my face into the leather couch. I wrestled his hand free from my neck so that I could breathe; but when I turned my face from the couch it was met with more blows to the front of my face. I was punching him back in the face and we were blow for blow but his body weight of over 200 lbs on my chest was taking my breath away. I had to get him off of me. I had to think fast. I yelled, "you're a punk fighting a woman like this." "Get up and fight me face to face like a real man." Then he jumped up, squared up, and said, "come on, come on bitch". "Fight me like a man." In the heat of the moment I yelled again, "look!" I pointed at the mirror. Will looked at the big mirror on our living room wall. Then I said in a soft voice, "Look at yourself; look at you telling your wife, the mother of your son, "come on bitch and fight you like a man." "Look at our son watching what you are doing to his mother." Then he walks up to me and spits in my face, goes into the bedroom, and closes the door.

    I dressed my children and took them to my grandma's house before I left for work that night. I was not going to leave them there with him. I left early but he did not question me; actually we said nothing else to each other after that fight. He had hit me before but he would act like he was just playing; and he would hit me like he was in a brawl with a man. I would have bruises on me from how hard he would hit me but he would say that I was just being sensitive. After this fight, I went to the hospital not because I was hurt so bad but because I wanted to get documentation of what happened. He dug the skin from my neck when I was trying to pry his hand away. The abrasions on my neck looked like tiger claw scratches. My ribs were bruised purple and blue from his stomps and kicks. My jaw was double in size, black and blue in color from the consistent pounding in nearly the same location. I couldn't chew on that side of my mouth. That was the last straw for me. He didn't know that I had been planning to leave him anyway.

When he was at work, my homeboy, my sister Kim, and her boyfriend helped me move out. I heard that one of his friends called and asked him, "hey are you getting new furniture?" He said, "no why?" "Cause your wife moving all y'all shit out." I was only getting my children's beds and some of our clothes. Even if I did, I bought everything in the house. When he pulled the stunt of leaving to go work in Iraq and lying to come back, he broke his contract. His daughter Laquandra told me that he broke his contract to come back and be with Emma because he heard she had a new man. He used me and our unborn child to say that I had complications with the pregnancy so that he could get back to her. The joke was on him though. He didn't read the fine print of his contract. When you break the contract as a civilian worker you have to pay the taxes on the initially tax free money that you had already been paid. He drew his retirement down from his job before he left, so he had to start all over on his job also. He was paying her alimony and child support from the already heavily taxed money. So, I was the breadwinner. However, to add insult to injury, when I went to get my bank statements to give to the apartment complex where I was moving, I saw where he had been taking other women to the hotels with my money because we had joint accounts. The sad part about it was that while he was disrespecting our marriage he could have at least respected me enough by paying cash for the room instead of swiping the debit card from our joint accounts to take women to hotels with my money. I knew that no relationship was perfect. I had been advised by some older ladies before, "pick your poison". That meant choosing which flaw of your mate you would deal with because none of them were perfect. Well, I wasn't going to deal with being beat on, cheated on, disrespected, and him spending my money on other women. I was done with him.

By the time Will made it to the house, we were gone. I had been putting money aside and had furniture on layaway long before I left him. I knew I was going to leave him. I really wanted to raise my children in a two parent household and I thought he was a good father. Being a good father was just another one of his many lies. I had many older women coming up to me telling me, "he's a good man" or "you just have to let him get it out of his system". I am not my mama or my grandmama. Those generations of women allowed their husbands to cheat and abuse them and they remained in the marriage. Not me. Those very words were why black women at one time had the leading cases of HIV because we allowed men to go "get it out of his system", and waited for them to return to us. I hadn't realized it yet but I deserved better than someone that would go out and use themselves all up with all the women that they wanted. Then bring back to me what's left of him; and I'm supposed to accept him and love him. However, he told everyone I was cheating and left him for another man. He told everyone that his Emma and Rosie Mae were correct that I was a whore. What he didn't realize was that my daddy called me a whore, Devonte called me a whore, his mama called me a whore, and his last wife called me a whore. I was numb to it by now. You can call me what you want but no one can call me his wife anymore because I was going to file for a divorce.

While at work on my birthday, November 11th, Tequilla told me that I had a visitor. I thought maybe it was James because he was the only one who would stop by to visit sometimes. It was the Constable from the neighboring town and county. He said, "happy birthday and you have been served". I said, "wait a minute". I looked at the papers and handed them back to him and said, "don't get yourself in trouble serving fraudulent documents outside of your jurisdiction." "Before you serve something for a so-called friend that has not gone through an attorney or court, it might be wise to take a look at them." "They are the divorce papers from his last marriage to which he had white-ed out Emma's name and written in my name and some of the pages are missing." "I'm not signing that." "Tell him I will file for the divorce the correct way."

The ladies at work and my friends were telling me to give my marriage one last shot before I completely give up. Everybody was saying he's doing all of this because he wants you back. So against my better judgement, I answered his call and I met him at our old house to stay the night. He tried to be intimate with me. I declined his advances. I told him, "I don't know what you've been doing and who you've been doing it with since I left you." " You won't be getting anything from me until you get tested." I had gone to the clinic about two hours away from Lafayette to get tested. Nothing's confidential in this town; so if he gave me anything, I could deal with it in private. I told the nurse, "I would like to be tested for everything." She looked in shock and said, "have you been exposed to something?" I said, "I found out my husband has been cheating, so I don't know what I've been exposed to." She said, "I'm sorry to hear that but I understand and I'm glad you are taking your health into your own hands." Lucky for him everything turned out negative, because it would have been ugly if I had any different results. That was another reason I gave him a second chance. I was telling myself that maybe he wasn't sleeping with the other women.

     While we were in bed, his phone rang at 3:00 in the morning. He declined the call; then I could hear text messages. I asked who it was. He said, "it's my kids saying goodnight". I knew he was still lying but I did not feel like getting out of bed and leaving at that time. The next morning, whoever was on the other end of his phone last night had put all of the tires on flat on my new white Honda Accord. I didn't even get mad. I just said, "I want them fixed and fixed today". He waited all day to get them fixed because he had planned a barbecue and invited the entire town to the house. He knew that if he had gotten them fixed earlier, I would have been gone. He said the barbecue was to let everyone know that he won his wife back. It was a celebration of a new start for us. He invited the Mayor, the police chief, the fire chief, all of the important people in town. William was what I called a people pleaser. He would mow the lawns of the elderly for free, rub elbows with the city officials, but come home and not even speak to his wife. Everybody that was anybody was at this cookout.

I was in the house fixing the twins a plate and I heard the screen door open, it was Rosie Mae. I hadn't seen her since my wedding. She put her purse on the table and said, "when I see you, you son of a bitch you, didn't I tell you I was going to get you?" "What are you doing back here anyway?" I asked, "why do you want to get me?" "Have you not noticed that I never disrespected you or said anything back to you after all of the ugly things you said to me?" "What did I ever do to you?" "Get to know me for yourself and be your own judge of character; and don't listen to Emma." "Ma'am you are old enough to be my grandma and I would never disrespect you." "I am not the person that Emma describes; give me a chance." Then she walked up to me and punched me in my left eye. I did not hit her back initially. I bent down to take off my zebra print pumps and she rushed me, knocking me into the counter. When I looked up she had hit my twins and knocked them on the floor. Before I knew it, I punched her in the face so many times I lost count. Her glasses and watch went flying. I thought about what she did at my wedding, calling me when I was pregnant saying my unborn child should die, and hitting my children and me. Someone outside yelled to Will, "do you hear that bumping in your house?" At that moment, I pushed Rosie Mae down the stairs. Will picked up his mama and took her outside and for the first time told her she had no right to come to his house and fight his wife. She was wrong. When we got outside everyone knew we had been fighting and Emma was sitting in the front yard. She had called and set it all up. Even though Will stood up for me. It was too late. I wanted nothing more with this family.

When Will returned from Iraq, he did not get his job back in Lafayette. He had to become a police officer in the neighboring town of Arkdale. After he would get off work, Will started waiting on me in the parking lot after my shift. He called my cell phone all the time. He started calling the work phone when I didn't answer the cell phone. I would find flowers delivered to the station to me all the time. I worked the 2-10 shift and had my children in night daycare. After picking up the kids, when I arrived at my apartment from work one night, he jumped from behind the dumpster and walked up to my window. I didn't get out because I knew I couldn't run with the children. He said, "I want you to come home; I'm sorry for everything I did." "I'm sorry for what my mama did." "I just sent those fake divorce papers to try to scare you into coming back home." "I want to show you that I'm not like your stepdad, I want to protect you, and I will never let anyone hurt you." I said to him through the window, "how dare you try to use that to get me back!" "How dare you try to use something so hurtful that happened to me as a child, to try and spin this in your favor!" "Well I'm not that little girl anymore." "I'm not hurt anymore and I don't need anybody to protect me, especially not you." " I am a woman that can protect herself." He said, "if I were at the crossroads and had to choose between the devil and God and the devil would give you back to me, I would go with the devil." "If we can't be together then we might as well be dead." Then he pulled out his gun. I said, "shoot yourself first then fool", and sat there and looked at him through the driver side window. It was foolish of me to say that, but I knew he was trying to intimidate me and scare me into doing what he wanted. It would have been better to be dead than to go back to him anyway. Everything in life prepares us for the next obstacle in life. My experience in the hospital and being told that I could die, made me no longer fear death. I had conquered that fear and I was not afraid of his threats.

    I knew my apartment was on the outskirts of town but nobody knew where it was. I wondered how he found where I lived. Anna, who worked at Arkdale Police Department with Will called Lafayette one day to warn me. She said, "I overheard your husband talking to someone named Anthony that works at the PD with you." "Will paid him to follow you and find out where you live." "He also asked him to call him when he saw you and James together because he knew that you and James were messing around." James and I were only friends. I was attracted to him but James was married. Will just couldn't accept that I left him for me and wasn't coming back. No woman had ever left him. It was like a game for him. I knew and he knew that he didn't want me, but he wanted to be the person to leave the marriage not me. He was the one that divorced all of his wives. Emma got wind that I left him and told him he could come back home with her. She said she kept his bed warm for him. I thought it was crazy that she still wanted him back after all he had put her through. She told me that he had cheated on her plenty of times but he wasn't going anywhere and he would never be mine. To her dismay, he did leave her but it was sad that she was waiting on him. Laquandra told me that he used to whip Emma with belts like she was a child or an animal. She said she also remembered that he would hit and fight her mother as well. There is no way I would want to go back to anyone that treated me that bad. However, when you're done with someone you don't care who they date. Emma can have him. But more importantly, Anthony was so wrong for following me and reporting back to my husband.. He was my fellow police officer at the same PD and he put my life and my children's lives in danger. I knew that Anthony probably did that to me because I did not give him any play. He tried to date me when I first started at the PD and because I rejected his advances, he became really nasty acting to me. It's sad that men will search for your demise out of vengeance because you choose not to be with them. He was married anyway.

    I soon found out that Anthony was not the only person stabbing me in the back. Thursday, we had a dispatcher training at Magnolia State University, about four hours from Lafayette. I told the ladies what was going on with me so no one knew where our training was but the chief. When the ladies and I got back from dinner, I saw Will, walking across the parking lot towards us. He had to have been waiting in the parking lot for hours because we went to the mall then to dinner for a couple of hours. He tried to make me let him up to my hotel room. I refused. He said, "you must have James up there?" I said, "there is no one there but I'm not going to let you in my room." He said, "we need to talk so you need to let me up". We went back and forth and I texted the ladies to stay with me in the lobby. He asked, "why won't these ladies leave?" "You must have told them something bad about me?" He was so angry. He hated for people to get a bad impression of him, the "people pleaser". I told him he had to leave and it was over. We were never getting back together. He said, "just let me stay the night and tomorrow I'll go home and never bother you again; I'm too tired to drive back tonight." "I'll give you the divorce." I said, "you being tired is not my problem". "I never told you I was here or knew you were coming." "If you can't drive back, go and get yourself a hotel, and get some rest until the morning." He was furious. We watched as he drove off. He was in a vehicle I had never seen before. I knew he had something else planned for me but it didn't workout for him. After he left I filed a report with the Magnolia State University Police Department.

  When we returned to Lafayette, I decided to file for a restraining order. Too many things have happened and I need to keep him away from us. On my lunch break, I walked around to the Office of Domestic Violence and filed the paperwork to initiate a restraining order. After I finished I returned to my office and started back working. About an hour later, an officer came in to relieve me and told me that the chief wanted to see me. I went into the chief's office and he said, "Sgt. Daisy brought this to my attention". "Why hadn't you told me about this?" I replied, "I just followed the proper process by filing the reports each time an incident happened; I didn't think I needed to report it to you." Then Chief Kelly responded, "well I told you when you first started here that these men are dogs and don't get involved with any of them." "I told you that they would pass you around like a dirty rag, but you didn't listen, now you have cheated on your husband and ruined your marriage." I replied, "with all due respect Chief, how did you get that idea from me filing a restraining order?" He responded, "I'm asking the questions here." "Sgt. Daisy also provided me with these reports that you filed." "Why wasn't I told that you had an incident when I sent you all off to training?" "And you say in your report at Magnolia State University Police Department that he came there unannounced and tried to force you to allow him to stay in your room, is that correct?" I said, "yes". Then he said, "I have done my own investigation on the matter and I heard that you invited him to come as a vacation or get away for the two of you." "I believe that is true instead of what you're saying; if not, how did he even find out you all were there?" I said I don't know; I didn't tell him. The chief insisted, "oh yeah you know, I believe you invited him then tried to invite this fireman you date so you had to get rid of your husband." I objected to what the chief said, "I never told him where I was, I hadn't talked to him, and we no longer live together, so I really don't know how he found out where we were!" I was astonished at the accusations by the chief. Then the Chief asked the Assistant Chief for his input because unknowing to me, he had him to investigate my situation. Assistant Chief Winston said, "I called the Arkdale and talked to their chief." "He said that her husband was at work that day then came in about an hour after his shift had begun and said he had a family emergency and needed to leave work." "I believe that if they planned to go to Magnolia State University together, he would have taken off work prior to that day and not have had to call in." "Some other officers stated that they saw Officer William Blake talking to you, chief and the log book shows that you traveled to Arkdale that day prior to Officer Blake taking off work." "I believe this young lady." Chief Kelly looked at his assistant chief with disguised anger underneath a silly smirk on his face. Then he admitted, "maybe I did accidentally say something about the dispatchers going to training." "Your husband has proven to be nothing but a standup guy to me." "Your actions are the ones that are in question; so you need to be really careful because nothing should have been happening with my employees right underneath my nose and I know nothing about it." " You need to report any and everything from this day forward directly to me." I responded, "my soon to be ex-husband and your friend will report everything to you". "You'll believe him anyway." Then I got up and walked out.

When I left the office, I figured Assistant Chief Winston would probably get in trouble so I told him, "you didn't have to do that and I really appreciate you for just being honest." He is usually a very stern man of little words and I never heard him say much more than hello. I was so accustomed to people seeing and knowing bad things had happened and they turned a blind eye to it. People will see things and gossip about it but nobody will speak up for what's right. In this case, Sgt. Daisy and the chief did more than ignore my husband's wrongs, they really aided Will in his shenanigans. Sgt. Daisy was just being messy by reporting my situation to the chief. All she had to do was her job. Instead, she opted to tell everyone what was in my report. People don't realize how talking about other people's business and being nosey could cause harm to people's lives. Mind your own business. Then the Chief chose to take sides with that demon and it corroborated with his evil antics. However, it took a lot of courage for Assistant Chief Winston to stand up, challenge his boss, and call him out. I later found out that my husband Will and my chief had been talking, hanging out, and picking up women together. Now it made sense that he would accuse me of being a liar.

James started coming by checking on the kids and I more often. We got closer. He was the opposite of Will in every way. James was not very tall and dark skinned. Will was 6'4 and looked biracial but he wasn't. He was a splitting image of his mother, a red faced, hazel eyed mean looking woman. James also looked like he could have been my step father's son. They both fit the redbone pretty boy perception. James was everything I would want in a husband except he was married. Everyone knew James and I were friends and just like any other cheating person, my husband accused me of having an affair with James. The cheater always expects and accuses you of doing what they are doing; and he was on a mission to try and find out.

Meanwhile, I had called Sister Linda Green to start my Bible study again. It had been years since I attended the Kingdom Hall. Difficult situations sometimes make people look to God for direction. Separating and divorcing is one of the most difficult situations a person can experience. I often feel that I have been experiencing a lot of these bad things because I made choices outside of God's arrangement. I have tried living my life the way I thought was best, now I think it is time that I try doing it the way God says is best. Each week Sister Greene over for my Bible study and my children and I attend all meetings and services at the Kingdom Hall.

During the time I was trying to fix my life through God, my soon to be ex-husband was trying to destroy it by dragging my name through the mud. We had phones on the same account. I totally forgot when I left him. He got detailed billing on my phone and called all the unfamiliar numbers to find out to whom they belonged. I got a call from James. He sounded frantic and upset. He said, "I just left the City Council meeting and your husband was there." "He had his name added to the docket to voice some concerns he had in the community." "When it was his time to speak, he stood up and said, "how does a citizen address the issue of the assistant fire chief messing around with his wife." "The entire room gasped in shock." "Then he pulled out your phone bill and said, I have proof that he and my wife have been talking to each other all the time." "I'm trying to make my marriage work but your husband won't leave my wife alone." "She gets out of bed with me at night to go talk to him on the phone." "They must be in love or something." "The sheriff escorted him out yet he was still yelling things as he exited, but the damage was done." "Then everyone looked at me because the mayor is my wife." "I'm gonna get him but I just don't know how."James was livid. He said, "now I have a worse situation to deal with at home." I apologized to James, "I'm sorry, I got you in this." "I will call your wife and explain everything." James said, "don't you call her." "I will talk to my own wife." I stayed in my place because I didn't want to make matters worse. Now the whole town of Lafayette believes we are having an affair. Will knew that we both worked for the city and his sole purpose was to cause problems for us both. He couldn't handle the idea of me cheating but I was supposed to forgive his cheating. What's good for the goose is good for the gander. I wished I was cheating and could give him a dose of his own medicine. However, I always believed that you cannot get even with someone cheating on you. I was not about to ruin my reputation or my body trying to get even with him. Will wanted to destroy me for leaving him. He said that no woman ever leaves him and he wasn't letting me go.

    I finally filed for divorce and along with that, I filed for a restraining order. William had shown me that he would stop at nothing to get me back or "get me back" for leaving him. I was referred to the services of the domestic violence shelter called Safe Home. At the initial intake, they told me that I would have to participate in counseling, attend group sessions and speak about my experiences at the Safe Homes events. I agreed because I felt like it was time for me to address some of the things I had experienced and learn to heal.

    At the first session, I was asked questions to detail my experiences with my husband. Then I was asked if I had ever been abused when I was a child. I answered yes and I was asked to elaborate on those experiences as well. I went through a series of exercises at each session that made me open up about my past. As I recounted things from my past, I noticed that it was like reliving them all over again. The feelings and emotions of everything that happened were fresh like it were brand new. I sank into a deep depression. I stopped bathing, barely ate, and couldn't sleep. Ms. Jennette, the director over Safe House, threw another wrench in the situation that made me even more depressed by believing the gossip of the streets. She said, "I heard that your husband contested the restraining order." "He said he wanted counseling, to keep his marriage, and that the reason you all were separated was because you were having an affair with the mayor's husband." "I just wanted to tell you that the Bible forbids adultery and you brought this all on yourself by cheating with that woman's husband." "She is a good woman and doesn't deserve that." I responded, "he and I are just friends, my husband is lying". Ms. Jennette said, "you have no business being friends with a married man and you still brought this on yourself because the Bible says to abstain from even the look of evil." "You shouldn't do anything that could be perceived as wrong; that includes as a married woman yourself, being friends with a man and especially men that have wives." I couldn't understand how I could control the perceptions of others. The actions of any person could be totally innocent yet be perceived differently by whomever was looking. I perceived all them at Safe Home as "men hating" women. They were all single women of varying ages that frequently participated in male bashing. They often talked about how men will do you so wrong, you have to be careful about having your children around them because many of them are pedophiles, they all cheat, and you can't trust them. I noticed how I was required to divulge so much about myself; then they used the Bible to gauge how my life's choices were incorrect. They psychologically broke me down to then try and build me back up to the person they thought I should be, just like them. They did all of the clients like that. Most of the ladies that worked there were survivors of domestic violence and had gone through the Safe Home program as well. So they could relate to us, knew our triggers, and knew how to mentally conquer each one of us. We were them.

The next counseling session was group therapy and I was glad to not be alone with Ms. Jennette. She makes me feel so bad. When we went to the session, instead of the clients being there, it was all the workers there and Ms. Jennette. They asked me to sit down in a chair placed in the center of the room. Then Ms. Jennette asked us to all bow our heads and she started to pray. "God forgive this sinner and help her to repent of her adulterous ways." "Forgive her for ruining her marriage and the marriage of others." "Help her to let go of her evil ways and accept your ways Lord God." Then all the ladies started walking around me speaking in tongues as if they all were in a trance. Each one of them was throwing Holy Water on me. One older lady held my head back and marked a cross in my forehead with anointing oil. What I noticed about each one of those ladies that worked at Safe Home is that none of them had a husband or mate. Each one was single and overactive in the church. God is what they used to fix their brokenness and they were trying to force it into me as well. It only broke me more. I felt like I failed God. I made all of these poor decisions and I deserved what had happened to me. I felt so low when I left there that night.

When I went home that night, I was so downhearted; I felt like I was to blame for everything bad that happened in my life. I thought about the fact that I brought children in this world to a broken mother that has repeated the cycle of a single parent home with an absent father. I tried to stay with this man through all of the problems to prevent being a single mother again. I learned that the thing we try hardest to not become will be the very thing that we will become. What you focus on, good or bad is what you manifest in life. I knew that once the relationship was over, the father of my children wouldn't take care of my children like they deserve. Usually when the relationship is over, the father becomes more absent from the child's life. It's my fault that now my son's dad is leaving his life too, just like my other three children. I'm making a pattern of leaving these men and ruining my children's lives. Maybe Ms. Jennette was correct, I shouldn't have been friends with James. I have ruined my life, another child's life, James life, and his wife. I think the best way to resolve it all is to just kill myself. It will save everyone from further heartbreak and disappointment. I got the razor blade from my bathroom and sat down on the couch. Since I caused all of this mess in everybody's life, the only way I can see out of it is to give my life as a sacrifice. I put the razor blade to my wrist. I had come to peace with my decision. There was no other way. This is what I have to do. I started to press the blade into my wrist, and felt the cool steel press against my skin. Then my phone rings. It was my older sister Berniece. I told her what was going on and what I had experienced that night at Safe Home. Berniece said, "remember where we came from." " We have experienced worse than that in our lives and we have overcome it." "Those people don't know you so their opinion of you doesn't matter. " "Get whatever you need to get from them and keep it moving." " Keep your interactions only on an as needed basis." "Don't let what they say affect you." "We are bendable but we are not breakable." Those few words that my sister said, literally saved my life. To recognize that my experiences and my mistakes did not define me, was a pivotal point in my life. They may have figuratively bent me but they can't break me. I can recover. I can heal. I can start over. I am not who anybody says I am; I am who I believe I am.

Since I have been living on my own, I have a peace of mind that I never experienced with my husband. It's a peace of not having to worry where he is when he's not home, a peace of going when and where I want without any resistance, and not worrying about any women cutting up my tires or calling my phone blocked and private. That peace also came with a loneliness that I never experienced. I thought about going back to him. I missed him when I recalled the good times we had experienced. My sole desire was to raise my children in a two parent household. Our son was asking for his daddy and it really broke my heart because I felt like I was taking my son away from his dad. It was my responsibility to provide for the emotional needs of my children as well and that included I asked my Bible study conductor what she thought about divorce and she had me read two scriptures aloud. Matthew 5:32 said, *"But I say to you that everyone who divorces his wife, except on the ground of sexual immorality, makes her commit adultery, and whoever marries a divorced woman commits adultery."* And I read Romans 7:2, *"For a married woman is bound by law to her husband while he lives, but if her husband dies she is released from the law of marriage."* Then Sister Green explained, "from these scriptures you can see that the Bible only gives two reasons for divorce and that is adultery or death." "If you forgive him for adultery and don't leave him, you can't go back and decide later to divorce him." I asked, "well what about abuse?" She said the Bible didn't say abuse. "We must pray to Jehovah for strength to endure and that Jehovah can help your husband change his ways." "My husband was abusive but I did what the Bible said and I just prayed for us both; and it's hard trying to raise kids alone so I decided to stay until my kids grew up." "Actually I stayed until he died from cancer so I abided by God's laws." "You also have to consider how people will view you as a single mother." I told her thank you and I considered what the scriptures and what she said. I wanted to give in and answer his calls; but I started to remind myself of the bad times. The bad outweighed the good. I realized listening to her, that she was like many women in my life. They experienced infidelity but stayed with their husbands because they thought that they didn't have the strength to raise their children alone. They also were concerned with how people looked down on single mothers, viewed them as weak or blemished and they didn't want to be seen that way. I didn't think much of myself but I knew that I deserved better than him. I didn't go back to him.

    Not going back to him turned him into another kind of monster. That Saturday night that he forced himself into my apartment and raped me, made me feel so disgusting but I was kind of used to it. That's why I just lied in bed and stopped fighting him. I just let him have his way. Most people that came into my life used me and my body some kind of way. I started being used as somebody's fleshpot at eight years old. It changed my feelings about sex and I never associated it love. I actually never really desired sex and never wanted affection. I wasn't affectionate with my children and I felt so bad about it. I wanted to be affectionate because I knew children needed that from their mothers, but I didn't know how. When I tried hugging them it made me so uncomfortable. I felt like I was violating them like people violated me so I didn't touch them unless absolutely necessary. I hated bathtime and changing diapers because it made me uncomfortable seeing nude children and babies. I looked at them as little as possible. I breastfeed them because I wanted to give them the most beneficial things for them but I would sometimes silently cry while nursing because a baby was touching an intimate part of me, my breast; and it felt so unnatural. I was uncomfortable being touched by anyone. I was never hugged and kissed by my mother or father and when I was touched, it was by some man fulfilling his sexual desires though my body. This time it was my husband, the police officer, not only fulfilling his desires but dually trying to dismantle what was left of my composure as punishment for leaving him.

    A couple of weeks later, Safe Home held their annual "A Walk in Her Shoes" Domestic Violence Awareness walkathon. I took my sister Berneice's advice and I didn't attend anything that wasn't mandatory. I learned that you have to protect your spirit and your energy from negativity. I stayed away from those ladies as much as possible because they emotionally took me to a very dark place. Distancing myself helped me remain positive about myself and mentally heal from my separation and the abuse I had experienced. The walkathon's purpose was to raise awareness and money for the cause of preventing domestic violence and supporting women that had been victims of domestic violence. High heels and pumps were donated and men wore those heels and walked in them in the walkathon to support the cause. On the 6:00 pm news, everyone appeared to have had a good time. A lot of people came out to support the event. The reporter interviewed the most charismatic participant and largest contributor to the event; it was my husband William. There he was on display, a pig in high heels. Then the director of Safe Home, Ms. Jeanette was in the interview with Will with her arm around him saying how much she appreciated his support. I was outdone. She was well aware of who he was and what he had done but according to everyone else's perspective, I was the culprit in this situation. I'm glad I didn't attend because as a victim, that was a slap in my face. The Safe Home staff was glorifying the abuser.

The time I was spending alone was allowing me to get to know myself. I started realizing that to fix things in my life, my focus should be on fixing myself and not trying to understand the people that had done and said those terrible things to me. It bothered me for so many years what people said about me, how they viewed me, and the false names they called me. I always had a comeback. I was always defensive. I realized that I was upset because I subliminally believed those disturbing things about myself. When I consistently heard degrading things from the people closest to me, I unconsciously started to believe them. Fighting everyone that offended me was just a manifestation of the battle I was fighting within myself about who I was. I discovered that it only mattered what I thought of myself and not what others thought of me and my decisions. I also realized what I thought I was, how I viewed others, and how they viewed me was defined by tradition and society's conditioning of what defines us. I started to redefine in my mind who and what I was. I am not who anyone says that I am. I am who I choose to be. I didn't know what that was yet but I did know what it wasn't. I wasn't a whore. I wasn't weak for deciding to be a single mother instead of staying in a bad marriage. I couldn't understand how so many people thought that it was not justifiable to leave your husband for abuse but I could leave him for adultery, if I wanted to but I didn't have to. I could not accept that women stayed because of fear of judgement. Many of our mothers and grandmothers experienced the same things because it was acceptable for men to cheat and beat their wives and we were supposed to stay to keep the family together.

Chapter Thirteen: The Unholy Pastor and Unprofessional Mayor

I quit the police department. I wanted to distance myself from those negative people, like the chief that supported William. I started working as a secretary for a nonprofit community service agency in Lafayette that provided low income families with assistance with housing, food, and childcare. The day for our first board meeting had arrived. My office was located directly across the hall from the board room. I had my door cracked as the board members were arriving. I could feel eyes on me. Someone was watching me. When I looked up, I made eye contact with the mayor, James's wife. I had no idea that she was on the board. I no longer liked this job. After entering the meeting, it was so uncomfortable. You could cut the tension in the air with a knife. I said very few words to anyone. I just passed out the agenda for the meeting and directed everyone to the lunch that was served. I recorded the meeting minutes and returned to my office. The older white lady, Ruth, who was a director called me back to the boardroom after most board members were gone.

She said, "Leia, I would like to introduce you to Mayor Robin Mitchell." We shook hands and I said, "nice to meet you". Ruth was so talkative and was really just telling all of my business. "Leia has four kids but still looks so young and doesn't look like she has borne one child." "I have been encouraging her to go back to school because she is so smart." "I wanted to introduce you all because I know it helps sometimes to see someone like yourself being successful and maybe the mayor could be a mentor for you Leia." "Just an idea." Mayor Mitchell started bragging about her education, accomplishments, and how much money she had. She talked about how she traveled the world, experienced so much, and how she had so much money that she was bored and didn't know what to do now. The city engineer overheard the conversation, started laughing, and said, "so much for your bucket list, there's nothing left for you to do." Then he said, "let somebody else help a little bit; don't just lay on your own horn, let someone else toot it for you." Then he walked out continuing to laugh.

I knew that Mayor Mitchell felt insecure because she was finally faced with the woman that her husband was publicly accused of having an affair. She was trying to size me up and let me know that she was superior to me. It was actually pathetic and obvious to all present that she was bragging on herself. It was counter effective and made her look weak. What was really sad yet very common was that when men are unfaithful we compare ourselves to the other woman. She was very accomplished and should not have felt less of a woman or the need to compare herself to me or anyone else if her husband cheated. Any person's choice to cheat is a personal decision and has nothing to do with the worth and value of the spouse. I didn't care what she had accomplished or what she had. No one cared. I couldn't tell her that all of what she was doing was in vain because I didn't cheat with her husband. I learned a long time ago that people would rather believe juicy lies than the boring truth because it's more interesting. So I just let her continue to make a fool of herself. She continued, "People find me intimidating because I am a strong black woman." I couldn't believe that she said that to a white woman but she was directing it at me. I guess thought or wanted me to be intimidated but she wasn't. That conversation became even more embarrassing and disturbing. Honestly, we didn't know what Ruth had experienced and overcame from which she could have delineated her strength. Race had nothing to do with this situation. Just because she was white didn't mean she wasn't strong. Simply being a woman could have proven many challenges for her. I found the mayor's conversation now insulting.

    I think that comment went over Ruth's head because she didn't address it. She just continued in her thwarted efforts to try and connect us. She said, "Leia, do you know Mayor Mitchell's husband?" "I know you used to dispatch and he is the assistant fire chief; you may have talked to him before." Oh boy! That moment became even more awkward. I wished Ruth would stop talking. I said, "yes I know him and I need to get back to work completing the meeting minutes, while the meeting is fresh on my mind".

    After that initial encounter, I saw the mayor many more times. Each encounter was more volatile than the last. Then she got her friends on board. The tax assessor, Martha, the city attorney, Laura, and the vice president of Lafayette Farmers Bank, Patty, were her clique. They would come to the after hours events hosted by my agency and pick at me. Patty and Robin walked up to me at the tour downtown event and called me a home wrecking whore in front of everyone. They laughed and giggled and talked about me to my face as if I wasn't standing there. I didn't say a word. I acted unbothered. Then Martha walked up and joined them in conversation. She started describing my clothes and the lack of labels and name brands that I was wearing.

They took turns shooting insults at me. Martha's husband walked up, snatched her by the arm, pulled her away, and told her to behave herself. What she didn't know was that a while back, I had to meet her husband to pick up a check that he was donating to the agency. He was a wealthy business owner and often made contributions. Martha's husband had been texting me about how beautiful I was and he wanted to take me out ever since I met him to pick up the first check. I never entertained his invitations but I still remained friendly and professional. He texted me after he made his wife leave and said, "I'm sorry for their behavior." "You are the most beautiful woman here and they are all just jealous, including my wife." People need to be really careful trying to fight the battles of others. Martha could have had her own battle with me because her husband had lurking eyes too. Lucky for her, I wasn't the woman they were trying to portray. The rest of them continued with the taunts and unpleasantries. I finally responded to Mayor Robin Mitchell. "Maybe if you were more of a whore like me, then you could keep your husband at home at night." "All of your money can't buy you any class and all your education didn't give you any wisdom." "If I were you, I wouldn't let the mistress know that her presence bothered me." "Please take your money and buy yourself some friends with sense because none of you have any." "And go home to your husband so he won't be waiting at my house for me." Her friends grabbed her because she was ready to punch me in the mouth, but she created this situation.

 The day had finally arrived for my divorce hearing. I arrived with my attorney and the director of

Safe Home. I received some grant funds to pay for my restraining order. That's why I had to deal with Safe Home. After the hearing was over, I wanted nothing more to do with any of them. William has arrived with his attorney. The judge is hearing the case about our divorce and restraining order. When she asked about the allegations of abuse, William said, "I've never touched her; she's a liar". "She just made up those stories to get rid of me so that she can be with her lover, the mayor's husband." He knew James's name but his tactic was to continue to abuse me by trying to humiliate me. That's why he identified him as the mayor's husband instead of his name. William continued, "ask her why she got out of bed with her husband at 3:00 in the morning to talk to that man." "Are you in love with him?" I couldn't understand why the judge would allow him to go on with the rants that didn't address the question that she asked. She seemed to be amused at the hot gossip about the mayor's husband and I. The judge was just like the other messy people in our town. Finally she said, "that's enough", and asked if our side had any evidence.

Then my attorney asked Will if he punched me in the face, stomped and kicked me in the torso around the date of May 8th. He said no. He asked Will if he stalked me and followed me to Magnolia State University. Will said, "no she's lying". He asked if he had followed me home on numerous dates, kicked in my door to my apartment, and waited for me in the parking lot at my job. Will said no to them all. Then my attorney said, "will the court please accept into evidence, exhibit 1, 2, 3, 4, 5, 6, 7, and 8." "These are various police reports and medical records indicating the abuse and stalking to which my client has been subjected." Will said, "she made those up because she is sleeping with an officer that works with her and he told her to do that." "Yes, we had one fight but she sprained my wrist and blacked my eye too." My attorney stated, "Judge, you can see on the documentation that the reports are from other police departments from other towns and cities that Mr. Blake followed Mrs. Leia Blake". William's lawyer told him to stop talking then. The judge said, "sir you are the liar here and I will grant her a restraining order." He was shocked to know that I had been documenting everything he had been doing by filing information reports everytime he did something. I documented everything except the rape. I was too ashamed and embarrassed to talk about it; how could I argue that it was rape if it was my husband. I just kept it to myself. However, I created a paper trail about all of the other incidents just in case something happened. I had to take measures to protect myself and it was beneficial for me this time. The best witness for yourself is yourself. Everyone doesn't have the courage to speak up for you so it's best to let the documentation speak for you.

Regarding the divorce and custody of our son, William asked the judge to give him custody of all of my children and asked that I keep his last name. He also stated that he wanted to contest the restraining order. The judge said, "you sir are a joke." "I've never had anyone contest a restraining order in my court." "You have accessibility to your child and that's all you need." "You don't need contact with this woman and I'm not forcing her to keep your last name if she doesn't want it." "You must be crazy if you think I am going to award custody for her other children to you and you are not their biological father." "Furthermore their father would have to relinquish their rights for you to attempt to have custody of them." "Get this man out of my court." "You are using my court to continue to abuse this woman and I won't have it." She granted me custody of our son with visitation rights to William, the right to return to my maiden name of Devine, the restraining order, and allowed me to return to our house to get the rest of my things.

When I went to the house with a police escort the officer had already warned William that I was coming to retrieve the rest of my items. As I pulled up to the front yard, he had all of my clothes thrown out on the lawn. He had broken my washer and dryer and sat them in the driveway. He stood there joking and talking with the officer that escorted me to the house. I just picked up my clothes as cars slowly passed with their windows down, eavesdropping on my continued humiliation. I left the appliances that he deliberately destroyed. I didn't report that officer because I was tired of fighting. I didn't have the energy to endure another battle of reporting someone and trying to prove how I had been wronged again. I learned to pick my battles and I was tired of fighting. I left this one alone because I had more in store for me.

I walked into work this Monday morning feeling relieved. Of course William had talked about everything all over town so my boss knew that I had finally gotten divorced. My boss and CEO Luther Jackson walked up to me and asked, "can I give you a hug." "I need one and I know you probably do as well."

I didn't want to hug him but I was intimidated by his position and was afraid if I said no, I would lose my job. He said, "your husband is a crazy man to let a beautiful young lady like you get away." He pointed to a picture of his wife on the mantle in his office and said, "I would do anything for that woman right there." He had a beautiful wife as well and often talked about her so I didn't initially think of him asking for a hug as being flirtatious. He was also a pastor of a church and would ask me into his office each morning to start the day with prayer. I wasn't a Jehovah's Witness yet but in studying with the Jehovah's Witness, I was taught that I should not pray with any other religion so I just bowed my head in respect but I didn't say Amen to his prayer.

Mr. Jackson asked me one evening what my plans were when I got off of work. I said, "I'm going to the gym". "I go five days a week." He said oh ok and I thought nothing else about it. The following day, I was wearing a loose fitting, calf-length skirt. I didn't dress provocatively because I didn't want to be perceived as an easy woman nor did I want to entice Mr. Jackson. Mr. Jackson said, "good morning, you look pretty good." "I can tell you have been working out by the definition in your calves." "Can I touch them?" I was so very uncomfortable with that request but I didn't want to lose my job so I reluctantly said yes. I was relieved that he wasn't sexual with his touch. He just grabbed my calf and squeezed it. He said, "you know I work out too so I just wanted to feel your leg to see your progress; it's pretty hard." "Appears that you might know what you're doing." I said, "yes I do." Then he asked, "well can I touch your butt?" That "can I touch your calf" was just an icebreaker to see what my response would be and a filler for him to see how far I would let him go with me. I was always respectful to him because he was my boss but now he crossed the line. I'm so tired of men treating me like I'm an object for their sexual gratification rather than a person. I went off on him. "Don't you dare touch my butt!" "You're gonna see real soon some other places that I have muscles when I knock you out."

He said, "I'm sorry I didn't mean to offend you." "I was just going to give you my professional opinion." I said, "no thank you", and walked back to my office with both fear and anger. Fearful that I may lose my job because I spoke to him in that manner, yet angry that he would put me in that situation. I sat at my desk and tried to calm down and regain my composure. Then after lunch he called me back to his office again. He pulled out his Bible and asked me to read a scripture that he had highlighted. "Read aloud John 1:9". I read, *"if we confess our sins, he is faithful and just and will forgive us our sins and purify us from all unrighteousness."* Then I looked up from the scriptures at him with this sassy, disgruntled look on my face and said, "okay and why did you want me to read this scripture?" He responded, " I wanted you to know that this scripture teaches us that if we confess our sins then God will forgive us." "He will purify us as if we did nothing at all." Again I said, "okay and what are you referring to?" He said, "I see your Jehovah's Witness friends coming by and you reading your Bible on your breaks." "I really find Godly women attractive especially since I am a preacher myself; we have in common the desire to please God." "I'm an attractive man and you're an attractive woman." "I know you want to do what's right and I just wanted to let you know that if you let me touch you and if we just happened to have sex, God will forgive us." "Immediately after we have sex we just need to get down on our knees and pray for forgiveness and the situation will be forgiven." "We would only need to confess it to God and keep that between us." "You know I have a wife and I would never want something like that to get back to my wife." "I really value my marriage and family so it couldn't get back to her." "There actually wouldn't need to be a reason to tell anyone because as the scripture states, God will forgive us our sins and purify us from all unrighteousness so it would be like it never happened."

    I sat quietly and stared him in his eyes for a moment. I stared at him in complete silence until he felt my energy. Then when I noticed his uncomfortableness I asked, "can I share a couple of scriptures with you?" He said yes. I read aloud for him, "This is Hebrews 10:26 and it says, *"If we deliberately go on sinning after we have received the knowledge of the truth, no further sacrifice for sins remains"* " And Proverbs 5:15-16 says, *"Drink water from your own cistern, and running water from your own well. Why should your springs flow in the streets, your streams of water in the public squares?."* "May I explain?" "You already know that adultery is wrong according to the Bible so if you have accurate knowledge and still willfully sin, there is no sacrifice left for your sin.". "And drinking from your OWN cistern implies having sex with your wife and not letting your SPRINGS flow in the streets." "Pastor, the Bible also tells us that all scripture is beneficial for teaching, reproving, and setting things straight in righteousness." "Please consider all the scriptures and not just the ones applicable to situations that benefit you."

He said, "you're a smart woman and I didn't expect that from you". I asked, "did you expect any less?" He said, "I just didn't think you were that smart." I asked, "why is that?" He said, "Well I know you got all them kids with different daddies, you're divorced, and uneducated; and look at you, walking around with a body like that, you're more like a trophy wife." I replied, "most people here think that of me but I'm not what people perceive me to be". He said, "It actually turned me on that you gave me a challenge and put up a fight." I thought you would be easier." "Men don't like everything easy." I then knew that he was sick or stupid because he said that knowing he was my supervisor.

Over the next few months, he consistently made comments about my body and talked about his fantasies of what sex would feel like with me. I didn't say a word. I just prayed every time for strength to contain myself; but I had other things going on in my life that were far more critical than dealing with this pervert.

Years ago when my son and I had nowhere to live, I applied for Section 8. I couldn't understand why a homeless mother and son could not get immediate help but I was put on a waiting list. They contacted me seven years later and said that they had finally made it to my name. I went to my appointment and satisfied the obligations to receive the voucher. I did have an apartment at the time but if I could get a house for my children to play in the yard and rental assistance to free up financial obligation, I would return to school to work toward my degree.

After I got it, I only had a couple of months to find a house, get it inspected and move in. I found a house in just the nick of time and moved in. After two months, the landlord told me that she had not gotten any follow up information nor had she been paid. I told her that I had not gotten any further information either.

I decided not to leave for lunch this particular day and just make personal calls from my office to try and get to the bottom of where the rental assistance checks were. I had to call several times before finally reaching some rude black woman that talked to me as if I was taking her personal Section 8 voucher. Then she tells me, "you weren't approved to receive a voucher". I said, "yes ma'am I was". "I have received it, found a house, your staff came out, inspected it, and approved it, and I have moved in." "I followed all of the instructions that were given to me." "The landlord is just waiting on her check for two months rent and I need to know the portion to which I am responsible." She responded, "I'm looking at your file now and it says that you are not approved". In a louder, more aggressive tone she states, "you were DENIED". "So I will call the landlord and tell them to put you out or you can move out." "If you don't want to do that, you can pay her the past two months rent."

I got so upset and tried to explain my situation to the case worker. I told her, "ma'am I'm trying to get you to understand that I did everything expected of me to satisfy the requirements to receive the voucher." I have double checked everything and compared my total net income and child support allotments with the income limits to qualify and I do qualify." "I have four children that reside with me, but you all were the ones that contacted me and told me that I qualified." "When did this change?" "Ma'am I left my apartment and moved in this house with the expectation that you would fulfil your part." "I can't afford this rent; it's double what I paid at the apartment and the apartment is no longer available." "What am I supposed to do?" She replied with a funky attitude, "we use the gross income not the net income and I don't know who told you that but it wasn't me". I could just imagine her nose turning up and her rolling her eyes when she said that. I said, "but why ma'am, you can't count money that I don't have." "I can't pay rent or feed my children with gross income." "And I thought qualification was determined by your office prior to sending out notices of approval, so why wasn't this determined before you all had me go through all of this process to just deny me after the fact." "Then no one sent me or the landlord any notification of the denial." "Can't we work something out since this is not my fault?" "My children and I have nowhere else to go." She responded, "where you go ain't my problem and I'll put your letter and the landlord letter of denial in the mail today." As I started to beg, "please ma'am". She hung up in my face.

    I just put my head down on the desk and started to cry. I couldn't afford to pay $750 for each month's rent that I was now behind and the next month's rent was coming due in a week. That was $2,250 I had to come up with in a week and I lived paycheck to paycheck with nothing left each month. My income was

$21,000 a year, which was pretty good around here. Realistically, I made enough to starve to death. I made a penny over to not qualify for any governmental assistance and not enough to assist myself. I was thinking, "I need to return and finish school so that I, at least, had a fighting chance to make some decent money; but I needed to work extra just to maintain daily needs for my family." "If I worked a second job, I would need child care assistance but wouldn't qualify for that because I'd be over the income to get that help from the government and be working just to pay daycare." "I wouldn't have any money left." "I can't get their dads to baby sit because they don't help me at all and I can't get my mama or grandma to babysit for me to go to school because Jehovah's Witnesses don't believe in attainment of secular education." "Our focus should be on only serving God and trying to spread the Bible truths and the fast approaching end of this world."

I couldn't say this but, I thought it was logical that we should not be solely focused on what's after this life and lose sight of how to function in this present life. Don't be so heavenly bound that we are no earthly good. I need to feed my children today. At my low time, some of the witnesses would share the scripture Matthew 6:26-34 with me. "*6 Look at the birds of the air, for they neither sow nor reap nor gather into barns; yet your heavenly Father feeds them. Are you not of more value than they? 27 Which of you by worrying can add one [a]cubit to his [b]stature? 28 "So why do you worry about clothing? Consider the lilies of the field, how they grow: they neither toil nor spin; 29 and yet I say to you that even Solomon in all his glory was not [c]arrayed like one of these. 30 Now if God so*

clothes the grass of the field, which today is, and tomorrow is thrown into the oven, will He not much more clothe you, O you of little faith?
31 "Therefore do not worry, saying, 'What shall we eat?' or 'What shall we drink?' or 'What shall we wear?' 32 For after all these things the Gentiles seek. For your heavenly Father knows that you need all these things. 33 But seek first the kingdom of God and His righteousness, and all these things shall be added to you. 34 Therefore do not worry about tomorrow, for tomorrow will worry about its own things. Sufficient for the day is its own trouble. The lesson here was to just pray to God about what I needed and have faith that He would provide it for me.

But then, I thought about the scripture in James 2:18-20 and 24. *"But someone will say, "You have faith and I have works." Show me your faith apart from your works, and I will show you my faith by my works. 19 You believe that God is one; you do well. Even the demons believe—and shudder! 20 Do you want to be shown, you foolish person, that faith apart from works is useless?* This meant to me that I needed to work towards whatever I wanted, pray, and have faith that God would bless it to be successful. I had to give Him something to bless, not just have faith that it would appear out of thin air. I was so confused on what I should do. Oftentimes, what I learned about Bible teachings confused me. I would learn of one scripture then understand another scripture that contradicted what I previously learned. I was taught at the Kingdom Hall to not question what came down from the Governing Body but have trust and faith that it was under the direction of God. I was under the impression that I knew nothing and I just needed to trust. What I did know without any doubt is that I would not get support from my family to go to college. I was stuck between a rock and a hard place. This was exactly one reason that I was so indecisive for so many years about going to college and finishing college. Was I displeasing God by not focusing on serving Him? Yet, because I committed other sins, should I add this to the list, make this sacrifice and pursue a career? Either way, right now I am suffering and struggling to make it every day, to provide for myself and my family.

    At that moment while my mind was all over the place and still crying, I felt a hand rub softly across my back. It startled me. I popped my head up and it was my boss, Luther Jackson. I pulled away from him and he said, "go to the bathroom and clean your face, then come to my office." I did as he requested. I washed my face in cold water to try and reduce my swollen eyes and rosy cheeks from the crying. I sat in the chair in front of his desk as I usually did. He said, "I heard you on the phone". "I'm sorry to hear that you are going through a tough time." "Are you dating anyone right now?" I answered no but I started to get angry because I wondered what that had to do with my situation. He continued, "well, I can only imagine how difficult it must be to be divorced and not have a significant other to help provide that financial support that you once had." I started to calm down when I noticed the point he was making was that I was doing it all alone. Then he said, "I would like to offer you some help because I feel sorry for you and your situation." Then he pulled a check from the drawer of his desk and slid it to me. I opened it and it was a personal check in the amount of $500. Before I could answer, he said, " you can have this if you can do something for me". I looked at him with a long blink and rolling my neck like, "what the hell is the "something"? He said, "it will be just between us and we can leave work early and go to the hotel." I asked, "So you want me to sleep with you?" He said, "you can do whatever you want". "You can give me that down there or that right there.", pointing at my mouth. I said, "I'm not for sale", and pushed the envelope with the check back across the desk to him. He replied, "I sign your checks, so I know what you make; you could use it". I replied, "we're in a recession and I answer the phones for the bill collectors that you owe; you could use it too, pastor."

After that incident, Mr. Jackson got even more aggressive and often talked under my clothes. He said things like, "your round but looks good walking away and it would look better on my lap" or he wondered how moist I was. I started recording him every time he or I were in a room together. The lawn man asked me one day when I was outside how it was working with Mr. Jackson. I said, "its work", because I didn't know who to trust with what I was experiencing. He said, "you don't have to say, I understand." "I just wanted to let you know that my bossman's daughter used to work in your place and she got fired because she wouldn't sleep with him." "She's my god daughter and I just wanted to give you her number and maybe y'all need to talk." "I'm just putting it out there and do with it what you want." I took the number, called and left her a message. We talked and her story was so similar to mine. We met up for lunch and she presented me with the recordings she had of him as well.

After that, I started looking through personnel files and gathering contact information for all the women that worked there prior to me. I called them all and they all had the same stories. I convinced most of them to write a letter about their experiences with Mr. Jackson and to send them to me. The others were afraid because they knew that victims were scrutinized like they did something wrong or they caused the inappropriate behavior and they were afraid. I knew that I could not go to the board with my story alone but having the other women's stories would support my efforts to expose how he had been ruining our lives. I knew that in his defense he would try and bring up the things people in this small town said about me but having several women with the same stories would help all of us. I collected all of the letters and uploaded all of the recordings and emailed them to all of the board members along with my letter.

The board president called me on behalf of the board the following day, apologized, and thanked me for spearheading the efforts to expose him and protecting the agency from sexual harassment lawsuits. The board was composed of five white males, one white with woman, and one black male. I learned that day, that black women were disposable and the least valued by this world despite our contributions. I understand now why no one wanted to speak up. All of the women he harassed and fired were all black. Mr. Jackson got a $5,000 reduction in pay, $1,000 per woman he harassed, and a letter of reprimand. I didn't ask for anything but I got promoted from secretary to executive administrative assistant. The president said, "we notice all of the hard work you do around here and keeping this place afloat." "So the board voted to give you a promotion to executive administrative assistant." I didn't care if they called me custodian. That "promotion" didn't come with a pay raise. I'm not hung up on titles. That title change was supposed to pacify me. It didn't. I only want to be financially comfortable. Give me my money. For my protection and to ensure that I would have little time alone with Mr. Jackson anymore, the board also hired a white male as my assistant IT person/secretary and paid him $12,480 a year more than me. They stopped me from picking up the checks so that I wouldn't see it but forgot that I completed the budget reports and saw it on the financials. I was done. I quit without notice and moved to Fort Chapel, Alabama with my dad.

Chapter Fourteen: False Restart

Over the past few months my dad and I started talking to each other more. Since I had been studying the Bible more, I knew that I had to forgive him in order to be forgiven for my sins. I couldn't go back and make him be in my life as a child or change any of the bad things he said about me but I could try to establish a relationship with him as an adult and move on. When I quit my job, I moved with my dad. He had been asking me for a long time for the kids and I to move with him. He said, "I know you want to return to school and I want that for you too." "Let me pay all your bills, take care of you and the kids, and you just focus on school." "That's the least I can do since I wasn't there for you growing up." "I feel like if I had been in your life, you never would have been raped." "Give me a chance to be the dad I never was to you and a granddad to my grandkids." I never had anybody to take care of me, I was reluctant but I said, okay with stipulations. I told him that I had to at least have a partime job so that I had some pocket money, if he paid my bills. He said no, he would give me a weekly allowance. I said, "A woman over 30 years old who's been working since 15 years old is not about to get a weekly allowance; I'm not a kid, I need my own money." He said he could deal with that and would give me money until I found a job. Then I said that I also needed my own place eventually because I was not accustomed to living with someone. He said, "I'll buy a house for you ." My dad had plenty of money and didn't care about letting everyone know it. He was a hard worker and I admired that about him. I moved there the very weekend that I quit my job solely on his promise to do right by me.

I found a Kingdom Hall in Fort Chapel and my children and I started attending service every week there. I started a Bible study with one of the ladies there. My children love the schools and are performing very well. My dad was paying my car payment, cell phone bill, and insurance and I applied to school. He gave me a hundred dollars and my four children fifty dollars each week for spending money as well. Everything was going well, just as discussed.

He lived alone because his long time girlfriend of over thirty years had passed away. She never married him because he was always cheating but she never left him. He took care of her daughter and son more than he did his own children. He paid all the bills in the house and paid for everything for them, their education, their cars, everything. He used his money to rectify his wrong doings with their mother. I didn't understand how men could take care of step children but neglect their biological children. He did my mama wrong too but he didn't give us money to mitigate his wrongs. I guess time alone and old age has afforded him time to reflect on that and he has had a change of heart with his biological children. I'm open to this fresh start for our relationship, the opportunity to escape the disappointments and misfortunes in Mississippi, and a chance to regain the lost years of my life.

Everyday I'm cooking, cleaning, applying for jobs, and studying for this placement exam to get into college. I've met two consistent women who date my dad. He told me that if I met someone, let him know. He said that he was going to buy a trailer and put it in the yard. "If we want to have sex, we can go out there and have sex in the trailer; neither one of us will have sex in the house with kids the here." I bucked my eyes in disbelief and shock because I didn't expect that conversation. However, I shouldn't have been shocked. He had always been known as a man with little tact and restraint with his tongue. I said, "well, I'm celebate because I'm trying to get my life right with God and live by Bible principles." "Besides, I have enough children with absent fathers, no job, or career." "And another thing, I can't get aroused anyway with no money in my pocket." "I wouldn't dare layup with somebody and I have nothing; and they have nothing to offer me." "I'm good." "I'm focused on bettering myself, not focusing on a man." "But, if that's what you want to do, it's your money, your house, and your prerogative." "The kids and I can just leave and go skating or to the movies or something and leave you alone with your lady friends."

My cell phone rang. It was Anna from the Arkdale police department. We kept in touch after she had my back. I answered, "hello". Anna said, " you were right to leave things alone when Anthony told Will where to find you." "God says, vengeance is mine, and I will repay said the Lord, and God has repaid." I said, "really, what happened?" Anna said, "Anthony is in the hospital and has attempted suicide." I said, "what!" Anna continued, "yeah, he was sending ringtones to himself from his wife's phone and received a text while he was on the phone." "It was a naked picture of your ex-husband Will." "I heard he looked through the photos and found more naked pictures of his wife and Will together and videos of them having sex." "You do know that Will is now Antony's supervisor too?" "The chief hired Will back here after you left." I said, "OH MY GOODNESS!" "I'm sorry to hear that; I wouldn't wish that on anyone." "Who is his wife?" "You know Olivia, that's the manager at B&W's Burger Spot." I said, "GIRL!" "My stepdaughter told me about an Olivia that Will was seeing and I figured he was seeing someone that worked at B&W's Burger Spot because he frequented the place when he wasn't with me." "Then when I went to the restaurant she had such a nasty attitude with me but she was messing around with my husband." "I'm so glad I'm out of that mess and away from there." "Thank you girl for letting me know." "I'll talk to you later."

    By the third week, things started to change with my dad. He was no longer voluntarily giving us the weekly allowance. When I mentioned it to him, he said, "all you have to do is ask me." When I did ask, he only gave me a little and no longer gave the children anything. He began expecting his clothes washed, ironed, the house cleaned, and dinner ready when he got home from work. I realized that I was not here in the capacity of a daughter attempting to develop a relationship with her father. My daddy made me his henhussy. Since his longtime girlfriend died, he needed a woman here to continue her household duties and take care of him. I didn't mind cleaning and cooking when I wanted to do it; but having it demanded of me was a different story. He wanted to do nothing around the house. He even expected me to fix his plate and serve him. I didn't do this when I was married. I'm not about to start now.

One of his lady friends, Earline, told me of a position that was vacant at her job. It paid $18 an hour and she said she was sure she could help me get it. I was excited and anticipated further details about applying for it. I had never even thought of making that much money and not having a degree. Meanwhile, Earline and my dad were bringing to the house, a lot of garbage bags each week, full of second hand clothes for my children and I to choose from. I didn't mind because I got, if not new, practically new clothes for free. I always loved a bargain. Then Earline started buying clothes, shoes and toys all the time for my children and I. Every other day, a shoe box, bag, or toys. I noticed it was done in an effort to try and convince my dad to be with her. If she could prove that she cared about his children and grandchildren, then he would choose her. I thought older women knew better than that but I was wrong. Wisdom has no age. There are old fools ignorant of the obvious and young luminaress aware and wise beyond their earthly years. I have seen so many times where women go above and beyond to do things for the children of men they date in order to win them over. I told Earline, "keep your money." "My children don't need anything else." "You seem to be a very nice woman and you should really focus on making yourself happy not my dad." Of course she didn't listen.

Still didn't listen even when she arrived at his house and another woman, Mable was there. My dad was cooking on the grill for Mable. Earline was riding by my dad's house like usual when he didn't answer his phone. It was an ugly scene when Earline spotted Mable and tried to fight her. I didn't understand that either because Mable knew nothing about Earline. She shouldn't have been mad at that woman. She should have been angry with my dad. He knew Earline was at our house last night and Mable is here the next night. Mable knew nothing. She was totally innocent. After mushing her in the face, throwing Earline out, and throwing her purse in the street, I thought she wouldn't come back anymore. He told Mable that Earline was his ex and was crazy. Later, he told Earline that he loved her and Mabel meant nothing to him. I got to see first hand from my dad how men have lied and played me.

    They both were very intelligent women with really good jobs and made plenty of money. Both were really beautiful in their own way. Earline with dark cocoa colored skin, full lips, and short natural curly fro has a shape like a pear with wide curvy hips and full bottom. Mable is a caramel colored, short, petite woman with long, straight permed hair. She seemed more mentally stable and self-aware than Earline but she was new to the shenanigans of my dad. I feel like she won't be around very long. I actually got pretty close with Mable because she was around more and we conversed more. Earline just dropped stuff off and came at night to sleep with my dad. Mable started calling my dad out on his stuff. Every time he talked about his money or what he could buy for her she said I can do it for myself. Then she got really angry one day and told him, "I make $150,000 a year, double what you make." "I never told you before because I was trying not to hurt feelings since you constantly brag about your salary;but you will not continue to verbally abuse me, cheat on me, and think you can pay for my forgiveness." "I don't need your money."

He didn't know but my kids and I would sneak over to her house and spend time with her just to get a break from him. She told me one day. "You and the kids look nothing like I imagined." I said, "really, elaborate please". She continued, "Well your dad said that his daughter from Mississippi and four children were moving with him because you couldn't take care of them." "He asked my opinion about adopting your kids until you got on your feet." "He said your kids had different daddies because you slept around and that you may have been prostituting to make ends meet." "He said he was paying all of your bills and had bought you a car so it would be easier to move you here with him so he can help you more." "After meeting you and your children, I knew those were all lies." "You all were so well dressed, well spoken, beautiful people; and the children are so smart." "I couldn't believe you would want to give up your children for adoption." "He asked me and some other people if we knew anyone that wanted to donate some clothes to his daughter and grandchildren." "I collected some from people at work." "People had gone out and purchased clothes for you guys because your dad pitched a believable story." "I'm so sorry."

I said, "it makes sense to me now why he and other people kept coming by the house dropping off garbage bags of clothes and shoes." "I'm so embarrassed." "I moved here for a fresh start in my life and to leave a place that had given me an unwarranted reputation only to begin a new life with an unjustifiable opinion of me." Mable said, "after the first conversation with you, I didn't believe him." "Don't be embarrassed, when people meet you, they will know that what he said isn't true." "Show people who you are." I told her, "I left a place where I was always trying to prove the truth about myself." "I don't have the energy to start that again."

When I returned to his house, I didn't want to say anything to him, not even look at him. I just focused on studying for my entrance exam. I researched study guides and did practice problems to prepare me for the test. While I was reading, I was interrupted by one of the twins crying and running into the living room where I was sitting. Then I heard my dad yelling at her. I asked, "What's wrong baby?" She said, "paw paw was trying to whip me". I asked him as he entered the room, "twin said you were trying to whip her." "Why?" He responded, "I told her ass to stop leaving that light on in the bathroom." I responded in a calm voice, "well she is only five and will make mistakes, but I will make sure it's turned off next time." He continued ranting, "y'all don't pay no damn bills around here, so it's okay to just leave lights on around here." I said, "it's not okay but she is just a child and that is not a good reason to whip her." "Actually you can't whip her or any of my children." "You are a stranger to them that goes by the name PawPaw." "If they don't know you or have a relationship with you, then it's not right for you to discipline them." "Plus it's not appropriate to spank them for everything; the punishment needs to fit the crime." "I'm the mama and I will be doing the disciplining."

He began to yell even more. "Well I'm their daddy and y'all are in my house so everybody gotta do what I say." I said, "you are not their daddy; they have fathers." He said, "they ain't got no daddies." "That's why they're fucked up." "Look at the oldest boy; he ain't gone be shit." "Look at how he walks with his head down, all slouched over." "He walks like he ain't gone be shit." "Why you walk like that boy?" "You trying to make sure you don't trip?" Then he answered for my son, "naw, you just in the making of being nothing when you grow up." I sat there in anger, yet pain. Hurting for my son because the things said were so damaging for a child to hear. Then my dad continued. "The twins are just stupid. I never seen kids more stupid and then it's two of them; double the stupid." "And that baby, I know he's gonna be a punk or sissy." "All he does is cry all the time and follows you everywhere you go." "He follows you to the bathroom." "These kids are messed up and all of y'all need me."

    I let him finish; then I responded. "You have no right to talk to my children that way." "My son can walk whatever way he chooses." "He is a good child with plenty of potential." Then I looked at my son, "you can be whatever you choose to be." "Don't listen to this man, he doesn't know you." "I will be there to support you." "Which is more than I can say for my deadbeat daddy." "How are you going to all the twins stupid because they forget to turn the bathroom light off, SOMETIMES?" "You forgot about your kids which sounds like the epitome of stupid." "And my baby is one years old, he is in a new place and has not gotten accustomed to living here." "It's normal for him to stick close to his mama." "But you wouldn't know that because you left all of your kids when our mamas were pregnant." "Now I don't mean to disrespect you but you have to know that you will hurt my children physically or emotionally." "I will not stand by and let you tear them down." "Not gonna happen." "I will make sure that they abide by your rules and I would like you to be conscious of how you talk to them." He responded, "they messed up because you won't let anybody say anything to them." I replied, "well nobody will say stuff like that to them."

Over the next few weeks, things continued to get worse with him. He just found things to yell and curse about. If family or friends called to talk to me, I couldn't talk on the phone without him interrogating me about who was on the phone, listening in on the conversation, and chiming in as if he was included in the conversation. Of course he wouldn't do that when I was having my Bible study on the phone, he was nowhere to be found then. With everyone else, he would even say really loudly so the person on the phone could hear, "how long are you going to be on the phone", or "I'm ready to eat." Sometimes he told me it's time to get off the phone as if I was a child. After I took my placement test, the academic advisor called me to give me the results. When I answered, I said, "Hello". She said, "may I speak with Leia Devine." I said, "this is she". She started telling me who she was and then he started yelling, "who is that?" I kept holding up my finger trying to tell him to wait because he was so loud I couldn't hear what she was saying. He just kept yelling for me to answer because his personality was that everything had to be about him. He had to know right now while I was on the phone, who called me. He was such a narcissist. I finally said, "it's the school and

I can't hear." Then he shrugged his shoulders and said, "oh, I didn't know but what are they saying?" I didn't respond then; I just continued to listen to the academic advisor. When I hung up, he said, "what did she say?" I said, "she told me that I made a perfect score and I was able to test out of having to take some classes." He said, "a perfect score?" "That's good, the reason you got a perfect score was because you have my blood in you and I'm perfect." This man never ceases to amaze me. He can't be my daddy.

    I left the house to go buy a lottery at the convenience store around the corner and I ran into Earline. "Ugh." I hate seeing her because all she does is talk about my dad, talk about how she loves him so much, talk about how he does her wrong, and how he cheats on her. Technically he's not cheating because she's not his girlfriend. She was the side chick for 16 years when he and his common law wife/long time girlfriend lived together. After she died, Earline didn't automatically become the main chick. She was still the side chick and he moved on to dating other people. I actually felt bad for her because she has not realized the stronghold this situation has on her. She finally asked about me. "What have you been up to?" I said, "I just got accepted into community college and I'm still looking for a job." Earline looked surprised and said, "your dad told me that you no longer wanted a job and was focusing on school." "I saw him at the bank a couple weeks ago and told him to give you my number because my supervisor wanted to hire you." "I gave you a good recommendation." I said, "wow, I never told him that." "I really need a job because he no longer voluntarily gives me money." "He wants me to ask him for money." "He gave me $40 a month ago and I refuse to keep asking him." "I have a little child support that I just tried to stretch out." "I just put gas in my car to take the kids to school and go to the Kingdom Hall." "I don't go anywhere else to avoid unnecessary spending." Earline handed me a hundred dollars and said, "I'll help you, let me know when you need more." I told her, "thank you but I'm gonna go find myself a job."

    I started getting up and dressed like I was going to an interview each day. I dropped off my children at school and was at the Alabama job center each day when it opened, five days a week. I made a personal goal to apply for at least ten jobs a day or drop off my resume to at least ten employers each week. If I apply for 50 jobs per week, 20 may call me for a first interview, 10 may call me back for a second interview, and 5 may offer me a job. When I ran out of jobs for which I qualified to apply for, then I went to the resource center of the job center. I utilized everything they had to offer. I took my resume to be assessed and I was instructed on how to revise it to better my chances of landing the right job. I did this for about six weeks. I started to get discouraged.

    Then one day the director of the Alabama job center came out. He was a tall, well dressed brown skin black man with a salt and pepper beard and low hair cut. He asked me to come here. He asked my name, and I said, "Leia Devine, sir". He asked, "what are you doing here, what are you trying to do?" "I have seen you here everyday and in the parking lot when we open for over a month now." "You are always dressed like you work in this office." I said, "sir, I'm trying to get a job." "If I happen to be called for an impromptu interview, I will be ready." "Dressed to part and a polished resume." "I don't want to miss the opportunity because I wasn't prepared." "Meanwhile, I continue to apply for everything that I qualify for and someone will eventually hire me." He asked where I lived. I said, "I'm from the Mississippi Delta but I've been living here for a few months." He responded with a look of surprise, "Mississippi?" "I never would have expected that you would be from Mississippi; you don't look or act like what I expected of people from Mississippi." I said, "well, I hope I can change the perception of how people from Mississippi are viewed." He said, "you have, keep up the good work and I know your ideal job will be meeting you soon." "I'd love to help someone like you, a person that's determined and prepared." "Please let me know if there is anything I can do for you." I left my resume with him and he helped me revise it more.

I became more discouraged and wanted to give up after another week of hearing nothing. It had been a total of two months of applying to no avail. Finally, that Friday, I was called for an interview. Then Monday, another interview. Over the next few weeks I was being called for interviews left and right. Then the job offers started, I was able to now choose which jobs fit me. Just when you feel like giving up, is the very moment when God will deliver a breakthrough. When I told my dad I had a job he was surprised to know that I accomplished getting a pretty good job as an account supervisor when he recommended that I apply for a cashier at a grocery store. He used his money to control me and now he would be losing his grip because I'm becoming independent. He wanted to control me. He needed to be needed to feel important even if it meant tearing me and my children down, isolating us, and limiting my resources. He wanted me to ask for his help, that made him feel like a man and somehow made him feel better for abandoning me. What he didn't know was that he didn't know me and being left by him and my mama left me to learn to fend for myself. It taught me to only depend on God and myself. It taught me to fight in some type of fashion, verbally, physically, or to never give up. I've had to fight for my life, fight to preserve my body from greedy men, fight my husband, fight his mistresses, fight public scrutiny, fight for my reputation, and fight all the embedded insecurities that tell me I won't make it as a single black mother. I am a fighter and no one even understands why. Unbeknown to me, my fighting has just begun.

    The Saturday before Thanksgiving, my dad has his newest woman over to the house. Her name was Sandra and she was from Florida. They met at the club. He's been seeing her for a couple of weeks. Mable ditched my dad shortly after the incident with Earline. She was smart to do so. Poor Earline is still calling and buying stuff, trying to make him love her. Like always he has been putting on a show in front of Sandra. He decides to throw his weight around and starts cursing at one of the twins. "I told your stupid ass don't eat in my living room." I intervened, "she wasn't eating in the living room". He said, "I'm looking right at her running to the living room and her plate is right here." I said, "she takes a bite at the table then returns to the living room." As I'm speaking, twin runs in the dining room to the table to get another bite. This time she remains sitting at the table. He grabs her by the arm and pulls her out of her chair. I ran over and pulled my daughter from him and said, "she's not taking the food into the living room ." "And can you please not yell and curse at my children like that?" He said, "bitch, so you're just gonna lie for these kids like that?" "If I can't say nothing to them and I can't whip them then y'all can get the hell out of my house." Then he picked up her plate and threw it at me. I picked up his ashtray and threw it at him. As he threw a chair at me, Sandra grabbed him and said, "calm down". Then I ran up and got in his face, standing toe to toe, eye to eye, and said with the coldest, sternest look in my eyes, "if you put your hands on my kids, I'll kill you dead." There was complete silence then because he never saw that side of me before. I had rage in my eyes and fearlessness in my heart. I was ready for him. I was always a little reluctant to take up for myself, but never hesitant to protect my children. He was gonna feel me today.

 The following day, I packed all of our things and put them in my car. I took some to my Bible study conductor's house and got us a hotel room. As I was walking out of the door, I placed the key to his house on the kitchen table: Sandra emerged from his bedroom, down the hall and stopped me. " Please don't leave your dad." "You have to understand his point of view." "You all need to talk." I responded, "I hope you tell yourself the same thing when he's cheating on you and beating your butt." "Stay out of stuff that you know nothing about."

 I continued to work and was now paying my own cell phone bill and car payment. I had to let the insurance lapse because I couldn't afford to pay it, with my other bills, food, laundromats, and hotel. After a few weeks, when my money ran out, I started to look for homeless shelters. This week I could not find anywhere for my children and I to stay. They did not have enough beds where children and their mothers could go. Then there was enough room for just the kids at one location but they didn't allow adults. I wasn't about to leave my children there alone. So we just parked in the hospital's parking lot because I knew they had security and we slept in my car that week. I washed their clothes on the weekend at the laundromats. I only had to pay for dinner and meals on the weekend because I made sure they ate at school. I still had my Bible study over the phone. It gave me strength to go on and peace from being afraid of sleeping in my car. I looked for apartments that weren't in the bad neighborhoods but I couldn't afford any. I had no choice but to again go back to Mississippi. The week the kids got out for the Christmas break, I quit my job and returned to Lafayette to live with my grandma.

Chapter Fourteen: You Can't Get Apple Juice From an Orange

I returned to Lafayette to no job, no home, and no hope. The only thing I had to look forward to was continuing to study the Bible and becoming a baptized Jehovah's Witness. My first Sunday back, during service, I ran into Martha at the restrooms. I smiled and reached out to hug her because I hadn't seen her in many years. She used to be in another congregation but I heard her and her husband were moved here. Their children were around my age, so Martha was close to my mother's age. I used to play with her children at gatherings when we were kids. Our families had known each other for years. Instead of Martha greeting me back, she put her finger up and said, "you're the one that used to dispatch to the fire department, right?" I said, "yes", and she responded to me, being very short, "that's what I thought". Then walked off. I knew what she was implying. She was letting me know that she believed the rumors about me and the mayor's husband and acting as if she didn't know who I was. I told my grandma about the situation and she said, "don't mind Martha, she always talked too much." I had more to focus on than her so I just disregarded it.

Sister Alice Peoples came up to me and hugged me. She said she enjoyed my comments and my children's comments and asked had I been studying with someone. I told her that I had been studying with someone in Alabama before I moved here; and I studied with my children. Then she asked, "if no one has offered, can I study with you?" I said yes, I was happy to study with her because she seemed smart, always gave good comments using Bible scriptures, and she was an elder's wife. She was really respected. I actually studied with her when I was 12 years old but she stopped studying with me because my mama didn't bring me to the Kingdom Hall for every meeting of service. She would say, "you know Hebrews 10:25 says, *"not giving up meeting together, as some are in the habit of doing, but encouraging one another—and all the more as you see the Day approaching"*. "That is Jehovah God telling you the importance of attending all meetings." "If you miss a Bible study or a meeting then you're going to die." After missing several over a matter of a couple years, she stopped studying with me. I didn't like that she stopped studying with me but I understood. I had no control because my mama was not a Jehovah's witness. She studied on and off for years but never made that commitment so she didn't hold me to a commitment of attending meetings. Now as an adult, I have control over my attendance. God has shown me so many times how He has saved me, protected me, and provided for me. I want to be at every meeting and teach my children about Him. So studying with her would not be a problem.

    We started my bible study every Friday. I didn't have a social life because I wasn't dating anyone and I didn't have any money but my child support and that was not enough to even cover my entire car payment. I was always $78 short. I would keep $150 dollars a month to cover gas, cell phone, pampers, and feminie products. I breastfeed to save money from having to buy formula because I learned from my first child that WIC would run out and I did not have $22 a week to pay for a can of milk for my baby.

    After the mid-week meeting had been eliminated, we began doing family worship at home on

Thursdays. So my Bible study changed from Friday to Saturday. We had weekly meetings on Tuesday, and service on Sunday. I had to study on Monday for Tuesday meetings, study on Wednesdays for family worship on Thursdays, study on Fridays for personal Bible study on Saturdays, and I would study wherever I could fit it in for the meetings on Sundays. I had a really busy schedule with spiritual things. I was still applying for jobs when I could fit that in also.

     One Sunday, Sister Alice and her bosom buddy Sister Grace. Came up to me as we were leaving the meeting and commended me on how well I had been doing. Before and especially after the meetings are when people get to fellowship. Sisters Alice and Grace were snickering and looking me up and down then Alice said, "those must be your favorite boots and favorite skirt". "You wear them all the time." Then looked at each other and laughed. They were making fun of me wearing the same skirt and boots often. I would switch up my blouses or suit jackets but I only had a couple of skirts that were long and loose fitting. I noticed how they looked at the girls and women that wore clothing that accentuated their figures; and I was always told that I must be modest in dress. They would turn their noses up, roll their eyes, and whisper to each other when they would walk by. There was even a picture of acceptable attire for women and men posted on the bulletin board above the contribution box. Our skirts had to be mid-calf, loose fitting, and no cleavage could be showing. My couple of skirts were the only thing that I had that fit that criteria and I didn't have money to buy anything else. I actually had quite a few pencil skirts that didn't fit tight, but you could definitely tell that I was curvy. I didn't wear those because I just didn't want to make any women uncomfortable and I didn't want any men looking at me and undressing with their eyes. You know when a woman has a certain shape and is kind of attractive, she has to put forth effort to cover up and be more moderate in dress. Otherwise she gets labeled as a Jezebel. I had enough labels and I was trying to erase some of them.

I responded, "well you know I haven't had a job since I moved back so this is all that I have to wear that is modest, but it's clean." Then Alice said, "and why do you have those white socks on that baby with dress shoes?" "Does he not have any dress socks?" "You know what, I'll buy your baby some socks", while patting me on the back. They were so focused on the attire of my children that they neglected to see the bigger picture, that I was a young woman, attractive woman, whose only focus was dedicating her life to God. I wanted to do what was right, work hard, and make an honest living. I had been told so many times, "you ain't gotta work for nothing, use what you got to get what you want." "I know some men that will take care of you and pay all of you bills." I didn't want that. I just wanted my own, without having to sacrifice my body or dignity to get it; but people couldn't see past my appearance to discern my spirit.

We were taught to not pursue materialistic endeavors and to keep spiritual matters in the forefront. Hence why most Jehovah's Witnesses worked menial jobs and many wives didn't work at all. However, I found it contradictory that the people that were valued in the congregation were those that had more money, dressed better, and drove nice cars. That reminded me of the scriptures James 2:1-4, *"My brothers and sisters, believers in our glorious Lord Jesus Christ must not show favoritism. 2 Suppose a man comes into your meeting wearing a gold ring and fine clothes, and a poor man in filthy old clothes also comes in. 3 If you show special attention to the man wearing fine clothes and say, "Here's a good seat for you," but say to the poor man, "You stand there" or "Sit on the floor by my feet," 4 have you not discriminated among yourselves and become judges with evil thoughts?"* That is why I always treated everyone the same, the janitor and the principal got the same respect from me. That is how a Christian was supposed to treat people.

    I noticed a lot of things but as my grandma always told me, "all of us are still striving for perfection until the end of this world when God restores us to perfection." "We all still have some things that we are working on." "God's organization is perfect but it is filled with imperfect people so we must not take their shortcomings personally." So I just let it roll off my back and kept my focus on getting baptized and becoming a Jehovah's Witness.

    After months of sticking to the rigorous study schedule, I texted Alice early one Saturday morning to let her know that I would have to reschedule. She texted me back in response, "please read Philippians 1:10". So I did and it said, *"For I want you to understand what really matters, so that you may live pure and blameless lives until the day of Christ's return."* I couldn't believe it so I showed it to my grandmother. I was rescheduling my personal Bible study not canceling, because I had to take my grandma to the doctor and frankly I really was tired. I just needed a day to rest when I returned from the clinic. I had finally found a job as a cashier in the cafeteria at the high school and I was juggling a lot between working, studying, my children, and my car had been repo'ed right after starting that job. I had gotten my taxes and gave half of it to a man that bought me a small truck from an auction that had a million problems. I did not have the energy for her but I actually got pissed off this time. I told Sister Alice that I needed to talk to her in person.

    I was told that I was perceived by many as a very timid, naive bimbo. I often did not initially speak up about things that offended me because I would hope that they would go away and I really hated confrontation. I had had enough fights in my life. I guess that's why people thought they were getting over on me. I notice everything; I just didn't address it many times. I left a lot of things in God's hands. This time it was just too much. She had actually been saying a lot of things and this just pushed me to the point of addressing it.

    We met that Monday by surprise. She did like she often did and popped up unannounced with Sister Grace at my grandma's house. She had popped up at my job unannounced a couple weeks prior. She asked the dishwasher, who was an older man, "is she being a good girl up here?" "Is he flirting with any of the men or dating any of them?" He said no, she is a nice young lady. I was 34 years old and not anybody's girl; definitely not needing to be checked up on. As I understood, *"The eyes of the Lord are everywhere, keeping watch on the wicked and the good."* I didn't need anybody checking up on me; the only one to whom I was accountable was watching me.

Just as she and Grace got out of the car at my grandma's house, my ex-husband pulled up unexpectedly also. I was thinking, "what the heck!" "Perfect timing." I hadn't seen or heard from him in over a year. He said he came by to see his son. I let him speak because I didn't want to make a scene and he left after about 10 minutes. Then Alice asked me, "Do you know what 1Corinthians 15:33 says?" I said yes and recited it, *"Do not be misled. Bad associations spoil useful habits."* "Right so even though you are not a baptized Witness yet, would it be wise to start back dating your husband?" I said, "no, I'm not dating him, I'm not interested in dating him." She interrupted me, "I saw how you looked when he pulled up." "You looked surprised, like you had been caught doing something wrong and I just want to help you stay on the right path to everlasting life." "You don't need to explain anything to me, I'm just giving you some scriptural advice." That infuriated me. One thing I hated is for anyone to assume and accuse me of anything when I have given you the truth. This man spit in my face and raped me. I would never go back to him. I don't even speak to him when I see him. I never said anything because people look at women that have been raped and find every reason why she deserved it, consented to it, or asked for it. It takes courage to come forward and talk about the demeaning and disgraceful things that happened to you; and it takes strength to deal with everyone's judgements about you and the situation.

I finally responded, "let me go ahead and address the issues I have with you." "This is one." "I just told you that I'm not interested in him and you assume that we are dating again." "You asked me during my Bible study last week was I celibate." "I said, no and you asked me am I sure." " I am grown with four children and an ex husband." "I ain't gotta lie about having sex." "I CHOSE to come here and to serve Jehovah." "If I want to have sex, I can stay out in the "world" and do what I want and not have to prove myself to any of you." "And when you sent me the scripture Philippians 1:10, you were implying that I did not have my priorities straight saying, 'be sure of the more important things." "You don't know what I was doing for you to assume it wasn't important and I didn't owe you an explanation about it either." "I have been consistent with all of my study and meeting for several months, if I just wanted to rest, the Bible tells us to be balanced in Psalm 127:2 "It is useless for you to work so hard from early morning until late at night, anxiously working for food to eat; for God gives rest to his loved ones." "You seem to have a problem with me not believing anything I say and talking about how my children and I dress." Then it dawned on me and I remembered something she said from fifteen years ago. "Are you still upset because I dated Dorothy's son?" "I recall hearing that you said that you would have me arrested for statutory rape if I were dating your son." "Is that why you don't like me?" She wasn't ready for everything I had just said; but she woke the sleeping bear. Then I asked, "do I just need someone else to study the Bible with me since you obviously have a problem with me?"

She responded, "do you want another Bible study conductor because it seems that you have a problem with me?" I told her, " I don't need another conductor". "I have addressed my problems with you, I expect you to correct it, and we will move on." She said, fine, got in her car and left. That night until the early morning, I was bombarded with text messages and emails of scriptures and publications where she had circled certain words with the intent to insult me. This went on until Sunday. She highlighted from one publication, "that we have weaknesses that other do not admire", "clothes yourselves with love and keep putting up with one another", "he who hates reproof is stupid". She just went on and on. I responded to one email and said, "thanks for the spiritual food." "I'll read it and I love you too sister." It damaged her ego that I stood up to her because she did that to everyone and most people were intimidated by her and I wasn't. She was a real bully.

That Sunday after the meeting, I told her husband the elder, that I needed a new Bible study conductor because I didn't think his wife wanted to study with me any longer. He said wait let me get her so I can get to the bottom of what's going on. I put my children in the truck, turned the air conditioner on, and went to talk to them. When he asked her what was going on, she said, "I don't know what Leia's talking about." I said, "she sent me all of these emails and texts insulting me because I told her about how she offended me." He said, "you seem to be the one with the problem, not my wife." I said, "I can show you." Then I pulled out my phone. He pushed my hand down and said I don't need to see your phone. I told him that we needed to have a meeting and I would like another elder to present so that all decisions would be unbiased and I can present the evidence to everyone. He told me to call an elder and we would meet back up at 3:00 that afternoon at the Kingdom Hall.

I called one elder; he said that he would not be available. The next one said, he was going out of town. The next one said he didn't want to get involved, and the last one, Brother Hartsell, said, "I'm not gonna be able to make it." He continued, "I know of people having similar issues with the same sister but we are going to pray and trust that he will put Jehovah God first and not his wife and make the best scripturally based decisions." "Call me back and let me know how it goes."

When I arrived, Brother Peoples and his wife Alice peoples were there early awaiting my arrival. I sat down and he asked, "where is the other elder you were supposed to call?" I said, "they weren't available or just didn't want to come". He smirked and said, "I knew it." "I knew no one else would come." "It is for your best interest that it is just me." "They were going to have her side not yours because you are just an unbaptized publisher." "What you need to understand is that my wife has already made it, you're trying to get there." That changed my whole demeanor and killed any chance of hope for him to be unbiased and act in a christian way. So immediately, I was on the defense and turned into the Comeback Queen. I asked him a question, "Are we at the end of this system of things?" He looked bewildered but said no. I know he was wondering where I was going with this. Then I said, "your wife taught me, Matthew 24:13 *"But the one who endures to the end will be saved."* "So since we have yet to reach the end, none of us have made it." "None of us are saved." "Whether you serve God for 50 years and fall short the day before or just start serving God wholeheartedly the day before, it is those that endure to the end."

He disregarded what I said and moved on to, "so why are we here?" I said, "ask your wife because I don't think she wants to study with me anymore." Alice said, "this precious young lady started accusing me of rumors she heard from the past and I never said anything to her or about her." "I just tried to help her but she doesn't seem to want help." I recanted everything that transpired between us and then pulled up all the correspondence from her over the past week. I tried to show it to him but again he refused. Alice lied about everything and even broke out in tears. I couldn't believe it. She said I was lying about everything and created a problem with her because she found out that my ex husband and I were dating again. I just shut down, then. I no longer tried to resolve anything with her because I knew what I was dealing with now. Then Brother Peoples told me, "to apologize to his wife". I laughed because I was like, "you gotta be kidding me." I responded, "at this point just let me go with someone else to do my Bible study because this isn't going to work." He said, "I will, but we will be right back in the same seat in the next few months with the new person because you are stubborn and unforgiving." "You need to allow the Holy Spirit to help you change your ways."

I recited to them both Luke 6:43-45, 43 "For no good tree bears bad fruit, nor again does a bad tree bear good fruit, 44 for each tree is known by its own fruit. For figs are not gathered from thornbushes, nor are grapes picked from a bramble bush. 45 The good person out of the good treasure of his heart produces good, and the evil person out of his evil treasure produces evil, for out of the abundance of the heart his mouth speaks." Then I said, "if you squeeze an orange, you'll get orange juice and an apple, apple juice." "Applying pressure brings out who we truly are." "The pressure from this situation showed her to be a liar and you to support the lies; you all are not what you want to be perceived to be." "You've been squeezed and I see what's inside of you; orange juice didn't come from your orange."

Chapter Sixteen: All Truths Don't Set You Free

I started studying with another person, Sister Evelyn Clara. She aided on into the Truth and I got baptized. Jehovah's Witnesses believe that our religion is the truth and call it such. Sister Alice Peoples did not give up. She was always looking and lurking for something to report on me. I even had a sister from another congregation that was visiting to pull me aside and tell me, "be careful". "I overheard a conversation of some sisters talking and they are watching you and looking for you to fail." "You have been doing a great job and keep up the good work." I asked her, "who were the ladies?" She said, "I didn't want to sew contentions in the congregation so I'm not going to tell you but know that I'm here to support you." I really appreciated her for telling me that.

I was still maintaining my studies, studying with my children, and now going out in field service. We encountered a lot of hate and rejection as we knocked on the doors of people's houses. Despite what I had experienced, I knew that God had delivered me from many things and he would continue to deliver me. That motivated me to want to go out and face those that hated us. Matthew 5:10 says, *"Blessed are those who are persecuted because of righteousness, for theirs is the kingdom of heaven."* What also motivated me was this song that stuck in my head from a child called, *Make the Truth Your Own*. I knew that I could not piggyback off of my grandmother's faith, I had to have my own faith and I had to teach my children how to find a relationship with Jehovah and develop their own faith. No one should deter my efforts to pursue a relationship with God.

While out in field service, I ran across James. I hadn't seen him or talked to him since I moved back. I happened to go to his parents house to offer a magazine and he was there. He and his mom accepted the magazines and let me share a couple of scriptures with him. He told me to call him later but I told him that I couldn't. If he was interested in a Bible study I would have to refer him to a brother because I could not associate with people that were not Jehovah's Witnesses unless I was studying the Bible with them and I couldn't study with him because he was a man at all. I actually still only had a couple friends left and I was only allowed to associate with them because I did informal witnessing with them and shared scriptures with them.

I never had a social life because I wasn't invited to gatherings or to feed the speaker very often. I heard one of the younger sisters in the Kingdom Hall stated that no one invites me to the singles stuff because the men are slim pickings and I would take their men; and my children and I are not invited when the speaker is fed, because no one wants to invite four children to their homes to mess up and eat up everything." So, I still talked to Necy and Sophia just to have some kind of adult association.

Sophia invited me to go to Dallas for her birthday. I was excited because I had never gone before and excited to finally have some adult time and recreation. My mama and grandma agreed to babysit. I accidentally said, "we're going for her birthday." The night before we were scheduled to leave, they told me I couldn't go because she was not a Jehovah's Witness and not good association because she was celebrating her birthday. I was so disappointed. I did not sleep the entire night. I kept replaying in my head, different ways to tell her that I could no longer go with her without hurting her feelings. She was one of few friends that was always there for me over the years. She was a beautiful soul, inside and out, and I didn't want to let her down. Then early that morning, she texted, then called, and called again. I was holding the phone in my hand still trying to figure out how to let her down without letting her down. After all I had experienced in life, the few people that loved me, I dreaded letting them down. After a while she stopped calling and texting. I told myself over and over again. "I'll call her and explain when she gets back", or "I'll call her tomorrow". I kept putting it off because I didn't know how to explain it and tomorrow never came. I wanted to tell her how sorry I was but I couldn't go back. I couldn't explain to her that the very people that I was trying to get her to join were the ones that wanted me to isolate myself from her. They wanted that to happen though. I wasn't supposed to have any friends outside of the organization but I didn't have any inside of the organization. I was truly alone.

  I already knew the fate for a friendship with James and I so I left it alone; but his mother welcomed me to come back on a return visit and share some scriptures with her again. When I saw James there again, he said that he and his wife were separated and in the process of a divorce so he had moved back in with his parents.

  One Friday evening when I was coming back

from the clinic, James texted me. I had a sinus infection and I went to get a shot. He asked what I was doing. I said just made it back in town. He said, "stop by the house". Against my better judgement, I went by the house. When I arrived, I saw all of the vehicles there so I knew his parents were home. So I felt better about going because I knew we weren't alone. He invited me in and I walked to the house. Then he hugged and kissed my neck. I pushed him back and asked, "what are you doing?" "Where are your parents?" He said, "everybody's gone and I know you like me." I did like him a long time ago but I no longer desired him or anyone and I definitely wasn't about to fornicate. He picked me up, threw me over his shoulder, and took me to the sofa. I was kicking and punching but didn't put me down until we reached the sofa. He held my arms down, unbuttoned my jeans, and proceeded to have intercourse with me. I fought at first but this was a very familiar nightmare that I kept reliving. Then I just laid there, motionless. When he finished he kissed my cheek and asked, "what's wrong?" I didn't say anything. Then he asked, "you didn't want it?" I said no. "I told you no." He said, "I thought you were just playing hard to get." "I didn't know you really meant no." I said, "fornication is not allowed in my religion." "I told you that." "I told you a long time ago when I first started studying that I would be celebate until I married again." James said, "I didn't know that you were for real." "I didn't know people do that." "Plus you already got four kids, I didn't think you were trying to save nothing." I told him, "having children doesn't mean I can't stop having sex." "This is my body and I can choose at any time, what I want to do with it." "I never want to speak to you again.

I went home and had to act like nothing happened, just like all the other times something happened to me. I walked into the house, and went straight to the bathroom. I bathed and went to bed not even greeting my children. I told my grandma that I still wasn't feeling well and just got in bed. I felt like it was my fault because I never should have gone there. I never should have answered his text. I never should have gone in the house. He may have been living with his parents but he was still married too. His divorce wasn't final. I could never say anything about this to anyone. I already know that it would just confirm the rumors of us already having slept together.

The following night, I attended the surprise engagement party at Sister Martha's house. Her daughter's soon to be fiance, who was from a neighboring congregation, had invited the people around our age in the congregation to be in attendance as he proposed to her. This was one of few invitations I received to attend gatherings so I was excited to go. It would also take my mind off of what happened last night.

I celebrated with everyone but I was still emotionally weighed down from reliving what had happened. I was thinking about what I could have done differently to have prevented it. How could I have been so naive to believe that a man could really have been my friend. I brought this one on myself. As I was standing in Martha's kitchen, in a daze, Sister Cecely from another congregation, walked up to me and hugged me. She said, "you have really been a good sport". I asked, "what do you mean?" She said, "I can see it all over you that you are jealous because you're not the one getting married." "I can read people." I looked at her in disbelief. This woman is so far in left field. Even if she thought she could read people, she couldn't read me. I responded, "no i'm not jealous". She interrupted, "yes you are". "You just don't realize it." "I know that all of y'all young sisters desire a husband." "You come to the conventions and assemblies looking all extra cute, trying to catch some brother's eye." "You don't have to try to fool me, I can see it all over you." "It's okay, your time is coming." I just let her keep talking because I know that when someone thinks that they have you figured out, you cannot convince them otherwise.

"You just need to follow Jesus's admonishment and advice in 1Corinthians, "to the unmarried and the widows, I say that it is good for them to remain single as I am." "Jesus said that singleness is a gift so you shouldn't take it for granted." "Now cheer up." I told her, "Sister Cecely, I appreciate the advice, but I've been married and divorced." "I don't desire a husband." "I'm not like the other single sisters." Most sisters and brothers at least 18 years old, are eager to marry because their sexual desires have aroused and they are ready to experience intercourse. They usually marry the first fellow Jehovah's Witness that is as eager to have sex as them. That's the only way they can have sex and not commit sin against God. They justify it by 1Corinthians 7:9, *"But if they cannot control themselves, they should marry, for it is better to marry than to burn with passion."* This often leads to many unhappy marriages shortly after. Once sexual urges are fulfilled, reality sets in and people realize that they didn't want to be married to this person eternally. They can't get a divorce unless it's a scripturally acceptable basis for a divorce. I guess Cecely didn't realize that I wasn't that young and sex had succumb to the law of diminishing marginal utility for me. I had had enough sex, voluntarily and involuntarily, and I did not desire it. I had had enough of men using me and did not want one even close to me. I only wanted my solitude to heal emotionally, mentally, and spiritually.

A little less than two months later, I missed my period. I already had children and just knew that I was pregnant. I took a test to confirm it. Then, I texted James out of the blue, after not even an attempt of communication from either of us since the incident. "I'm pregnant." He immediately said, "I'm so sorry." I texted back, "you have ruined my life." I never even told anyone what happened, how was I going to explain that I was pregnant. Sister Alice has tainted my reputation within the congregation and this made it even more difficult to consider talking to the elders about my situation. She reminded the congregation of what the whole town knew about the situation with my ex husband accusing me of an affair with James, the mayor's husband. How could I say he raped me? Everyone believed we had already had an affair. Was it really rape when I did like him at one time? In my mind I dismissed it as unwanted sex with someone I onced desired, like having sex with my boyfriend or husband when they wanted it and I didn't. Plenty of my old friends and I had talked about many times being in relationships and marriages, obligating our bodies to men out of duty not consensuality. Was it consent when

I stopped fighting? It wasn't rape, I just didn't want it then. This rationale allowed me to take responsibility and control of what happened. It was my fault so I'm going to get an abortion and not tell anyone about it. I'll never be alone with a man again.

    Over the next couple of weeks, I went back and forth with myself about the abortion. I prayed and prayed about what I should do. I texted James and asked him what he wanted. He said, "whatever you choose, I will support you." He sounded again like the friend I first met. After more prayer and consulting the Bible, a few scriptures gave me the answer to which I was searching. I sat down, digging into God's word, looking for resolution and began to read Psalm 139:15, *"My frame was not hidden from you when I was made in the secret place, when I was woven together in the depths of the earth."* Then I began to cry. I went back and read the scripture before that, *"My frame was not hidden from you when I was made in the secret place, when I was woven together in the depths of the earth."* I knew then that Jehovah God purposed this baby to be here and I would not abort it.

    I continue to attend the meetings but I mostly stopped going out in field service. That was more time out with other Jehovah's Witnesses and it made it more difficult to hide the emerging baby bump. I still had not told anyone I was expecting. Not going out in service put you on the radar as being spiritually in trouble. So I was being watched more now. Many of the other witnesses and "friends", friends are also what other fellow Jehovah's Witnesses called each other, began to ostracize and criticize me because of what Sister Alice was saying about me. Then her other partner in crime, Sister Blackmon's daughter, Sister Katherine wanted to remind everyone of the rumors she got from her co-worker Emma, Will's ex wife. You know how one person says, "girl I heard she was like this." Then the other person says, "I believe it because I heard she did that with so-and-so's husband too." You know, good christian people gossiping about what they got from the street committee. Then their elder husbands started to keep tabs on my children and I tried to find things for which to discipline me. "You cannot go out in field service because your son doesn't have on a tie.". "Your son needs a lower haircut." "We heard that you allow your children to watch inappropriate shows on cable tv." "We were told that you had a picture on social media with an alcoholic beverage on the table in front of you." "We need to meet with you Leia about your consistent tardiness for the meetings and service." I couldn't sleep at night. I was suffering guilt and depression.

    The fact that I was still coming was because of my dedication to God. People didn't even realize that I was in battle pushing myself to go anywhere, especially the Kingdom Hall. I didn't want to sit next to anyone that questioned my loyalty to God, talked behind my back about my alleged past, but offered me scriptural encouragement to help transform me, a fellow Christian from my "homewrecking adulterous ways". On top of all of that, James reneged on his promise to support me and I hadn't heard from him anymore. He ignored my calls. I was all alone. As instructed, I had to cut off my "worldly" friends that weren't Jehovah's witnesses. There was only one person that sometimes I talked to in the organization and it was the lady from another congregation that warned me of them "looking for me to fail." It was Sister Hope. She was the epitome of what a Christian should be. The kindest person I had ever met. I had to distance myself from her also because if she knew I was pregnant, she would have to tell on me. Another rule at the Kingdom Hall and among Jehovah's Witnesses was that if you saw your fellow spiritual sister or brother stumble, then you were obligated to tell on them. The purpose was to protect the reputation of God's organization and to get help for the spiritually sick person.

I was still struggling financially but it did make a little more money. I had applied for a secretary job at the school and got it. I continued to do informal witnessing at the school to the teachers I encountered. As I got further along in my pregnancy, I had to stop attending the Kingdom Hall because my belly was too big to hide. I decided to move to a neighboring town called Cromwell, away from everyone. Cromwell was bigger than Lafayette. It had a bigger Walmart, some shopping centers, and more restaurants. We gauged the size of a town by the number of restaurants, size of their Walmart, and number of traffic lights. Some people from Lafayette come to Cromwell, typically on the weekends to shop. I made sure that I was home out of sight so no one would see me.

I was pumping gas at the Walmart one Friday evening when I thought I recognized the vehicle of a young lady from Lafayette that was studying to become a Jehovah's Witness. She circled around the gas station but by the time she got near my truck, I had gotten in and was driving away. I know she was trying to see if it was me because that was the tea. Where has Leia moved? The Jehovah's Witnesses couldn't pop up at my house unannounced and demand a meeting between the elders and myself without knowing where I lived. The newer members and Bible students are the most eager to prove themselves to the organization so that they can fit in. These are the main ones that seek out troubled ones like me, and want to report us to the elders to make themselves seem genuinely invested in upholding God's law. In actuality, what they get is a temporary pat on the back for being the snitch and an invitation to join the cliques within the congregation only to later have the same things done to them. It was just a cycle of mess in the name of keeping the organization clean of ones committing unholy acts. So many times people don't see what they think they saw but run and tell it all.

    I cut off communication with my family because if the elders questioned them about me, they could be honest and say they didn't know. Not telling them about me or where I lived was to protect my family. However that didn't even work. That young lady's vehicle I saw was indeed Shaquitta Tipton from the Lafayette Congregation. She confirmed to everyone that I was pregnant. Sister Hope told me that she heard that my mom and grandma had been questioned by the elders and because they said that they didn't know anything, they were removed from the Ministerial School. They were being punished because the elders thought they were lying and taking up for me. When I called out Sister Alice Peoples and asked her about the rumors she said about me, she shared the scripture

1Corinthians 13:7, "*Love bears all things, believes all things, hopes all things, endures all things.*" Then she analyzed it and told me that I should have not believed the rumors I heard because Jehovah says that we are supposed to believe the best first of our fellow christians, hope for the best from them, and even if they may have offended us, turn the other cheek and endure through the offense. Yet, my family gave them the truth and christian agape love wasn't exercised toward them by believing them first and hoping they were honest. That was the very thing that made me want to come become a Jehovah's Witness. I would hear my friends talk about the church gossip, who was doing what with who, who got in trouble, and who got spared out of favoritism because of what they did or paid to the church. I thought the Kingdom Hall was different. I thought when I joined the Truth and told the truth, things would be different. I thought that the Truth would set me free. I was wrong. All truths don't set you free. After becoming a Jehovah's Witness, I have never felt more in bondage, more restricted, and more internal conflict than ever in my life.

    I was barely making ends meet. Before work this Friday day, I got all of my old purses and asked my children to collect all of the change from the purses. We went to a gas station and I had the seven year old twins go in together to pay for the gas with the change we scraped out of the purses. We collected $5.38. I was too embarrassed to go pay with all that change. It was the middle of summer and scorching hot. The air conditioner did not work in my truck, one of the back windows didn't roll down, and the passenger window doesn't roll down either. I couldn't afford to get any of it fixed. People often yell at me or blow the horn when I'm riding in traffic because my doors were open. I would make sure all the kids were strapped down well and my oldest son and I would crack the door open with one of our feet so we could have some air. This particular day, not having any gas money, looking in the rear view mirrors seeing my babies sweating, and looking down at my belly at the baby on the way, that I clearly couldn't take care of, took me to rock bottom.

When I made it home, I went into my room and closed the door. I cried and cried. I couldn't do anything else. My son made dinner for himself and his siblings because he knew I wasn't well. Everything I had experienced in my life had reached a climax. It was all too much for me. All the things that had bothered me from my past had resurfaced. All the suppressed feelings of each traumatic experience had been unleashed. I soon learned that simply letting go of bad experiences don't heal them. Moving away doesn't escape them. It takes just one catastrophic event in your life and it brings them all back to the surface and slaps you in the face. Being bullied as a child, being molested, being raped, being abandoned, being judged, being poor, being accused, being cheated and cheated on, and being alone created this dirt that I had gradually been settling into since I came into this world. Over the years, being buried in that dirt combined with my sweat, my tears, and the figurative Holy Water that was supposed to be used to cleanse my soul only devised that Mississippi Mud that I couldn't seem to escape.

I remained in that depressed state for another week. I wasn't eating or sleeping. I went to work, smiled, and helped everyone like usual. We don't know the burdens that each person carries on their shoulder, and I carried a lot in secret. No one knew the great effort it took to be functional each day. When I returned home each day, I removed the mask that I wore all day and retreated back to my bedroom and my low place. I was reliving the feelings of responsibility of falling asleep in my mama's bed and putting myself in position to be molested. That's why my mama didn't love me because of what happened with her man. It was my fault. It's my fault I got pregnant by Bud and was irresponsible and lost my baby. I should have listened to everyone and not dated Devonte. It's my fault Dorothy doesn't like and Shantella hated me. I never should have dated Will. Maybe he and Emma would still be married. Then maybe I never would have met James and maybe I wouldn't have all these children to take care of alone. I ruined my own life.

    I was only sleeping one to two hours per night. When I would fall asleep, I would be awakened by a loud boom, like a door slamming or a gunshot. I would go into my children's rooms, wake them as ask if they heard that. They always said no. Other times I would jump up from my sleep, startled because I had a feeling of someone standing over me, watching me. I would look out all of the windows to see if anyone was lurking outside my house. There was never anyone there. I had started hallucinating. Hearing things and feeling someone watching me while I slept drove me crazy. Until now, I wasn't conscious that I had been this way for many years.

    Thursday, I went to work still trying to

camouflage the pain I was carrying. Two male teachers stopped by the office for some supplies. As I walked into the supply room, they followed me. One of them said, "you don't look pregnant from the back". "I'd still hit that." I responded, "that's so disrespectful". "Please don't speak to me that way." When I exited the supply room, I sat the items on my desk to check them off of the inventory. Then that same teacher touched my back pocket. I felt my pocket and he had put something in it. I pulled it out and it was gum paper. I opened it but nothing was on it. I said, "why would you put that in my pocket?" "There is the trash can". He replied, "I put garbage with the other garbage." Then they both laughed and walked out with their supplies in hand. People don't realize that the small insult they gave you, the rudeness that they showed you, and the act of being inconsiderate may be just the final indignity that pushes them over the edge.

    After picking my children up from school, I went home and retreated to my room again. As I was lying on my bed, I heard a ding sound from my purse on the floor. I was surprised to see it was a message from James. I hadn't heard from him or seen him my entire pregnancy. I opened the text and it said, "my wife and I decided on the best thing for us to do." "I need a DNA test first." "If it comes back that it's mine, I am going to relinquish my rights." I texted back, "you knew I was celibate and I didn't want to sleep with you." "You took it from me!" "Now you are questioning me?!?!" He texted back, "I don't know what you're talking about." "Everyone knows how you are." "We both know that you came to my parents' house and seduced me." I didn't text anything back after that because I had no more fight or argument left in me. I didn't think I could feel any lower but after those texts, I felt my lowest.

    I called out for work the following day. I didn't take my children to school either. I got a few phone calls and text messages from some ladies that worked with me but I didn't want to talk to anyone. I didn't bathe or brush my teeth. I never left my room the entire day. My children came in every once in a while to ask for permission to eat snacks or go outside to play but I never left my room. I finally slept Friday night. I came to peace with many things. Saturday morning, I had a solution for everything and I was going to save us. I got up, cooked for my family, ate, took a bath, and got dressed. I told everyone to get dressed and I dressed my youngest.

    We all got in the car, I made sure that everyone was strapped in. The kids sang songs in the car and I took them to get ice cream. I drove about an hour to the Mississippi River bridge. As the bridge got in sight, I locked the doors. I was going to drive into the Mississippi River. I wanted all of my children locked and strapped in so that they could not escape the truck. We are going to die together. I can't live here anymore and I refuse to leave my children with my family, people that did hurt me and didn't take care of me; and their daddies don't want them. Just as I approached the roadway leading to the bridge, I took a deep breath and started to speed up. My youngest son called me, "ma", and I looked at him through my rearview mirror. He said, "you are a great mama and I love you." I slammed on the brakes, right at the base of the bridge, and burst into tears. He was so innocent. They all were. I was all that they had and I had resolved to take their lives. I was about to take the life of my unborn baby before he even had a chance. It was like God was speaking to me through my son. Letting me know that all of my efforts were not in vain and that I was of value to someone, my children. I wasn't trash, I wasn't dirty, and I wasn't damaged to the little people that valued me the most. Psalm 34:18, *"The Lord is close to the brokenhearted and saves those who are crushed in spirit."* God saved me through the people that I thought I was saving, my children.

Chapter Seventeen: The Lonely Road to Freedom

I gave birth a couple weeks later, alone. Of course James wasn't there. One of my coworkers stayed at my house and kept my kids while I gave birth. I didn't have many friends because I cut them all off when I became a Jehovah's Witness. I didn't have any at the Kingdom Hall because I had sinned and would have been considered a bad influence. If anyone did get close to me they would have been counseled to watch their association within the congregation. Surprisingly, the coworkers that I initially studied with stuck around and we became pretty close. I consider them friends now. I was always taught to not associate or trust "worldly"people. What I learned from them was that everyone that wasn't part of my religion or any religion weren't all bad people; and everyone claiming to be devout Christians and religious people were not all good people.

I finally told my family where I lived. I cooked dinner and invited them over to see the kids and meet the new baby. I only have a few months left on my lease here so I was considering moving back. For the first time in my life I was ready to move back to Lafayette. I realized that of all the years I spent trying to escape problems the only solution to fixing them was to face them. I told my grandma that James was my youngest son's father but I didn't expect him to be in my son's life. I told her the entire story of how I conceived this child. Retelling it helped me realize that it wasn't my fault. That also helped me to realize that a lot of things that I took responsibility for were not my fault either. I was not blameless for my lot in life but I had been a victim in a few of those horrible situations.

When my lease ended, I moved back in with my grandma to save some money. I also started back studying the Bible. My time alone helped me to see myself. I noticed that no one can truly heal until they spend time alone. Always being on the phone with people and being around people, whether discussing my past or current problems or not, was just a distraction from dealing with my own stuff. Seeking everybody's advice, support, and condemnation of culprits that wronged me was just a way to continue to be a victim and epitomize helplessness. Throughout my lowest point, I continued to pray and lean on God for understanding. For me to become whole, to heal, I needed to forgive everyone that violated me in any kind of way. I also discerned that I consistently attracted the same types of people and types of situations because I had not healed from the first violation. The first encounters of the ominous spirits created a home for themselves inside of me and they just invited more of their kind. I recognized that all of the people that caused me problems were all the same types of problems or spirits just manifested in different people. Yes, I did need to identify and acknowledge what spirits I had been battling. I can't win a fight when I can't see my opponent. Using God's word helped me to see who my opponents were.

Living with her allowed my grandma and I more time to talk about why I stopped going to the Kingdom Hall and my last baby. She told me that I needed to confess my sins to the elders, get counseled or disciplined, and come back to Jehovah. I said, "you're talking like you now believe the street committee and don't believe that I didn't consent to sex". She said, "I hear what you saying but my opinion about it doesn't matter." "I mean you have found yourself in this situation more than once, but I'm just leaving it up to elders and the arrangement to make the right decisions so you and the kids can come on back to Kingdom Hall and in the Truth." "We are living in the last days and I don't want you all to lose your life." I knew then that my grandma had been influenced by what other witnesses said but I wanted to serve God. I also had time to reflect on how He had delivered me so many times and like always wanted to dedicate my life to Him. So, I told my grandma that I would go talk to the elders.

Saturday, my grandma had been out in field service and left her bag in Sister Katherine's car but my grandma was gone with my uncle to the hardware store. Sister Katherine stopped by my grandma's house to drop it off. I was in the back of the house but I heard the doorbell. One of the twins answered the door with the baby in her arms. They knew not to let anyone in the house but like many of the women Jehovah's Witnesses, Sister Katherine was aggressive and relentless. My daughter reached for the bag then Katherine said, "oh let me see the baby", while pushing the door open and inviting herself in. She grabbed the baby from my daughter's arm just as I walked into the room. "Oh he is such a pretty baby." I walked up to her and grabbed my baby. I told her, "Don't touch him."

I had heard that Sister Katherine was the one that had the conversation with Shaquitta and she was the one that actually took the news of my pregnancy to the elders. The elders told her to get confirmation before they could do anything about it. Then Sister Katherine lied to my grandma and mama like she saw pregnant pictures of me on social media to get them to confirm or deny my pregnancy. I never took pictures because I was ashamed of my pregnancy. The fact that Katherine was seeking information on me and was conniving in her efforts to get information on me made me very angry. There was nothing Christian about the situation. I know I should have responded better, but I'm a work in progress and I ain't there yet. When I got home, I told my grandma about the situation. She told me, "yeah she was wrong for what she said and what she did before but Jehovah said we have to keep forgiving one another and that's your spiritual sister."

The next day after Sunday service, the elders called my grandma and mama to stay after for a meeting. Brother Peoples told them, "it's been brought to our attention that Leia is living with you." "Is she?" My grandma said yes. He continued, "well let me share a couple of scriptures with you both." "1 Corinthians 5:11, *"But now I am writing to you that you must not associate with anyone who claims to be a brother or sister but is sexually immoral or greedy, an idolater or slanderer, a drunkard or swindler. Do not even eat with such people.""* " And here at James 4:17 it says " *"If anyone, then, knows the good they ought to do and doesn't do it, it is sin for them."* "So sister, here in 1Corinthians, what is God telling us to do?" My grandma responded, "not to even eat with such a person." Brother Peoples responded, "and if we were to do such a thing, then what would that mean for us?" My grandma said, "it would mean sin for us." He said, "right". "So we need you to encourage your granddaughter and your daughter to come to us and confess her sins so that we can help her get back in good standing with the organization and Jehovah." "As long as she is not in good standing, she will not be allowed to live with either of you because that would be like supporting her fornication." "I don't think you all would like to be viewed as people that support fornication." "Then you all could have your privileges revoked and we don't want that to happen either."

My grandma came home infuriated. She yelled, "Leia come here." I walked in and she said, "you gonna have to find yourself somewhere to go cause I'm not gonna lose my position as a pioneer or get in no trouble for letting you stay here." "You gotta go talk to the elders or you gonna have to get out." I said, "Grandma, you mean to tell me that you are going to let some people that don't know the truth about me, convince you to put me and my children out because I won't do what they say when they say it?" She said, "it's Jehovah's arrangement and you have to abide by it." "You brought this on yourself." "You could have gone and talked to them in the very beginning and maybe you wouldn't have had to leave." I said fine. "I'll find somewhere to go."

The following Sunday my grandma home again telling me, "they questioned me again about you." "I done told you now, you gonna have to find you somewhere to go cause I'm not getting in no trouble for you." I packed some clothes for my children and I and I left. We went to a motel and stayed. I had already been looking and applying to properties. For the next month paid week by week to stay in a double bed room at the Lafayette Inn and Suites. I washed at the laundromat and we ate tv dinners. Finally an apartment became available for me and we moved in. It was dilapidated and many of the apartments were boarded up but it was my own place.

I had not seen any Jehovah's Witnesses in a few months with the exception of my family. Until early one Saturday morning, I got a knock at my door. I answered, not knowing who it was. They were out in field service. I was invited to a convention. I decided to attend. I still read my Bible and followed along with the magazines because I desired to have a relationship with God and this was all that I knew. A lot of us choose religions and choose churches because it is tradition. Our parents, grandparents, and even great grandparents introduced us and we continued with it because it is what we have grown accustomed to. In times of stress and despair, it is only right that we look for someone or something spiritual to relieve our spiritual ailments. We acknowledge a higher being and desire connection with it. Our route to the connection is usually predetermined by tradition until we become self aware, if we ever become aware. There was this song that always stuck with me from a child. It was a Kingdom Hall melody called "Make the Truth Own." I never knew until now why it stuck with me and what it meant.

I attended the three day convention the following weekend. The first day I came in late and sat at the back so that no one could talk to me. I just wanted to get some spiritual food and be left alone. I left early so there was no time or opportunity for anyone to say anything to me. Day two, I got caught at lunch by Sister Martha. She grabbed the twins and hugged them. She said, "I missed yall but now I need to whip y'all." "Leia, I need to whip you too." "You ought to be ashamed of yourself going out there and getting another baby." I told my children to come on and I got my stuff to leave. Then I was stopped by Sister Willerine just as I was going out the door and she said, "so this is the new baby I heard about." "Do you have enough children now?" I was thinking, "what about people greeting me with glad to see you back, a simple hello, or simply don't say anything ." I couldn't get out fast enough. After that I was bombarded with calls and texts from different sisters. They were sending scriptures telling me of how I need to repent of my sinful ways and return to Jehovah. Some took the more subtle approach by comparing me to the lost sheep in the parable that Jesus described in the Book of Luke. They said, "Jehovah will come and find just one lost sheep, you." "And He will call everyone and rejoice that you returned." "God cares about you." I had the workings of the "good cop, bad cop" tactic to try wear me down.

I tried one more time to go back. I went to a special meeting at the Lafayette Kingdom Hall on the last Sunday of the month.. Service was good but my children and I got a lot of interesting looks which kind of distracted our concentration on what was being said. We all were impeccably dressed and for once, I didn't try to wear anything that was too big and hide my figure. However, I was modestly dressed in my black skirt suit and unapologetic with my bow hips accentuated by my attire. I wanted to serve God but I stopped trying to conform who I was to fit what made everyone else comfortable with my presence. Sister Hope and her husband had since joined our Lafayette Congregation. It was good to see her because she was one of the good ones. She met me outside to talk to me as my children and I were leaving. She asked, "Are you going to meet with the elders so that you can come back?" "We really miss you." "I can ask my husband to be one of the elders that meets with you." I said, "yes, I am considering it because I do want my children to know God." She continues, "That is so encouraging to hear." "You know that you will have to stop seeing your baby's daddy and show the elders that you are repentant." I said, "I was never seeing him; what do you mean?" She said, "Oh I had heard that you and James had been dating since you had the baby." "Don't say anything but a couple of the sisters said they had passed by your place several times and always saw his car over there." "They said he was practically living there."

    I shook my head and said, " I didn't stop coming to the Kingdom Hall because I fornincated and didn't want to confess my sins." "I stopped coming because of that right there." "You I have been depressed for years." "I have experienced so many things in life intended to kill me." "I recognized God's hand in my life and how He saved me so many times." "I genuinely wanted to dedicate my life to God." "I didn't fornicate when I got this baby." "I didn't consent to sex." "I just happened to be in the wrong place at the wrong time." "I'm guilty of being in the wrong place, that's all." Then Sister Hope hugged me and said, "I'm so sorry." " I will admit that, I too, assumed that you fornicated." "I'm so sorry for what happened to you." "Did you call the police?" I responded, "For what?" "For them and everyone else to delve into my past?" "To put my mistakes and the things that have happened to me on display for the world to judge?" "To be transformed from the victim to the assailant trying to destroy this man's reputation?" "I rather not." She said, "I understand, I miss you alot and I want you to come back." "I just need to warn you." "The sisters had already been saying that you were promiscuous and this baby is just proof of what you had already been doing." "So just be ready for the gossip but I know you are strong and can overlook them." I grabbed my door handle and proceeded to get in my truck. She was standing there, bewildered at how abruptly I ended the conversation. I had had enough. I didn't want that negative energy, camouflaged as genuine concern, in my spirit. Then I said, "THAT is the reason I left." "Y'all told me that the world and the people in it were bad." "I needed to leave the world and join God's only true religion yet I get treated the same or worse by God's people." "This ain't right."

After that, every other week, I was getting unannounced visits from the elders at my house. I didn't answer the door. I did them the way people used to do us. I would see them outside and just be quiet and not answer the door. They left notes at the door saying, "please call Brother Peoples or Brother Lee it is urgent." The notes were coupled with magazines depicting the end of this world or system of things.

I had finally made the decision to return to school. I wasn't ready to talk to the elders and decided to channel my focus on bettering myself. I focused on college. I began meditation, affirmations, and reading self help books. I read required texts from school that enlightened me about other religions; and I listened to encouraging sermons and speeches online. I even listened to a few gospel songs I heard online. We were always forbidden from listening to gospel music, reading, watching, or learning anything about other religions. That was why we were encouraged not to attend weddings and funerals at churches. Never told we couldn't go but "encouraged" not to go. Then given examples and personal testimonials of how someone was saved from Satan, disasters, or violent people by avoiding family, events, and/or people in the church or in the world. Everyone in the audience would clap and praise that person for staying close to the organization and its traditions. It seemed as if you were making your own decision but actually you were not in control of your own life at all. It was all orchestrated. I even saw it in the church when I started going with my friend. The trick though was to select specific scriptures and draw out from those scriptures the understanding and interpretation they want you to get from those scriptures.Then use those scriptures to convict you for not adhering to their principals and laws, to convict you for not conforming to their standards, to condemn you for having individuality. You must be like them.

    And you did what they asked. These charismatic leaders like the preachers and the elders actually controlled us all. The fact that people believe that the Bible is truly God's word was the tool used against those vulnerable people seeking refuge from life's tribulations.We would do anything to fix a broken spirit and that was the opening to a takeover of my soul. Everyone wanted to belong. I wanted to belong. So no matter how irrational it sounded, I cut off my family, I cut off my friends, I gave them all of my money, I sacrificed my education and a career, I judged people and condemned them, and I devoted most of my time to a religion. I sacrificed my life in exchange for what I thought was a relationship with God. A lot of Jehovah's Witnesses didn't even have cable television in their homes in an effort to reduce the exposure to the outside world and its influences. Nothing was supposed to make us question our practices. We were not supposed to question the elders, the teachings, or the governing body. I started to realize that I should question anything and anyone that did not accept who I was.

      I often sat in my living room with the wooden door open, reading, and studying in the natural sunlight. A shadow suddenly covered my pages and I looked up and there were two elders at my door. They finally caught me slipping. I couldn't avoid them this time; but I didn't want to. I was ready to talk to them. Sister Alice had texted me a while back quoting the scripture in 2 Samuel 11-12 about King David setting up Uriah to be killed and how Nathan told David to confess and repent of his sins. I guess she alluded herself to Nathan and was trying to encourage me to confess my alleged fornication. Since I didn't, she sent her husband. Brother Peoples said, "we have been trying to get in touch with you". "We need you to come to the Kingdom Hall and meet with us for a judicial hearing about your fornication." I said, "Did you try calling me?" "I have had the same number for over ten years." He said, "We have called but you never answered so we thought we were blocked." I said, "No you're not, I never received a call but okay, I will be there." He said, "is Wednesday at 7:00 pm okay?" I said yes. He and Brother Lee looked at each other in surprise and well if can't make it call us and handed me their numbers. I said, "I don't need it; I have your numbers", and closed my door.

    The next day, I spent hours thinking, writing, pacing, then erasing on the letter that I decided to write to the elders. I wanted to tell them everything that led up to me wanting to leave the Kingdom Hall. No one is officially out until they write a letter to the organization stating their desire for dissociation or they are disfellowshipped. That's the only way anyone can leave. I had had some conversations with people that left the Truth and they told me that simply not coming back for any meetings didn't mean that you were out. You had to write the letter. While pondering on what to say, I had an epiphany, I thought about the lady Charlene that I met in Virginia. She was a complete stranger that came to my aid. I had prayed for help, when I was at one of my lowest moments, and God sent her to me. What I didn't realize until this very moment was she was disassociated. When I asked her if she was a Jehovah's Witness, she said she grew up there but hadn't been in a long time. That's a disassociated person. The very person God sent to help me was someone that had managed to leave that bondage. Some experiences in life are not meant for that moment, that's why we don't understand it then. It was meant for me, right now. I was meant to remember that, who God sent for me was not a Jehovah's Witness or a self proclaimed Christian, so that it would give me the confirmation I need at this very moment. I was meant to remember her from 11 years ago. This was the sign I needed to let go. I had made up my mind.

I went to my grandma and told her of my decision. I didn't tell my mama because I knew my grandma would and we weren't that close anyway. Matthew 5:23-24 states that *"Therefore, if you are offering your gift at the altar and there remember that your brother or sister has something against you, 24 leave your gift there in front of the altar. First go and be reconciled to them; then come and offer your gift.* So before you give your gift of service, your tithes, and sing praise to God, He said, mend the ought or reconcile the problems we have with each other first. That meant to me that all the time my mama was sacrificing going out in field service teaching people about the Bible and all the times she tried to encourage me to come back, the significant commandment that she should have followed from the Bible which just might have changed my heart, was to reconcile things with her daughter. Make peace with me; but I had made peace with myself about everything. I forgave her because she is my mother and I needed to move on with my life. Sometimes we never get I'm sorry, not even from Christians but that doesn't stop forgiveness. Forgiveness is a personal choice that benefits me. Everything happens for a reason. It was meant for her not to say I'm sorry because I didn't need to go back.

My grandma said, "Ohhh, I hate that you made that decision." "Now we won't be able to talk to you anymore." I said, "But you know everything I experienced there." "I know some things that you experienced which weren't right." "The people there that do you wrong get excused 'cause I should turn the other cheek and when I do something wrong, according to their standards, I'm disciplined because I'm not a part of the cliques." "They do things that are not right and are not held accountable by the organization but I am." My grandma said, "just leave it to God to take care of them." I said, "shouldn't the same courtesy be extended to me?" "Why do I have to be held accountable to these people when God made these rules?" "He sits high and looks low and sees both the good and bad." "Why can't He "take care" of me too?" "I don't think that's right." My grandma said, "that's Jehovah's arrangement and we have to abide by it." I said, "no grandma". "That's their arrangement, the Governing Body." "And who are they anyway for them to have so much power and authority?" She said, "They were anointed and selected by Jehovah." I said, "how do we know that I wasn't anointed?" "How do you know that they were anointed?" "She said, "because they said so and I don't question anything that comes from them because they get their direction from God." I said, "I could say the same thing." "But that's the problem right there." "No one questions anything." "If my life depends on it, shouldn't I question it?" Then there was a long pause. I continued, "I see you're getting upset and I'm not here to convince you to leave." "I just came to let you know of my decision." She said, "I'm so sorry to hear that and I think you need to think about it." "We won't be talking to you again." "You will be dead to us." I said, "I will be dead to y'all but I will just be starting to live." "I hope that you can start living too." I wiped a tear from my eye and said my goodbye.

It's Wednesday and I have been visualizing myself not even meeting with them and just taking them that letter and walking out. I mean, who are they to tell me that I have to come to a judicial hearing about my life. I walked into the Kingdom Hall with three of them sitting there around a chair in the center, designated for me. Brother Lee, Brother Hope, and Brother Peoples. I had the letter in my hand, palms sweating, waiting to get it over with. Brother Peoples told Brother Lee to open up with prayer.

Brother Lee started, "may we bow our heads?" We all lowered in anticipation for the prayer. He said, "Thank you Jehovah for allowing us to be here today, for providing this arrangement to help the lost sheep come back, and for providing this arrangement to help Leia." "God you know that she is spiritually sick and may you help her receive the plentiful counsel and discipline that you have provided to help her because she is spiritually weak." "God she so desperately needs strengthening and may this be the first step in restoring her morality." "Amen." They all said Amen. I didn't. By the first "spiritually sick" comment, my head was up, eyes open, and I was staring a hole in his bald head. I'm not saying Amen to those insults.

Then Brother Peoples said, "we want you to know that you cannot have any recording devices or record this meeting on your cell phone." I said, "I don't have my cell phone but okay." I was thinking, "what is going to be said that shouldn't be recorded?" Brother Peoples continued, "we are here today for the judicial hearing on fornication by Sister Leia Devine." "You can start by telling us what happened with this act of fornication and what led up to you leaving the congregation."

I painstakingly told them detail by detail what happened between James and I. He asked, "Well why didn't you come to us to tell us that?" I said, "you wanted to come in front of three men and tell you the most intimate and shameful things that happened to me." "I had to deal with my own feelings about what happened to me, my feelings about caring a baby that I didn't want to have with that person, and the lies and judgements from the people here." "Women don't often say anything because you scrutinize us as if we did something wrong; and I didn't." Brother Hope said, "I'm so sorry to hear that, we didn't know." Then Brother Peoples said, "We knew you had a baby and had heard that you and the child's father were together." I said, "Do you know what Proverbs 18:13 says?" As they went to their scriptures to read it, I recited it for them, *"When anyone replies to a matter before he hears the facts, it is foolish and humiliating."* "So you all assumed I fornicated and went as far as to have a judicial hearing based on your assumption."

Then Brother Hope said, "well you could have talked to us about what happened and trusted that we were going to help you." I said, "yeah the last I had an issue and asked the elders to meet with me no one would because my issue was with an elder's wife and none of you wanted to get involved." "I was told that since she had made it and I had not, no one would believe me." Brother Lee asked, "who would say something like that?" I said, "Do you want to tell them Brother Peoples, that it was you?" He said, "I don't recall that." I said, "I figured you say that, just like your wife, so I took the liberty of recording that meeting if y'all want to hear it." "But it's neither here nor there now; it doesn't matter anymore." "So you all do realize that you were asking me to trust you all to make sound, scriptural decisions on my life when you had already failed me." "You see, I didn't leave because of my perceived failures to uphold Godly standards." "I left because of many of you actually neglecting to uphold and adhere to Godly standards." "When I attempted to come back, I had sisters telling my children and I that we needed to be whipped and I should be ashamed for leaving." "I even had one of the elders wives tell me that the friends had been calling me promiscuous." Brother Hope looked with shock and asked, "who would tell you that?" I said, "your wife did." "And none of that was encouraging nor did it make me want to come back." Then everyone looked at me in disbelief and silence. I said, "We are taught that this is God's only true religion and John 13:35 says *By this all people will know that you are my disciples, if you have love for one another.*" "Love is not what I got from here."

    Then Brother Lee said, "well now that we know you didn't fornicate, do you know about the scriptures and the training given to women if they are raped?" I said, no. He said, "if you were paying attention, you would know." Then he read Deuteronomy 22:23-24, " *If a man happens to meet in a town a virgin pledged to be married and he sleeps with her, you shall take both of them to the gate of that town and stone them to death— the young woman because she was in a town and did not scream for help, and the man because he violated*

another man's wife. You must purge the evil from among you." Then he asked me, " did you scream?" " I said, "no". Then he said , "if you were back in those times, do you see what would have happened to you?" "You would have been stoned to death." I said, "I didn't scream when it happened and I was eight years old." "Am I to blame for it then too?" He said, "well yes, you bear some of the responsibility because you didn't scream." "Someone may have been able to help you had you followed God's instructions and screamed." I said, "it doesn't matter how much training you get, until you find yourself in that situation, you don't know what you will do." "All your training will be nowhere to be found." "But I refuse to entertain this conversion any longer." " I hope you all can see it's the people among you that talk like this, that run people away from trying to know God." "This meeting went left when you started this prayer off saying that I am spiritually sick." "1Samuel 16:7 says that *"For the Lord sees not as man sees: man looks on the outward appearance, but the Lord looks on the heart, and* John 4:24 says " *God is spirit, and those who worship Him must worship in spirit and truth."*
"So how can you, a man, look at my physical appearance and judge if my spirit is sick or not?" "You can't, that's between my God and I." "I could look at you and say the same things that you conclude about me." "Your logic is not rational or compassionate." "But I'm not here for a judicial hearing." "I came to bring some light into this darkness." "I won't be coming back here and don't need your decision to tell me if I can." "I choose to leave and never return."
"Here is my letter of disassociation." Then Brother Hope says, "I really hate to see you leave Jehovah

God." I said, "what you all have yet to realize is that my relationship with God is not attached to a particular place." "God is too big to be limited to the Kingdom Hall." "I don't have to go anywhere to get Him." "I appreciate you all for teaching me the Bible but since I left here, I found God." I walked away leaving them, their dynamic, arbitrary rules, and puzzled faces.

I finally did it. I was free. I no longer had to hide, run, and duck at the sight of any of them. As a matter of fact, when I saw Sister Hope in the store, I waved at her and she didn't speak. At first, I thought that maybe she didn't see me until I saw my mama and grandma at the gas station a few days later. They acted as if I was the wind, like they didn't see me at all. I was literally dead to them, and I was okay with that.

I reflected on the many things in my life that made me broken. It is the weakness created in me from broken homes, failed relationships, and abuse that provided an opportunity for the devil to use my desire to fill those broken places with the right thing, God. The devil knows the Bible too and he will manipulate it to turn God's people astray. That song, *Make the Truth Your Own*, meant to find the truth for myself. God showed me the truth. I tried to get out of the Mississippi Mud so many times for so many years. I always left and had to come back. I needed to come back and face what I thought were problems. I now realize that I was not buried at all. God planted me there. All the things meant to make me dirty, provided the opportunity for me to grow. This is only the Mississippi Mud while you fight it. Now I embrace it; it's my alluvial soil that nurtures my faith by allowing me to see the real God.

Author's Bio

Chinna Dunigan is writer, motivational speaker, and author of *Buried in the Mississippi Mud*. This old soul is a self-proclaimed "jack of all trades, master of few", versatile and savvy at many skills. Her friends and family know her as a walking search engine, ready to overwhelm you with knowledge from her research and daily reading, to her plethora of life experiences. Her research has led to a passion of sharing knowledge, experiences, and education to help transform self-image, cultural biases and perception of all mankind, especially women of color.

Chinna is a graduate of Mississippi Valley State University in Business Administration/Organizational Management and a current MBA student of Louisiana State University. This mother of five is a native of Indianola, Mississippi. She has always aspired to create thought provoking writings that promote healing by addressing the uncomfortable and shameful but necessary topics that plague women and black culture.

Acknowledgements

A lot of time, sweat, and tears were incorporated into each page of this book. I would like to thank Latonzia Evans, Kathy Brownlow, Temeka Jones, and Melissa Ivory-Brown for encouraging and supporting me over the years. Each of them has always told me that I had stories that needed to be shared and reminded me to stay on course. My sister Veronica Vargo for being an example of strength, courage, and perseverance to pursue her dreams and exceed her goals; and my sister Elizabeth Battle for her ingenuity, faith, optimism in that things will always work out or figure one out. I appreciate my children for always supporting me in all my crazy ideas including painting my own car and they say "ma that looks good", even though it was terrible. Shakia Bell, I could hear your words in my ear each time I was tired, "you better push through". Joseph Cotton you always engaged me with thought provoking intellectual and spiritual conversation that were the basis for many days of research. Roderick Woods thanks for dropping everything and being there when I needed you. So much gratitude and appreciation to Alex Miller for pushing me to keep going, checking on my status, and giving me the positive energy and whatever else I needed to finish this task and pursue my dreams when I wanted to give up.

I love you all very much.

Made in the USA
Monee, IL
23 July 2021